Finding Mallory
A Cash Delaney Novel

BEVERLEE HUGHES

Published by Cliff Street Books

ISBN-10: 0692328017
ISBN-13: 978-0692328019
Cover Photograph and Design by Joshua Adams
First Paperback Printing: November 2014
Printed in the United States of America

For Nanette Peterson

"For most of history, **Anonymous** was a woman."

Virginia Woolf

"Poverty is death in another form."

Latin Proverb

Finding Mallory

PROLOGUE

I was sleeping soundly in my comfortable queen-sized bed at the back of my rented cottage on Beach House Lane in Carolina Beach, on the southeastern shores of North Carolina, where I was directing a somewhat salacious dream that involved a fabulous meal of all kinds of things that are eaten with fingers rather than utensils. Things like oysters on the half shell and boiled shrimp and roast leg of lamb and ears of corn dripping with butter and mugs of cold beer and sweet cider and cherry tarts and my dinner companion was that guy who played the debauched TV Doctor House, and who was getting ready to ask me to participate in some of that debauchery when suddenly someone was trying to hijack my dream.

I resisted as long as I could but to no eventual avail. I opened my eyes and looked a bit groggily at my oldest friend and housemate Sarah Ehrenson, wearing what appeared to be a pair of pale yellow silk pajamas. She looked really beautiful, which she was, and totally grumpy, which she often was. I was thinking about how contradictory those two characteristics should be when I heard her exclaim,

"Damn it, Cash, wake up. Jesus Christ. Katherine Delaney, for heaven's sake WAKE UP." I woke up.

"You have just absolutely ruined the entire thing, Sarah," I muttered testily. "I was about to get jumped by…"

"I don't give a flying fuck," she countered, cutting me off from one of her least favorite subjects for mutual conversation, although her choice of words might have perfectly described what had been about to happen. "Stella's on the phone. She says it's important." And she turned away from me and quickly headed back to her suite of rooms on the other side of the cottage.

Stella Conroy is a fellow private investigator as well as my partner in a business we call C&D Investigations, so I knew it wasn't a frivolous call. I crawled out of bed and glanced at my little clock on the bedside table. Four in the morning on a Friday in November. By the time I'd reached the only land line in the place, which was in the kitchen, my feet were freezing. I'd forgotten to slip anything on them and it'd been an unseasonably chilly month for this part of the south, and anyhow I was worse than the natives when it came to the cold. I hated it.

"What's up?" I said into the phone.

"Well," said Stella Conroy, in that low, husky Kathleen Turner voice of hers, "I reckon we got ourselves a potentially serious situation to contend with and we gotta go take a look, see what we think, whether we even want to get involved, y'all get my drift. Might could be a cop thing. You okay with bein' picked up in a half hour or so?"

"Anything preventing you from giving me a hint about this potentially serious situation?"

"Husband says it's a kidnappin'. I am merely reservin' judgment knowin' him and his circumstances the way I do."

"I'll see you in thirty minutes," I said and headed for the shower.

I was sitting on the wide arm of one of the Adirondack chairs that lives on the patio in front of the cottage and finishing up one of Sarah's homemade scones slathered with butter and lemon curd when Stella pulled up in her shiny gold Mustang. Once I was in, she U-turned out of Beach House Lane and headed for Snow's Cut Bridge, so we were leaving the island, probably heading to Wilmington, a rather liberal southern city of about a hundred thousand souls that always has a bunch of people who fancy themselves brilliant criminals active at any given time. Clearly, tonight was no exception. I noticed a large cup of coffee sitting in the cup holder on my side of the car.

"Is that for me?" I asked.

"Sarah suggested it might be wise to ply you with coffee, I wanted y'all awake and alert," said Stella Conroy. "Besides, I never argue with Sarah."

"Nobody does," I said. "There's no percentage in it. But I'm particular about coffee. I like…"

"Three sugars, good dollop of cream," Stella said. "Drink up, Delaney. You need to be on your toes. Speakin' of which, whaddya'll dressed for? Welfare relief?"

I looked myself over. I had put on a pair of comfortable but presentable black slacks, although the fabric at the knees was wearing thin, and a red-and-white striped sweatshirt with a black windbreaker over it. There appeared to be several white blotches of something on the jacket that I had not noticed. Then I glanced at my feet. I had on one white sock and one black sock and the sneakers I had grabbed both had holes where the big toes should have fit snugly and therefore been unnoticeable. Instead, there they were in all their glory, one white, one black. I wiggled them.

"I dressed in the dark," was what I said by way of explanation. I easily could have added, "And I was semi-conscious." By way of contrast, I looked over at Stella who was wearing a pair a deep brown cargo pants with a tan turtleneck underneath a black cable-knit sweater. On her feet she wore a pair of brown leather ankle boots. On her right wrist, I could see a dazzling gold watch band. Her long

3

blond hair was a bit wind-tossed.

"Well," said Stella Conroy, "it's not like Alvie'll pay it any mind. By this time, I expect he's driven way past unsettled and is careenin' headlong into hysterical. He's always been a tad dramatic for a man."

"Alvie's the client, I take it," I said, still chagrined about my wardrobe malfunctions.

"Uh huh. Alvie Weather. I've known him all my life. He's a couple years older'n me but he failed two grades so we graduated together. We weren't exactly friends, but I kinda liked him. He was sweet and quiet and very polite, three qualities that should be beneficially injected into most men at birth."

"And his wife's been kidnapped?" I asked.

"What he says," Stella said. "We'll see. Her name's Mallory. She's younger than Alvie, but it's sorta hard accusin' him of bein' a trophy wife kind of man. He's just not the type. He's got no real arrogance about him at all. They been married seven or eight years."

"Is there enough money involved to make a kidnapping realistic?" I said.

"Yes," said Stella Conroy. "Now when Alvie and I were young, his family was so poor they thought dirt could constitute gravy. But Alvie wanted better and he found a way to get it. He started fiddling with old car wrecks when he was nothin' but a baby, fixin' 'em and sellin' 'em and then he got to where he had a little car lot; he bought and sold other people's wrecks after fixin' 'em all up, and over the years, he parlayed his mechanical and negotiatin' skills into what's today an international marketplace for custom classic and antique cars as well as reconditioned luxury vehicles of all makes and models. He's got a huge showroom somewhere down on Market Street. He is probably worth northwards of ten million dollars. And these days, he's dabblin' in producin', a word that, to my mind, simply means 'give me your money, sucker'. Sorta like a highway robber might say to you, you couldn't defend yourself."

"Producing what?"

"Who the hell knows," Stella said. "Television shows, movies, streamin' porn for DirecTV, even stage plays for all I know. I got no earthly idea. He'll tell us, we want him to. Not that it's necessarily pertinent."

"Hollywood's a long way from here," I said. "You'd think if he wanted to be a player, he'd move west."

Stella Conroy slowed down and looked over at me. "I thought you knew," she said. "Wilmington is Hollywood East. Has been for quite a while now. They're always filmin' somethin' or other around town, disruptin' traffic, cloggin' sidewalks, makin' people crazy. Last week, that guy played Chaplin was here filmin' Iron Man III, got himself hurt hanging over the Cape Fear River in a crane, some such nonsense. I guess they're also filmin' that new TV show Revolution. I've never seen it but it's supposed to be a big hit. There's more movie and TV people in town than you can shake a stick at.

One time, some fat cat tried to hire me to babysit an actress I never heard of; he wanted her off the sauce until she'd finished a movie he was producin'. I emphatically declined. Nothin' worse in this world than watchin' some fool's back. But y'all would not believe how good the money was he offered. I coulda' taken a year's vacation, I wanted."

"I had no idea," I said.

"I'm surprised Sarah didn't tell you," said Stella.

"Maybe she's unaware."

"Hard to accuse Sarah of that," she said and grinned at me. "Anyway, we're nearly there. He lives in Landfall, one of those planned communities just across from Wrightsville Beach. Lotta folks call it Landfill, but I expect that's due to the fact it was built on one; that, or envy. Only problem I see with the place is a lot of the structures are mostly ugly. They're really just big old houses that could be nice but instead the owners have hung a lot of architectural crap on them, like turrets and cupolas and pillars and pilasters and water fountains and falls. One guy had the builder put a widow's walk on his mcmansion.

Now understand, his house overlooks a parkin' lot with a large storage annex of the New Hanover Public Library. So, I guess if his wife happens to be standin' on that widow's walk one afternoon and sees her husband drop dead on the macadam as he's walkin' home from an afternoon lookin' at old books, y'all could contend that feature fulfilled its function."

I got laughing so hard at the absurdity of the picture she'd painted that the tears started streaming down my face and pretty soon Stella started laughing, too. After a minute, it was clear we'd both lost it and before we knew it, she'd veered a bit into somebody's hedge of Knock Out rosebushes, scattering a whole bunch of petals all over the road like a flower girl at a wedding before bringing herself and the Mustang back under control.

"Stop it now Cash," she said, between big gulps of air. "Here's his driveway. And sweet Jesus, there he is, waitin' on us. Well hell, if y'all can't stop laughin', then pretend you're not feelin' well and cough instead. Here he comes now Cash."

I started coughing in between laughing jags and stayed in the car while Stella Conroy got out, shook her head to release whatever tension she might be feeling, and opened and put her arms around a slight pale barefoot man with lank brown hair and a lean face that needed a shave. He was nearly her height and wearing a pair of loose pants that looked like army fatigues beneath a multi-striped smoking jacket. He was openly crying and clinging to her and saying in a desperate tone of voice,

"Y'all've gotta help me, Stella, please God. Help me. I can't abide this awful desolation." The man's face was a landscape of despair.

So there wasn't anything remotely funny anymore. I stopped laughing and exited the car, and Stella and I walked with Alvie

Weather between us, holding on to each of us up the driveway and over the walkway and into the house where he lived and from where his wife of seven years, Mallory, had been, according to her husband, kidnapped.

CHAPTER ONE

Once inside his house, Alvie Weather simply stopped moving, as though he was confounded by the challenges of motion. We were standing in a rather large foyer with a black and white terra-cotta floor and a center staircase at its far end. There was a room on either side of us; each was accessible through an arched entryway. The room to the left, which was dark, appeared to be a dining room; on the right, a living room or library or sitting room. Perhaps a combination of all three. All the walls that I could see were painted what I would have called foam green. Alvie had not turned on any electrical devices save a small lamp somewhere in the living room and the ambient light through a massive skylight above the foyer was dim. The house was full of shadows.

"Alvie," Stella said gently, and pressed her hand on his arm. "Where are we goin'?" Nothing. I looked at her. She looked at Alvie. He had broken out in a sweat. I could see the droplets on his forehead and neck, and I could feel them slippery on his forearm. He was hot, as though he had just gotten out of a steam bath. I thought the temperature in the house might be sixty-five. Then he started to fall. His knees just buckled, and Stella and I had to brace him on either side so he wouldn't slump to the floor.

"Let's get him into that room over there," said Stella, indicating the living room. So we steadied him, with his toes dragging along the tiles, and carried him to a large armchair that could have held three of him and set him down gently, and he simply closed his eyes and went to sleep. I finally recognized the scent that had been assaulting my senses since I'd walked into the house: overweening jasmine, accompanied by some kind of classical music playing softly in the background. Possibly, I thought, Mahler.

A frisson of dread went through me. I was as cold as Alvie was hot. I looked around the room. Everywhere I glanced, there were harlequins: paintings, representations in ceramic and bronze and brass and iron, photographs, designs on pillows and throw rugs, a tromp l'oeil painting which otherwise might have been a small exit at the rear of the room. There was even a full-length statue with a tragic mask on its face overlooking a grand piano in the far right corner of the room.

I felt as though I was in a sort of Southern gothic dream, with dark bayous and trees dripping with sheets of Spanish moss just beyond the boundaries of this house that felt inhabited by ghosts. I kept expecting Katharine Hepburn to materialize and declaim, "The Calla lilies are in bloom again; such a strange flower. Suitable for any occasion. I wore them on my wedding day." And then that camp phrase, with Montgomery Clift dead on a pile of rocks in Tennessee Williams' *Suddenly Last Summer.* "Goodbye Sebastian."

"What the hell," I said to Stella Conroy, who was lighting a cigarette.

"Mallory writes those books where the women are always bein' saved and carried off by big strong handsome men who are good at sexual acrobatics," she said laconically. "Whaddya call 'em. Romance novels. I don't have any idea if she's good at it, but she's persistent." She took a huge drag on her cigarette.

"Some romance," I said. "What do you think he took?" I asked, nodding at Alvie.

"Well, I've never known him to be a big drinker," Stella Conroy said. "My guess, he swallowed something like an Ambien. Those things'll take down a rhino. Speakin' of drinkin'," and she looked around the room until she saw a tray of bottles underneath a front window, "I could use one. How 'bout y'all?"

"I'll keep you company," I said.

A half hour later, Stella and I were at the rear of the house, in the kitchen, fixing sandwiches of fresh baked ham and onion relish on French rolls and homemade potato salad we found in the refrigerator. When we'd eaten, we walked back to the living room.

Alvie was still slumped in the big chair, but his eyes were open. Empty, but open. We each sat down in smaller chairs and looked at him.

"I guess I took somethin', Stella," he said so softly I had to strain to hear.

"I guess you did, Alvie," she said and smiled at him.

Alvie looked around his living room as though he were a visitor. Finally, he landed on me.

"Hello," he said to me. "Who're y'all?"

"I'm Cash," I said.

"You're what?" he asked politely.

"She's my partner, Alvie," Stella Conroy said, somewhat irritated. "Cash Delaney. Look here, we need to get to whatever has happened to Mallory. Can y'all focus?" Alvie Weather scowled, which gave his face a look of concentration.

"The note's on the computer," he said.

"What computer," said Stella. "Where is it?"

"That laptop," he said, "underneath the sofa cushion. I hid it so no one would find it." He sounded pleased with himself.

"Stella," I said, "he's still way out there in left field."

"I know that," she said.

There was no laptop underneath any of the four sofa cushions. "God damn it," she said to herself. "I oughta shake him, but that would do no good whatsoever. He'd just feel bad." Alvie had closed his eyes again.

"Look underneath the sofa," I said. So she did. And lo and behold, there it was. A skinny new notebook. Stella Conroy sighed with relief and lit a cigarette. I walked over and we both sat on the sofa and Stella put it down on a coffee table and opened it up. Alvie hadn't bothered to turn it off, so what we saw when we looked at the screen was this in caps and big bold type:

WE HAVE YOUR WIFE MALLORY. YOU WILL BE CONTACTED AT EIGHT O'CLOCK TOMORROW MORNING WITH FURTHER INSTRUCTIONS. THEY WILL ARRIVE ON THIS COMPUTER. THERE WILL BE NO PHONE CALLS. IF YOU CONTACT POLICE SHE WILL DIE.

Stella and I both looked at our watches. It was six-thirty in the morning.

"Well," I said, "they're either moving her out of the area and need time to do it or they want us to think that's what they're doing. Either way, we need Sarah."

"That's if this whole thing is real," Stella said.

"I'm not following," I said.

"Mallory makes outrageous things up," she said. "Just look at the kinds of books she writes. If Alvie's a tad dramatic, Mallory's a full blown opera. She's capable of pullin' a prank like this just to test its strength as a story."

"Prank?" I said, sounding incredulous. "Who the hell would put a person through something like this? Look at the poor man; he's a wreck. But really Stella, it doesn't matter either way. We've got to proceed on the assumption that this is real and we need Sarah before eight o'clock; otherwise whatever comes in we'll just have to accept as literal truth with no ability to trace the information or talk back to it. I'll call her. Why don't you work on rousing Alvie. Coffee with a lot of milk might help. Even food, if it's bland. He doesn't look very robust to me."

I walked back into the foyer and speed-dialed Sarah, who I knew would not be pleased to get another call at what she considered an ungodly hour. Her phone rang eight times before a voice said, "What?"

"Is she awake, Mick?" I asked. Mickey Huntley is Sarah's lover and a well-known lawyer in Wilmington, where her reputation as a tough-as-nails defense attorney keeps her in more clients than she knows what to do with.

"No," is all Mickey Huntley said. "The vibration woke me up," she added. "She keeps it under my pillow."

"Well," I said and sighed, "you've got to wake her. We need her and it's urgent. We've got until eight o'clock to get her over to Landfall, and she's got to be set up with the necessary trace equipment before then."

"Details," said Mickey Huntley.

"It's a kidnapping," I said and then I explained the rest of what we knew. "Stella's trying to bring Alvie around, but she thinks he took an Ambien and he's really out of it."

"There's no good antidote for Ambien," Mickey said. "If you can get him to throw up, it might help, depending on when he took the drug. Otherwise, time, and a little food, a little water, maybe coffee, and you've got to keep talking to him, walking him around. We'll be over there in awhile. What's the address?" I gave it to her and she hung up.

I walked back to the living room where Stella was feeding Alvie some milk through a straw and talking quietly to him. I thought he was nodding, but that could have just been his attempt to stay awake.

A half-eaten piece of toast was sitting on a plate in front of him. I raised my eyebrows at Stella.

"He's feelin' pretty tuckered still, but better," she said. "He thinks he took a whole pill. They're Mallory's."

"I'm a ambient virgin," Alvie Weather said to me and then he giggled. I tried and failed to remember when I had last heard a man giggle.

"Who are y'all?" he said again to me.

"Never mind that now, Alvie," Stella Conroy said. "She's a friend of mine and that's what you need to remember."

"Okay," he said and closed his eyes and went to sleep again.

Stella Conroy sighed with annoyance and lit a cigarette. "I don't know why the hell men fight wars," she said. "All they'd have to do, get over on each other, is spike a relevant water supply with this shit and their whole niggling difference of opinion'd be finished. Sarah comin'?"

"She's on her way," I said. An hour later, we heard the big Mercedes pull into Alvie Weather's driveway. The cavalry had arrived.

CHAPTER TWO

I opened the front door of the house and Sarah Ehrenson walked in carrying a laptop that was probably a computer fit for a wizard, and a lot of cords with different ends on them that I knew she would be sticking into various outlets to set up whatever she needed for tracking purposes. She was followed by Mickey Huntley, who was in possession of an unwieldy looking phone with a variety of lines going wherever the hell they would eventually go. Sarah looked unusually spectacular and incredibly displeased.

"That a new outfit, Sarah?" I asked, hoping to distract her from her mood, which I knew was due entirely to the hour. She is not an early morning person.

"Yes," she said. She was wearing a pair of tightly fitted winter white wool slacks. Her coat, which was open, was mid-calf length and dark brown suede. Beneath it, she wore a raw silk blouse in pale blue with a small form-fitted vest in black leather. A pair of black Ferragamo leather boots completed the ensemble. Her dark red hair was in the blunt cut she preferred and there did not appear to be one hair out of place. Her make-up was so impeccable you had to wonder, except for the deep red lipstick, if she was wearing any.

Mickey Huntley grinned at me. She didn't look so bad herself in her designer jeans, black turtleneck, drab olive pea jacket, and black leather loafers. "Nice shoes," she said, glancing at my sneakers. I grimaced. "Sarah's cranky. Is there coffee?"

"There's a fresh pot in the living room," I said, leading the way.

Stella Conroy had, by this time, sufficiently roused Alvie Weather so that there was a bit of animation in his eyes and he no longer slumped in his chair. In fact, he was displaying some signs of nervousness. His fingers drummed on the arms of the chair and his feet kept moving up and down, side to side, as though he were rehearsing a dance routine.

"Sarah needs coffee," I said to Stella.

By this time, Sarah had walked into the room, frowned, looked around at all the harlequins, and muttered, "Where am I? Clown school?"

Alvie Weather's eyes got huge and round, and he reached for Stella Conroy's arm like a drowning man reaches for a life raft. "Stella," he said just above a whisper, "I am hallucinatin'."

"Say what?" Stella said to him and moved a little closer to his side.

"She is not real," he said, and Stella and I could hear the distress in his voice. "She cannot be real."

"Who?" Stella Conroy asked him.

Alvie Weather stood up. He wrung his hands together and once again I could see sweat on his forehead. Unsteadily, he took small steps in Sarah's direction. She, however, was paying no attention to him or this particular tableau. Instead, she was shedding her coat, handing it to Mickey Huntley, and fussing with the computer stuff she needed to set up. Alvie kept taking small steps toward Sarah until he was only an arm's length away from her. She glanced at him, glanced away, and grabbed a cord she needed to link the two computers. Alvie reached toward her with his right hand, touched first her face, then her neck, and then her breasts, running his hand back and forth across them as though looking for something in the dark.

"She feels real," he whispered. Sarah was frozen in place.

Stella Conroy was on her feet and moving. Mickey Huntley, who was separating phone cords, had not noticed what had happened.

"What the hell's wrong with you, Alvie," Stella Conroy hollered, grabbing his arm away from Sarah and turning him around. "His eyes are glassy," she said to me, and she slapped him hard across the face with the flat of her hand. Whatever spell he'd been under broke.

"I'm sorry," he said to Stella. "Mallory said she was a dream. Y'all have any idea how many letters come in askin' about her?"

"I think you drank the cool aid, Alvie," Stella Conroy said harshly to him. "Nobody in this room has a fuckin' clue what the hell y'all are goin' on about. I've never known him to be rude," she said to Sarah. "You okay?" Sarah hadn't moved.

"That woman," he said, ignoring Stella and turning and pointing at Sarah, "isn't supposed to be real." Alvie Weather walked toward the rear of the living room and picked up a book that was lying on top of the grand piano. Then he walked back and handed the book to Stella, who looked at it, then held it up for the rest of us to see. There on the cover was an artist's ravishing idea of none other than Sarah, looking, well, like she'd just finished having highly erotic and exotic sex with somebody and also looking nearly as good as she did right now.

"Mallory spent months workin' with the artist to get this to where she wanted it. And now here she is in the flesh," he said to Stella. Then he looked at Sarah. "I am most sorry for my startling display of rudeness. I am deeply chagrined at my lapse in manners."

For the first time in all the years I've known her, Sarah was speechless. Mickey Huntley whispered something to Sarah, who finally turned and looked at her, then whispered something back. She rested for a moment against the lawyer's weight, her hand on Mickey's shoulder, then finally turned back and smiled at the slight pale man who had exhibited such untoward behavior.

"I accept your apology," Sarah said to him. "But we're here to help you. Now let's see if we can't begin to understand what has happened to your wife and how we'll go about remedying that situation." It was seven forty-five. Sarah had fifteen minutes to be in whatever place she wanted to be in before we heard from the kidnappers.

"I feel certain," said Alvie Weather quietly, "that this is somehow related to what has happened to Mallory." And he sat back down in the chair that swallowed him and fell back to sleep.

"He's still whacked," said Stella Conroy.

"Double whacked with Sarah and the Ambien." I said.

"I wish I could get you two to understand how disconcerting this sort of thing is to me," Sarah said without inflection, while she was busy setting up what she needed to trace whatever came across Alvie Weather's computer screen. "But all you ever do is laugh about it, dismiss it, and tease me."

"Sarah," said Mickey Huntley, "this has nothing, really, to do with you. It is disconcerting to see that artist's rendition on the cover of that book. It's uncanny and I distrust uncanny. No one could have imagined that out of whole cloth. You can't take the time to worry about it now, but you've got to file it under 'to be investigated.' I've got to run. Court's scheduled for nine this morning. I'll call you later."

Sarah nodded and got back to work. By the time she was satisfied that she had what she needed, it was eight o'clock and a little bell on Alvie's computer indicated that he had mail.

"Should we wake him up?" I asked.

"Let's see if we can do without him, he's so ridiculously scattered," Stella said. "Whoever we're dealin' with gets a whiff of his craziness, they might just knock off Mallory and walk away."

Sarah was sitting on the sofa with the two computers and the phone lines in front of her. She clicked on the incoming message for Alvie. On the subject line, we saw these words: "Look at the attachment before you read the message." Sarah clicked on the attachment to open it. What we saw was stark. A woman was sitting on a straight back chair. Her feet were bare and bound together with a length of what looked like bicycle chain.

There were two steel posts set in concrete on either side of her and each of her hands was tied to each of the posts, so that her arms were outstretched. Her head was being held back at a difficult angle that looked painful. Someone wearing a dark glove had grabbed a bunch of her long brown hair to hold it upright. It was clear she'd been beaten. One of her eyes was swollen shut; the other was wide open and full of terror. Her makeup had run and there were noticeable tears streaking along the few lines in her face. She was wearing an orange running outfit, and she looked quite young to me. A Star News with today's date was positioned on her lap where we could see it.

"That's Mallory," Stella Conroy said. "Print it Sarah, please."

Here is what the second message from the kidnappers said:

YOU NOW REALIZE THE SERIOUSNESS OF THE SITUATION. HERE ARE YOUR INSTRUCTIONS. YOU ARE TO PLACE TWO MILLION DOLLARS IN A CARRY ON. YOU WILL ACCOMPLISH THIS IN ONE DAY, BEGINNING NOW. ON THE SECOND DAY WE WILL CONTACT YOU AGAIN.

Sarah began immediately doing things with her computer and a lot of little dings began to sound between the two machines. Lines of type that were unreadable to me appeared on Sarah's screen. Then she brought the photograph of Mallory Weather back up on her screen and drew small boxes around parts of the picture, over and over, until she said to me, "It's not a cell phone. It's a Nikon. Old.

Maybe from the sixties." All the time she was working on the photograph, her computer was spitting out that unreadable text. Then it stopped.

Next, Sarah pulled up a map from Google Earth and an arc began to appear across the screen. It started in Wilmington, went across the Atlantic Ocean to Spain, then on to Latvia, then Denmark, then England, and back to the United States to Texas and finally to Maryland.

"They're clever," Sarah said. "They'd like us to think they're in Maryland."

"But," I said.

"I sincerely doubt it," Sarah said and looked up at Stella and me and smiled. "I think they are right where we'd prefer them to be. Right here in our own backyard. Anyone with this many cyber stops has probably not left home."

"What happens if you answer their email?" I asked.

"If I'm right, and they are here, then it's a dead drop that they access remotely," Sarah said. "And knowing what I now know, I might be able to get closer to where they actually are when they answer. What do you want to say?"

I looked at Stella Conroy. "How would Alvie say that this picture means nothing to him except that she might be dead and that he's got to hear his wife's voice before proceeding?"

"Well," she said, "he's flowery and kinda formal. How 'bout something like this: 'Sir, I am not persuaded, due to the hideousness of your attachment, that my wife is still living, so before I will agree to your monetary demand, I must insist on direct conversation to prove otherwise'."

"Okay," I said.

Sarah sent the reply and the three of us settled in to wait upon developments while Alvie Weather continued to sleep.

CHAPTER THREE

Jefferson Davis was standing on the shore of the well-protected inlet near Supply, North Carolina, surveying the floating cages that held what would become his first crop of cultivated oysters. He and his partner, Cooper Grey, had chosen this site and leased it from the owner, and constructed the cages while the oyster seedlings that had been delivered from the hatchery in two-pound bags had been planted in an upweller, a tank system "sorta like a greenhouse" he had explained to Cash Delaney, a couple months ago. Then, after two weeks in the tank, they had transferred the bags to these suspended cages in this inlet where they began to absorb plankton and saltwater nutrients.

They would stay here for another six weeks. Then he and Cooper Grey would load them on his boat and move them to the bottom of the inlet where they would live essentially free-range on mud for another year or so. Both he and Grey had been happy with the low level of salinity in the water as it would relate to the taste of the oyster. They expected a sweetness they hoped would be popular among oyster lovers in the area. Each two-pound bag of seedlings could, at the end of the year, yield 200,000 pounds of oysters. And North Carolina was still importing nearly seventy-five percent of the oysters consumed each year in the state, so the sky was the limit for their new venture. He was feeling very pleased with himself. Patience had always come easily to him, and he had finally discovered a business where patience was not only a virtue, it was a critical necessity. You couldn't produce oysters overnight.

"Hey boss," a young voice said. "Y'all got work needs doin'?"

Jeff Davis turned around and saw a scrawny white kid of about twelve looking at him, his hands in his pants pockets, and an unlit cigarette in the corner of his mouth. The shirt the kid was wearing was two sizes too big for him. His pants were an old pair of leisure slacks rolled up at the ankles and held up by a length of rope he'd tied around his waist. The shoes on his feet were a pair of what had been white high tops that were now the color of dirt. He had no socks. Jeff Davis guessed he might be about five feet tall, maybe seventy pounds. His hair was carrot top and looked like an inverted bowl on his small head. A heavy spray of freckles ran from his left cheek, over his nose, to his right cheek. There was a smear of mud on his chin. I am lookin' at Tom Sawyer Redux, Jeff Davis thought to himself.

"How y'all doin'?" he said to the kid.

"I'm all fired up, boss," the kid said, "ready to work." Jefferson Davis smiled. The kid took the cigarette out of his mouth, stuck it in his shirt pocket, and grinned back. Then he lifted his other hand from his pocket and held them both out beseechingly.

"What's your name, son," Jeff Davis said.

"Brad Pitt," said the kid, still grinning.

"I bet," said Davis. His cell phone began to ring, and he looked at the number and then answered. "I'm at the inlet, Coop. Where're you?" He paused, and then said, "Okay, I'll meet y'all for breakfast at Grannies. I might be hiring some help like we talked about." He ended the call and said again to the kid, "Your name?"

"It's just I don't like it," the kid said, scuffing his toe in the sand in front of him.

"Why? Am I gonna find it plastered on a wanted sign in the post office?"

The kid laughed. "I don't guess so, boss." he said. "Not right yet."

"Well, until y'all decide otherwise, you can be Brad Pitt, without, however, benefits."

"Huh?" the kid said.

"Nothin' y'all need to worry about right now," said Jefferson Davis. "Let's go get my truck and drive to Carolina Beach. We gotta meet a man and have some breakfast. You hungry?"

"Do ducks quack?"

When Jefferson Davis and the kid pulled into the parking lot at Grannies, Cooper Grey's Altima was already there.

Holding the front door of the restaurant open, Jeff Davis said, "Go wash up a bit, son. I'll be right around the corner." Then he walked into the restaurant and joined his friend Cooper Grey.

"We may have a runaway on our hands, Coop," he said as he was sitting down.

"Oh?"

"He approached me at the inlet and asked if I had any work. He's probably eleven or twelve but he's on the small side. He's obviously not in school, and he won't tell me his name. He says it's Brad Pitt and that he doesn't like his real name. I couldn't just leave him there and I didn't want to spook him so I brought him. See what y'all think. Here he comes now."

The kid who called himself Brad Pitt walked up to the table and then sat down next to Jeff Davis. He had washed his hands and face. He looked at Cooper Gray.

"You the guy on the phone boss was talkin' at?"

"That's right," said Cooper Grey. He studied the boy for a few seconds. "He tells me you don't like your name."

"You ain't from the south," the kid said accusingly

"Nope. So what's that make me? The evil enemy?" Cooper Grey said.

"Nah," the kid said and grinned. "Just a skosh not dependable. Whaddya gonna eat, boss."

"Whatever I want," said Jeff Davis, handing a menu to the boy. "Take a look and order what sounds good to you." A waitress had come up to the table and was pouring coffee.

"Y'all want some milk?" she said to the kid.

"Coffee," he said. The waitress looked at Jeff Davis, who nodded. He noticed that the boy was frowning at the menu. He looked at Cooper Grey, who mouthed, "Can't read," at him.

Jefferson Davis took the menu from the boy's hands and said, "I'll order for both of us, son."

"Okay, boss, I like everything," the kid said and poured a good shot of cream and a lot of sugar into his coffee. He took a sip and smacked his lips. "That's fine stuff," he said.

"Just like Cash," muttered Jeff Davis. "All that sugar."

They ate in companionable silence and when they were finished, the kid had devoured two eggs over easy, home fries, sausage, bacon, ham, two pancakes with maple syrup and an English muffin with strawberry jam. He burped softly and took his last swig of by now cold coffee. "That all there were gooder than grits," he said, "and I thank y'all boss. Where's the work needs doin'?"

"I think you need a uniform, if you're going to be working for us," Cooper Grey said. "Let's see what we can rustle up."

"Boss?" the kid said, looking at Jeff Davis

"Yep, let's go."

An hour later, they walked out of the Independence Mall in Wilmington. The kid was dressed in Levis, a heavy wool sweater in red, a winter jacket that was black and white stripe, black socks and purple and white designer sneakers. He looked good. Cooper Grey put the additional purchases in the trunk of his car, and they all drove back to the beach and parked in the lot closest to Jeff Davis's boat. Once they were onboard the fifty-foot Sea Ray, his cell phone rang.

"Katherine," said Jeff Davis, happily. "What's your pleasure and how may I help you realize it?"

"I've got a guy I need to drop off with you, Jefferson, and I'm in a hurry." Cash Delaney was sitting next to Sarah Ehrenson in the backseat of Stella Conroy's Mustang. Alvie Weather was sitting in the front passenger seat of the car and was asleep again, although he had managed to get dressed in street clothes.

"Well good Christ, woman," Jeff Davis said, "talk about a deflator. Who's the guy and why me?"

"His name's Alvie Weather," Cash Delaney said. "He sells a lot of expensive cars according to Stella and is worth a lot of money. But that's not the reason we're bringing him over to you."

"Hell, I know Alvie," said Jeff Davis. "He sold me a gorgeous Jaguar sedan years ago. I loved that car, all twelve cylinders. I spent more money on speeding tickets that year than I did on food. What's the problem?"

"His wife's been kidnapped and Stella and I have got to get hold of a couple million dollars of his money sometime today in case we can't find her and have to proceed with the ransom. And we can't leave Alvie alone. He took at least one Ambien. Stella thinks he may have swallowed two. Anyhow, he falls asleep on a dime, then wakes up and makes no sense most of the time. We were afraid if we left him at his house, he'd sleepwalk to god knows where or drive his car and end up dead or killing somebody else."

Jefferson Davis absorbed this information quickly. Then he said, "Well, that's not good. Okay. I'll see y'all when you get here."

"What's the story?" Cooper Grey asked. The kid was on the bow of the boat, looking through a pair of binoculars.

"Cash and Stella caught a kidnapping. They're dropping off the husband here. I've known him for years and I am here to tell y'all, he is a genuine oddball. Harmless, but odd nonetheless. Stella's convinced he took a couple Ambien, and his behavior's erratic. They can't take a chance on leavin' him alone."

The two men walked below decks and sat at a small table used for dining. "Well, they're right not to leave him to his own devices. People experience blackouts with Ambien and later have no idea what the hell they've done. Meantime, what should we be doing with our own oddball, that kid," Cooper Grey said to Jefferson Davis. "Reasonable people would call Social Services."

"Exactly," Jeff Davis said. "The real question? Are we reasonable? And when has Social Services ever done a child like this any good?"

"Well, I would suppose hardly ever. But there are rules in place to handle things like this. Besides, we're not a charity, Jefferson."

"Sure we are, Cooper. Sure we are. Just look at the women we choose to love. If that doesn't make us the most charitable men on the face of this earth, I don't know what does."

"You'd better forget you said that. If Stella or Cash ever heard you give voice to such an idea, neither one of us would ever get laid again," said Cooper Grey. "And I like having sex with Stella. I like it a lot, even though it hardly ever happens on my timetable."

"Hey boss," the kid shouted from the bow, "it looks like a whole bunch of tall, good lookin' womens is headin' this way, and a couple of 'em is haulin' a little skinny guy between 'em. I think he's sleepin'. That, or he died."

CHAPTER FOUR

"Y'all wanna give us a hand here Jefferson," Stella Conroy yelled. She and Cash Delaney were holding up Alvie Weather who looked comatose and was dressed in a gray pin-striped business suit without a shirt. Cooper Grey emerged from the galley and walked over to the side of the boat.

"At your service, darling," he said to Stella Conroy and reached down and lifted Alvie up and over the side rail and into the boat. He let go of him gently to help the women onboard. Alvie slumped to the deck like a sack of stones.

"Don't darlin' me, Cooper Grey," Stella Conroy said. "I hate that ridiculous word." Then she looked at her husband for a second and softened her tone. "Lookin' fine, baby," she said. "Where's Jefferson at?"

"Right here," Jeff Davis said, coming up from the galley. He was walking over to Alvie Weather, getting ready to lift him onto the one lounge chair he kept for Cash Delaney on the aft deck.

"Help Sarah set up the computer stuff, Stella," Cash said to her partner. "Please."

When Stella and Sarah had gone below deck, Cash Delaney said to Jefferson Davis and Cooper Grey, "Sarah cannot, I repeat, cannot handle Alvie Weather. That has got to be your job, at least for the moment. And unless you want nightmares, keep him away from her. I'll explain later. But we've got to keep all this computer stuff close to Alvie in case the people who have kidnapped Mallory want to see him on Skype. So far, they haven't asked for that. But we think they might.

If the poor bastard could just stay awake for an hour at a time, it would help. But so far, that's not proved to be possible. So Sarah's going to stay here with you. She's working on narrowing the parameters of where they might be, and we've been playing it fast and loose with them, making demands they don't care for, but they like the idea of the money more. So to a certain extent, they've been cooperating."

"Can we see what you've got so far?" asked Cooper Grey.

"Yes."

"Let's go."

"Boss?" said the kid, standing on the walkway just outside the aft deck.

Cash Delaney frowned. She looked at the kid, looked at Jefferson Davis, then at Cooper Grey. "What the hell," she said.

"Not now, Brad," said Jeff Davis. "Y'all just stand watch, let me know who's comin'. I'll be back up in awhile? Okay?"

"My name ain't really Brad, boss," the kid said shyly. "It's Jesse," he said. "Jesse Shine. Makes me out like a girl."

"Jefferson," said Cash Delaney, sounding as unhappy as he had ever heard her.

"What have I heard y'all say in the past?" said Jeff Davis, looking her straight in the eye. "It's complicated."

"He's a child," said Cash.

"And your point is?" he said to her.

"He's a damned child!" said Cash Delaney. "Whose child is he, BOSS?"

Jefferson Davis continued to hold her gaze. Then he said softly, out of the kid's hearing, "We don't know, Katherine. He looks to be a runaway. We are fixin' to find out. Please do not frighten the boy. We don't want him runnin' off."

Cash Delaney ran through a quick calculus of the situation and factored in what she knew to be true about Jefferson Davis. She nodded to herself. Then she turned to the boy and said in as even a tone as she could manage,

"Where's home, Jesse?"

"Y'all ain't from the south, either," he said. "Just like him," pointing at Cooper Grey.

"Well, thank God," Cash Delaney said to him, finally smiling. "Somebody has got to retain a modicum of sense around here."

"Your toes cold?" the kid asked.

Cash Delaney laughed. "You're a funny guy, Jesse," she said. "Touché." Then she turned to Jeff Davis and said, "I'd really like to see what you and Cooper think about the recording we took from Skype before Stella and I take off to see about the money."

"We are ready whenever y'all decide to join us," Stella Conroy yelled from below decks.

Stella had used Sarah's cell phone to record what had been sent to them on Skype. "It took them twenty minutes to get back to us on the email we sent, asking them for verbal proof that Mallory Weather was still among the living," Sarah said. "That is confirmation enough for me that the address they are using to generate their emails is a dead drop and that they are actually still in town, rather than in Maryland."

The picture looked distorted in the way that Skype often does. But it was clear enough. Once again, they were looking at a woman, feet bound, arms outstretched and tied to pillars, sitting in a straight backed chair. A voice that sounded computer generated said, "You have asked to hear from Mallory. So here she is in her own words."

And the chair was pulled away from her, a move that left her hanging in mid air, unable either to stand or otherwise rest in any way. She cried out in pain as the task of holding her weight fell to her shoulders.

"Alvie," she said, "please, please, please just give them whatever they want. Please, baby. I am truly beggin' you. They have already," and that was the last we heard from Mallory Weather.

Then the altered voice spoke again. "I trust this satisfies your sophomoric requirement and that you will now proceed to gather the amount of money requested. You will hear tomorrow to arrange for the exchange." The message ended. No one said anything when the cell phone screen went blank. Finally, Cooper Grey stood up and began to pace back and forth in the limited space the boat afforded.

"I don't believe it's computer generated," he said. "They've probably used a portable voice changer, but it sounds professional to me, so they know what they're doing. And they certainly appear to be literate."

"And if it's not done with a synthesis program on a computer, then they could even be choosing to alter their accent," Sarah said. "They could be from the backwoods of Louisiana, or the jungles of Manhattan, and we wouldn't know it."

"Let me see that room again," Jeff Davis said. Sarah pulled up the first email she'd received from the kidnappers.

"Whaddy'all thinkin', Jefferson?" Stella Conroy said.

"I'm thinkin' it reminds me of a boat hold," he said slowly. "Artificial light, concrete floor, steel jacks, and no clutter we can see. Can you bring up any background noise, Sarah?"

"Not with this computer equipment," she said. "It won't handle the spectrograph software."

"Do you have the equipment that will handle it?" Cash Delaney said to her.

"No," Sarah said. "But I know where I can get it. Mickey has a friend who's a sound engineer for Screen Gems Studios. He's been working for two years with the cast and crew of 'East Bound and Down' and they're on hiatus right now. We might even be able to break down the voice alteration, and get it closer to itself. I've met him a few times. Shall I give him a call?"

"Yes," Cash said.

"I'm going to have to tell him why I need to borrow his stuff," Sarah said. "These people are fanatical about their equipment. They are loath to let anyone else use it."

"Y'all go right ahead and tell him," Stella said.

Sarah looked up the number on a list she kept on her computer, dialed it and hit speaker phone. After four rings, a deep mellow voice said, "Yes, my dear Sarah, I'm always available to you for work. What do you need? A bartender for one of your costume parties? A protestor at one of Mickey's trials?"

Sarah cleared her throat. "Hi Dodge," she said. "Actually, I do need your help. We're working on a kidnapping and we need to be able to hear and separate the background and foreground noises on the messages we've received from the kidnappers; and we also need to see if we can strip a professionally altered voice to hear what the kidnapper who speaks actually sounds like."

For a few seconds she listened to nothing but silence. "Dodge?" Sarah said. "Will you help us?"

"Of course I'll help you, my darling," said the sound engineer named Dodge, suddenly serious. "I can meet you at Screen Gems on 23rd in an hour. We should pretty much have the place to ourselves now that Bobby's injured himself."

Sarah packed up the computer and the attachments she needed to take to the studio, and they all walked back up to the aft deck. It was breezy, but the sun was trying valiantly to warm the air. "Can we stop for five minutes so I can change into something that doesn't make me resemble a homeless person?" asked Cash Delaney.

"Sure we can," Stella said. Then she looked at the lounge chair where she had last seen Alvie Weather. "Where's Alvie?" she said.

The kid walked along the side of the boat and stopped when he was across from the others. "All done playin', boss?" he said. "Time to get to work?"

"Jesse," said Jefferson Davis, "have y'all seen the man who was sleepin' on this chair?"

"Sure, boss," said Jesse Shine.

"Well where the hell is he?" Stella Conroy said urgently.

"I don't know, lady," said the kid. "Alls he said to me was he were goin' out to find his wife."

CHAPTER FIVE

"What now?" Sarah said.

"Well, the short answer is we're screwed," Stella Conroy said. "Unless we can find Alvie, we can't continue. We need him to call that concierge banker of his to get the money together, we need him in case the people who've got Mallory want to see him, and we need to know he's safe, not somewhere wanderin' around when right now he don't have the sense god gave a gopher."

"Jesse," said Jefferson Davis, "did you see which way he went?"

"He weren't movin' too fast, boss. And he was listin' to the side, like a sailin' boat about to topple. Last I saw him, he was turnin' right by that corner up ahead where the stop light is."

"Canal Drive," said Cooper Grey.

"Or Carolina Beach Avenue. Y'all take Canal, Coop, we'll take Carolina," Stella said. "Let's go, Cash. Listen, Sarah, you'd best call and tell that friend of yours we have been unexpectedly delayed."

"Jesse, you stay here with Sarah. We'll be back," Jeff Davis said. The four of them left the boat and headed for their cars.

"Your name's Sarah?" Jesse Shine said to Sarah Ehrenson.

"It is," Sarah said.

"It's a fine name," the kid said.

"I've always thought so," said Sarah Ehrenson, wondering who this young boy was and where he came from.

"I got a sister name of Sara," said the kid.

"Is she here at the beach with you?"

"No Ma'am," said Jesse Shine. "I ain't seen her in quite a while."

"Tell me about her," Sarah said.

"She's a positive corker. A genuine high five. I had more good times with her than I expect to have again," he said and smiled.

"Well, I wouldn't worry about that if I were you," said Sarah. "There'll be more good times ahead. You're young."

"Not likely," said Jesse Shine.

"Why do you say that, Jesse? Where is she?" Sarah asked.

"Dead," the kid said.

We were driving slowly, halfway down Carolina Beach Avenue North, when I spotted a flash of something I thought might be Alvie Weather, moving between two houses on the waterfront. "Up there, Stella," I said. "Between that pink cottage and the blue condominium complex. I think I saw him. I know I saw something."

Stella pulled her Mustang over to the side of the street where I'd indicated. But all there was to see was a man walking toward a dock that protruded a good way into the Atlantic Ocean, not Alvie Weather looking for his wife.

In another few minutes, we came to the turnaround at the end of the Avenue. What lay ahead of us was a small parking lot below an old established bar and restaurant, and beyond that the public beach on the north end of this barrier island, where tourists and natives alike gathered to enjoy their summers. Off to my right and raised on high thick pilings was an old pedestrian pier that looked fragile to me and where serious fishermen who couldn't afford boats did their fishing all year round. Today it was deserted, probably because of the wind. Stella and I got out of her car and looked around. A few seconds later, Cooper Grey and Jefferson Davis pulled up in the truck and parked beside us.

"I'm going up on the pier," I said. "Maybe if he's wandering along north beach I'll be able to spot him."

"We'll all go," said Jeff Davis.

"No," I said. "If I see him, you're the one with four-wheel drive and you'll have to go get him."

"Well, then," Stella Conroy said, "I'll go with y'all."

So Stella and I went up the interior steps that led to both the restaurant, which was closed, and the pier. When we emerged from the stairway and walked a bit out on the rickety structure, we looked at the length of north beach and saw nothing, not even a seagull. The wind up here was bitter cold.

"Damn it," Stella said. "He's probably passed out in some dumpster. Well, we really got no choice now, Cash. We gotta call the cops."

I nodded in agreement. Stella was right. We'd come to the end of this particular line. Then I walked to the end of the pier, where, when I looked, the endless expanse of the Atlantic Ocean taunted me. I was trying to clear my head and trying to ignore the cold that was assaulting my body. We couldn't locate Alvie, we couldn't get the money for the ransom together, we couldn't find Mallory nor could we save her. We had run out of options, and I was experiencing the overwhelming sense of futility that always comes to me when my best efforts aren't going to be enough.

I bent my head and could see the rising tide below, between the planks of the pier.

There, bumping up against the pilings, was Alvie Weather. He was face down in the water. I moved so suddenly, leaping over the railing at the end of the pier and landing in the water below, that Stella

Conroy couldn't register. Then I heard her voice rising above the wind and riding the clipped white caps of the ocean.

"Cooper," she yelled at the top of her lungs, "Cash's in the water. Get over here. What the hell! Jefferson, move it. She will surely freeze to death, we don't get her out of there right now."

I had pulled Alvie Weather out from under the pier and was side stroking with my left arm and hauling Alvie out of the ocean by the collar of his suit coat with my right. I was nearly on shore when Jefferson Davis and Cooper Grey came to my assistance. The three of us dragged the drowning man up on safe ground and Cooper flipped him over. Alvie's eyes were half-closed, and he didn't appear to be breathing. His lips were blue. How long he had been face down in the water, I had no idea, but at the moment, I was experiencing my own set of problems.

My teeth were chattering out of control, and I was shivering with a sort of violence I had never experienced before. Jefferson Davis just picked me up and carried me to his truck, where he turned the heater on high and blasted the cabin with heat. He reached for an old woolen blanket that he kept in the locker behind the seat, ripped off my freezing clothes and wrapped me up. I wasn't warm, but neither was I freezing.

"I'm taking her back to the boat," he said to the others, "before her muscles cramp."

"Go," Stella Conroy said. "We'll finish up here. Alvie just convulsed and spit up half the ocean."

Once we were back at the municipal parking lot closest to Jefferson's boat, he parked and jumped out of his side of the truck and ran around to my side and interrupted me as I was trying to exit the vehicle.

"I can walk," I said while tightly clenching the blanket. The involuntary shaking of my body and chattering of my teeth was driving me crazy.

"No you can't" he said and picked me up again and carried me to his boat where he somehow managed to climb over the side rail while holding me. The kid was watching us from the bow of the boat. Sarah, who had been resting on the chaise longue that once held Alvie Weather, stood up in alarm.

"What's wrong?" she said to him. "What's happened?"

"She went in the ocean," he said cryptically, and took me below to his stateroom where he sat me down in a chair, pulled back the coverings on his bed, then picked me up, unwrapped the blanket he'd put around me in his truck and dried me off, threw a pair of his pajamas on me, and put me down on the bed and covered me with warm cotton sheets and a heavy ivory comforter I had given him because I liked it. Then he turned up the cabin's heat and stepped back and studied me like he might consider a critical experiment.

Sarah was standing behind him as he satisfied himself that I was warming up and would be safe enough.

"Why did she go in the ocean?" Sarah asked, looking worriedly at me.

"To save Alvie Weather," said Jefferson Davis. "The silly bastard had fallen in or jumped in or who knows what. I swear this woman wouldn't know the meanin' of the word caution if it strode in and hit her upside the head."

"Please do not talk about me as though I am not in the room," I said, my teeth still playing chopsticks in my mouth.

"Do you want some peppermint tea, Cash?" Sarah said. I nodded assent. "With lemon and honey?" she said. Again I nodded. I was trying to tame my teeth.

"Get her some food, too, Sarah," my blond and blue-eyed knight in shining armor said. "There's no tellin' how many calories she depleted during that little swim in the ocean or what it cost her. I've got Canadian bacon and eggs, and she likes those scone things that y'all are always makin'. The ones I have are store bought, but they're good. She needs a solid dose of fuel."

We heard a commotion on deck, and then it stopped. Sarah had walked into the galley to see about food and Stella Conroy burst into the stateroom. "Y'all okay?" she said to me. I nodded. It seemed to me that nodding might be in my future.

"Well, I can't say it's a wise thing you did, jumpin' into the Atlantic Ocean in November, but it was for certain productive. And there's at least one person who's more than a little beholdin' to you, even if he is a twit."

"Keep him away from me," Jefferson Davis said crossly to her. "I might level him." I reached out and took his hand and made him turn and look at me.

"Not his fault," I said. My teeth were quieting down. "He's dealing with the devil and isn't himself. He's a nice man."

"She's right, Jefferson." Stella Conroy said to her ex-brother-in-law in her most soothing tone of voice. "Alvie's not anythin' like how he's behavin' now. He's eccentric, I'll grant. But right this minute, he's stretched beyond his limits and damn it to hell he's got that disastrous Ambien creatin' havoc, runnin' through his system. Cooper threw him in a hot shower with his clothes still on, and he still has no idea where he is and what's really goin' on, although I expect that dip in the ocean did not help his sense of confusion any. We'll have all we can do to be certain he makes sense to that concierge banker of his."

Jesse Shine walked into the state room carrying a tray with a big cup of tea and a scone on it. "This here's from Miss Sarah, boss," he said to Jefferson. "She says to tell y'all it's a first stallment and it's for your girlfriend there." He nodded at me. "She's real good lookin' boss, even though she ain't a blond." As he made this preferential pronouncement, he turned and gave Stella Conroy a dazzling grin. "You look like that woman did Base Insinc," he said to her. "I had her picture once. She's my favorite. Y'all hooked up?" he asked.

Stella Conroy glanced at him absentmindedly and ran the fingers of her left hand through his hair. She seemed unconcerned that she had not a clue who the hell he was. Maybe, I thought to myself, this is another clear divide between the north and the south. Up where I was born and lived most of my life, we'd have been calling the cops and the social workers and screaming bloody murder if a child we did not know somehow wandered into our midst.. Here, they were, in Jefferson's words, fixing to find out who he was. It might have signaled a clue to sociologists who study the differences that geography and history provide, but to me it was unfathomable.

I looked at the kid and wondered all over again: whose child was he, where had he come from, were there people actively looking for him, and why had Jefferson Davis decided to get involved?

CHAPTER SIX

Mallory Weather had not heard the voice of a human being except her own in what felt like an eternity to her, although it was roughly a day and a half since she'd been kidnapped right out of her own house by what she assumed were at least two people. Someone had walked up behind her as she was about to pour herself a cup of coffee after her morning jog, knocked her unconscious, and taken her to wherever she was now.

Neither had she seen a human face, although there was one person around, who occasionally fed her bits of dry bread and cheese and water, and who had twice released her long enough to go to a bathroom somewhere behind a screen in this small room. That person was in some kind of black costume, she thought, and wore a mask that completely covered both the face and neck of whoever it was. She had wondered more than once if she were on a boat, but she'd been unable to detect any motion, so she'd concluded that she was not being held on water, although she hadn't completely dismissed the idea of a boat in storage.

Wherever she was, however, had no windows at all and no doors that she could see, and was not really what she'd ever call habitable space. And it was mostly dark, although there was one bare light bulb that hung from the ceiling to her left. Her right eye, the one that got hit by an elbow when she'd struggled against one of the kidnappers, was paining her. The pain seemed to burrow into her forehead like a sharp ache where it settled somewhere behind her bruised eyeball.

She hoped against hope that her somewhat scattered husband would carry through with what the people who had kidnapped her asked for. He had always suffered from what she'd come to call a disease of the attention span. He was a good man, she knew, but he wasn't always one who coped well with the stresses of life that came his way.

He wasn't what she'd characterize as weak, exactly. You didn't amass the kind of fortune that Alvie had by being a weakling. It was more that he needed to know there was support around, somewhere handy, in case he needed to lean on it. They had told him not to call the police, and he was a literal man and he always followed directions, so there'd be no cops for him to count on. Nevertheless, she knew he'd have to call on help from someone, and she truly hoped it wasn't her idiot brother who would only make things worse by making Alvie afraid, which might paralyze him and make inaction more than a possibility. Because she knew in her heart they would not think twice to kill her if they did not get what they wanted.

Maybe he'd chosen to rely on his manager at the dealership. Mallory liked him. He was smart and competent and well-spoken and he would be able to help Alvie navigate the instructions he had been given. She decided that yes, more than likely he had picked his manager to help him and that made her feel a bit better, and the ache behind her right eye seemed to ease a bit. All Alvie really needed was the help of a good man he could trust. She guessed that was all anybody really needed. I wonder if I can fall asleep, thought Mallory Weather, so she closed her eyes and quieted her mind as best she could, and hoped that sleep would come to her.

Jesse Shine's homestead outside of Varnumtown could have been mistaken for a landfill. The sprawling lot of sand held dozens of starving small scrub oaks, four car carcasses, five skeletal television antennas, an abandoned outhouse, three signs that admonished you to beware of dog, an empty cargo bed long abandoned by its truck, two dead chickens, and countless bicycle wheels without spokes. The backdrop to this stark art of poverty was a tar-paper shack with no discernable windows. A door that hung by one hinge flopped back and forth whenever a breeze hit it. A long-forgotten door knocker said "welcome." It might as well have said "welcome to hell."

Hollis Shine, the owner of this desolation, had a hangover he knew could surely kill him. He was lying on a wooden table that rested on the ground at the back of his house and he had no idea how he had come to be there. But Hollis was not an introspective man. He was an angry one. And he was thirsty. If he didn't get a drink right quick, he knew he was dead.

"Where in hell is that fuckin' slut," he muttered to himself as he slowly sat up on the old picnic table. He was speaking of his wife, whose given name was Rose. "Hey," he yelled. The stab of pain that shot through his temples made him lower his head to his hands.

A back door opened and a slight, pale woman peered out at him. "What's it, Hollis," she said.

"Gimme a beer," he said in a quiet voice. "Quick like." He was rubbing both of his temples, his head still bowed. He glanced to his left and saw his twenty-two lying half off the table bench. He had a momentary flash memory of shooting something or someone last night. He pushed the memory under his mental radar.

"There ain't but one," Rose said. "I gotta walk to the Scotchman store, see can I swipe that food stamp card for more. If Sally ain't on, likely I can't."

"Then you'd best be certain she is," he said, nudging his toe against his twenty-two. The indifference that animated his wife's face might have indicated she was a member of the walking dead. She turned and retreated into the shack. A minute later, she was back.

"Here," she said to him, handing him the last can of beer. "I'll be back in a bit."

"Send Jesse," he said to her. Then he raised the can and drained half of it in one gulp. "They look different on kids they do grownups. Besides which he is faster than you. He can steal it, he has to."

"He ain't here," she said matter of factly.

"What the hell does that mean," he said. "Where is the little bastard?"

"Gone," she said and turned to walk to the store.

Hollis Shine felt the effect the beer had on his psyche. "Fine," he said to her back. "Good riddance to bad rubbish." Then he cackled. "One less mouth to feed, anyways. Buy a bag of pork rinds go with that beer."

By the time I'd finally got my body temperature back to normal and had eaten enough food for two people and dressed in clothes that Stella had fetched from the cottage, I was once again ready to face the day. Cooper Grey and Jeff Davis had dealt with Alvie, even drying off his clothes in Jefferson's dryer, and Coop had told us a few minutes ago that Alvie was finally awake and aware enough to call his concierge banker to order the money be made available to Stella and me for pick up.

Sarah, meanwhile, had spoken with her sound engineer friend Dodge, who had volunteered to bring a portable version of the equipment over to the cottage, with the software we needed to access and assess background noises. He was due to arrive late in the afternoon. It was now nearly three o'clock, so Jefferson was getting ready to drive Sarah home to the cottage, along with Alvie and Jesse Shine. We would all convene there when Stella and I finished the bank run.

After thinking about it for a while, Cooper Grey had suggested to Stella Conroy that we might want to consider placing a small GPS tracking device in with the money if it became clear we'd be delivering the ransom. Both Stella and I were concerned that if the kidnappers somehow found the tracker and dumped it, they would conclude that police were somehow involved and decide to kill Mallory Weather before they disappeared with the money in hand. We agreed to weigh the question some more before making a final decision, so Cooper told us he'd drop by his condo on his way to the cottage and pick up a device that was left over from his bounty hunting days.

"They're so small now, they might go unnoticed for days," he said to us as he left the boat to get his car. "I'll see you later," and he gave his wife a little kiss on the cheek. Jefferson and Sarah disembarked right after he did, with Alvie and the kid carrying all her equipment. Alvie looked mostly awake for the first time since I'd met him. The kid looked happy.

Stella and I were headed back to the Landfall area of Wilmington. Alvie Weather's financial institution was a branch of First Bank, located on Eastwood Drive, quite close to where his home was. We pulled into the parking lot, then walked into the bank where Alvie had told us to ask for Michael Murphy. Once called, Mr. Murphy quickly hustled into the room carrying a black leather satchel and looking nervous.

"He looks like the quintessential poster boy for bankers," Stella said to me, "with that fat moon face and those jowls and eyeglasses without frames, and his white shirt and gray suit, and that mournful expression on his face like somebody died." She gave him a little wave. He nodded and headed over to us. I thought he looked like Karl Rove and felt a little sorry for him.

"May I see your identifications, ladies" he said quietly to us. "Especially your work and driver's licenses." We obliged, and he satisfied himself that we were who we said we were and that it would be safe for him to entrust us with two million dollars of his client's money. The exchange was made and we turned to leave the bank. I felt a tap on my right shoulder and looked back at him. "Is mum to be the word?" he said to me. I forced myself to avoid a laugh.

"Yes," I said seriously. "Mum is indeed the word."

"I have honored and will honor that request and tell no one," he said solemnly, "until and when I may hear otherwise."

"Thank you," I said. "We appreciate your discretion. There are lives at stake."

"Although impossibly compromised and clichéd," he said with the ghost of a smile, "discretion is, after all, the better part of valor." And with that, he turned and walked back to his office.

I dismissed my earlier, purely physical, comparison. Karl Rove would never have exhibited such an empathic concern to save his soul, assuming he had one.

By this time, Stella Conroy was back at the Mustang, putting the satchel with the money into the trunk of her car. I quickened my step and crossed the lot. We made good time driving back to the beach, and when we pulled up and parked at the cottage on Beach House Lane, I glanced at my watch. It was a little after four o'clock in the afternoon and we had a lot of work to do before tomorrow when we would again be hearing from the kidnappers.

When Stella and I walked into the great room, we saw only Sarah, who was sitting at the dining table peeling an orange and drinking what looked like club soda. She had changed her clothes and was now wearing a pair of jeans with a Georgetown University sweatshirt. She had a pair of flip-flops on her feet. Her hair needed combing.

"Minerva got away from me," she said. "She was chasing a big mouse and took off for the avenue so I had to run her down. Why are you staring at me, Cash? Is my hair a mess?"

Minerva is the calico cat who adopted us when we moved to the beach a year and a half ago, and she's got a mind of her own, by which I mean she keeps both of us on our toes all the time because she has the heart of a rebel and the stamina of a lion and the loudest yowl I have ever heard.

I have always maintained that by naming her after the Roman goddess of wisdom and war, I unknowingly released a warrior princess. But we love her, although I secretly believe that given a choice, Stella Conroy would happily drop her in the middle of the Atlantic Ocean or feed her to a shark. It isn't an idea I choose to share with anyone, especially Stella.

"It could use a comb," I said. "Where's the she-devil now?"

"I let that kid Jesse take an old computer of mine and load some games on it so he's back in my study playing and Minerva went with him. She seems to want to keep an eye on him for some reason."

"Where's Alvie at?" Stella said.

"He and the boys are sitting on the other side of the dune or walking on the beach. Now that Alvie's awake, he's so nervous he can't stay still. Cooper and Jefferson are trying to calm him down by wearing him out. The NIH ought to take a closer look at that Ambien," she said. "It's not safe for people."

I wandered into the kitchen area and looked around. There was a dish of shelled pistachios on the counter, and I grabbed a handful. Shelled pistachios are one of life's great luxuries. "How about a drink, Stella?" I said.

"I am due," she said. "Hell, I am overdue."

"What'll it be?" I asked.

"Surprise me," she said and walked outside to smoke a cigarette.

"Sarah?" I said.

"I wouldn't say no to a glass of zinfandel," she said.

I poured Sarah a glass of the wine and made two sweet manhattans from a bottle of bourbon that Tallahassee Bodine had dropped off from the Sawtelle still. "Enjoy," I said to Sarah, giving her the glass.

Then I walked outside and handed one of the drinks to Stella Conroy, touched glasses with her, said, "Up the Irish," which made her grin, and took a solid sip of a drink that ranks right up there with the best of them.

"How do you figure this to play out," she said to me, after putting out her cigarette in an ashtray that was on a little deck table.

"Well," I said, "I'm not really a cockeyed optimist. But neither am I a cynic. I've been thinking about Coop's suggestion of the GPS tracker."

"Yeah," she said. "Me too. It's true it's a gamble if they notice it. But how many people take time to dump a bunch of money out of a satchel to see if there's somethin' there that's gonna give them problems."

"There's an easy way to avoid that whole thing, Stella," I said. "We just put it on Alvie, if he's going to be delivering the ransom, and we follow him at a far enough distance that we aren't noticed."

"Uh huh," she said. "And that way we could take two cars, which makes it much easier to disguise a tail."

"Yes," I said.

We each turned at the sound of a vehicle travelling down Beach House Lane.

"Must be Sarah's friend Dodge," I said. A small yellow van was coming along at a slow pace.

"Well," said Stella Conroy, draining her drink, "let's go see can we decipher background noises enough to figure out where Mallory's at, make this ransom business moot. That would be an endin' we could all appreciate."

If either one of us considered that possibility to be highly unlikely, we chose, at this moment, to keep it to ourselves.

CHAPTER SEVEN

The guy who was most likely Sarah's friend climbed out of his van and walked over to us. "I'm Carlton Ball," he said to me and stuck out his hand. "Everybody calls me Dodge." He didn't smile, and his accent was nothing I recognized, it was so uninflected.

"I'm not surprised," I said and looked at him. He was a square-built, muscular guy about five-feet-six with a black crew cut and a nose that had been broken at least twice in his life. It wandered back and forth across his face until it stopped with a downward slant that almost made it touch his upper lip. In different lighting, it might have given him a sinister look. Now, it made him interesting to contemplate. That and his deep green eyes. He wore a pair of black corduroy slacks beneath a bulky sweater the color of oatmeal. His choice of footwear was a pair of tan construction boots.

"I'm Cash Delaney," I said and shook his hand, "and she's Stella Conroy."

"I like those earrings," Stella said to him. "What are they? A carat each?"

Dodge was sporting a sparkling diamond stud in each of his earlobes. "I guess," he said. "I didn't ask. They were a gift. Where's the divine Miss Ehrenson? I've got the stuff she needs." His voice was pleasantly deep and mellow.

"She's inside," I said to him. "Do you need a hand?"

"No thanks, I can handle it." He walked to the rear of his van and picked up a large square computer screen. I opened the front door for him, and Sarah stood up and said, "Thanks for doing this, Dodge. My study's in back. Just follow me."

A few minutes later, he came out and returned to his van. This time he carried a rectangular thing that was something or other into the cottage. He and Sarah again disappeared into the back where she did the bulk of her work.

"Why don't you see if you can scare up the boys," I said to Stella. "Cooper and Jefferson will want to be in on this for sure, whether or not Alvie does."

At that moment, all three of them sprinted up and over the dune. They looked chilly and windblown, and Alvie looked tired but alert, almost hyper. "That guy Dodge with the special software stuff we need is here," Stella said to them. "Y'all ready to take a look and a listen?"

When the five of us entered the cottage, the kid was standing in front of the television set. "Minnie and I are stayin' out here and watchin' a show on TV," he said. "Law'n Order SUV. Okay, boss? Miss Sarah allowed how she didn't cotton us bein' underfoot. Minnie's a pistol. She gets under everything." Minerva was sitting sedately on one of the wicker chairs that she sometimes tries to eat. Her ears twitched at the sound of the word "Minnie."

"That's fine," Jefferson said to him. "But don't let her out and don't y'all go out either. If you're hungry, take a look in the refrigerator. You comin' back to watch, Alvie?"

"I'll sit with the boy," said Alvie Weather. "I don't need another upheaval in my stomach or my mind."

We squeezed into Sarah's study as Dodge and Sarah were transferring the Skype video from Sarah's cell phone to the large computer screen that Dodge had brought. Then he hooked up the spectrographic software to the screen and began to fiddle with a bunch of dials.

"We'll start with the foreground sound," he said, "and move our way through to the deepest background noises. Sarah tells me you heard only voices in the foreground, but there may be other sounds we can identify with this software. So put your listening caps on. Here we go."

The first thing we heard was the voice-altered message that introduced us to what followed, the voice of Mallory Weather begging her husband to do as the kidnappers had asked. Then, the altered voice returned with its goodbye message. Everything was as clear as a bell, but the voices were all we heard.

"We'll deal with the voice alteration later," Dodge said, as he adjusted a couple of dials. "Let's listen to that again." The computer-like voice began to speak again. Before it finished, I heard a noise I couldn't immediately identify in the background.

"What was that?" I said.

"It sounded like compressed air," Sarah said.

I thought about that for a minute. "Play it again please," I said to Dodge. "Can you raise it above the voice?"

"Maybe," he said. "Skype does not deliver good sound quality." He turned another dial just slightly and replayed the sound. The voice receded and the noise increased.

"It's air brakes," Cooper Grey said suddenly. "Big cross-country multi-transport trucks come equipped with them."

"They're all over the Port of Wilmington," Jefferson said, looking at me. "Longshoremen must off-load four or five cargo ships a week at those docks."

"Well," Stella said, "unfortunately there's other places got 'em, too. They haul heavy equipment, aerospace products, construction debris, perishables, and a whole host of light manufacturing. They took over from when Wilmington quit the railroads. So the sound of an airbrake won't find us Mallory."

"It probably does mean your victim isn't stuck in some farmer's barn in the middle of a corn field," Dodge said. "Let's drill down and see if we can get closer to a likely location."

When Dodge had obscured the first two sound levels in favor of the third, a noise that sounded like a click, followed by something whirring, became audible. A thin pitch followed that.

"Someone turned on an interior fan," I said.

"I heard a whistle after that," Stella said.

"Can you isolate the whistle sound?" Jefferson asked.

We heard a short blast and then a longer one.

"Stella," Cooper Grey said, "I'm beginning to be convinced we really are listening to the life of the docks. That whistle sounded like a cargo ship's arrival coming into port."

"There's one last level," said Dodge. And he turned a small knob a quarter inch. And there it was in the vast distance: a fog horn.

"It's for certain the docks," Jefferson said.

"Well," said Stella, "we've got the night to take a look."

We all heard a loud crash from the great room. Jefferson Davis jumped up and ran out. Everybody followed. The kid and Alvie Weather were each on their hands and knees on the kitchen floor, carefully picking up what looked like big shards of glass. There was food all around them, and Minerva was helping herself to what appeared to be a carrot. The crazy cat loves carrots.

"What happened?" Jeff Davis asked.

"Alvie wouldn't give Minnie a treat," said Jesse Shine. "He said it weren't good a cat ate people food."

"Jesus Christ," said Sarah, sounding really annoyed.

"That doesn't answer my question," Jeff Davis said to the kid.

"Minnie tripped him up," said the kid, looking at Jefferson and grinning his approval. Alvie Weather was busily avoiding us and continued to gather up the broken pieces of a platter. The remains of yesterday's pot roast and vegetable dinner was still being enjoyed by Minerva.

"I'm sorry," Alvie finally whispered.

"Pick her up before she pukes and makes it worse," Sarah said to me.

I did what I was told and carried the cat back to the laundry room and shut the door. Minerva gave one of her most devastating yowls in protest.

As I was returning to the great room, Mickey Huntley walked into the cottage, noticed the gathering in the kitchen, stared at the mess on the floor, looked at Sarah and said, "I realize you are dedicated to trying the traditions of other cultures where different dining arrangements prevail. But this Pakistani notion of eating on the floor does not appeal to me at all."

"It was Minerva's idea," Sarah said. "She was hungry."

CHAPTER EIGHT

Once we had cleaned up the kitchen, we returned to Sarah's study, this time with Mickey Huntley in tow. We had also dragged Alvie Weather along, because Sarah didn't want to lock up Minerva for something she wasn't really responsible for, and she didn't want Alvie around the cat. Minerva rejoined the kid at the TV set.

"So you think they've got her stashed at the docks," the lawyer said to me.

"Yes," I said.

"Have you any idea what kind of ground the Port of Wilmington covers?" Mickey asked. "Hundreds of acres. It'd take a platoon of people about a week to do a proper search, and even then there are so many crevices and crannies all over that place they still might be unable to locate a person being held there."

"We can't be deterred by how unlikely our efforts may be, Mick," Stella Conroy said. "Y'all know somethin' about the futility of things, bein' a defense attorney. We just gotta give it our best shot."

"Most of my antique and collectible cars come to my showroom every month through the port," Alvie Weather said quietly. "I have rented a good bit of cargo space there for years because we do not always need all of the autos that come in and we have to store them.

We even keep a small office open there for matters of lading. My manager is often on site to see that things are progressin' as they should."

Everybody in the room, even Dodge, turned and stared at him. Then I looked at Stella Conroy and wondered could it really be that simple? Could we actually find Mallory among the automobiles being stored in the cargo space that her husband leased from the port?

"Can you pull up a map of the port?" Cooper Grey asked Dodge.

"Sure," he said. "Stand over here by me, Mr. Weather, and show us where your rented space is located."

Alvie was faltering and sweating again. I did not take this to be a good sign. "Are you feeling okay, Alvie?" I said to him.

"I think I am goin' to faint," he said, reaching awkwardly for Stella. She grabbed his shoulder just as he began to pitch forward and got in front of him to prevent him from falling on his face. Cooper Grey stepped behind him and lifted him out of Stella's arms and looked around, seeing a computer chair in a corner of the room. "Wheel that chair over here," he said to me. So I did.

Once Alvie was slumped in it, Cooper tilted his head back and braced it with his left hand. Then he started to pat Alvie's cheeks. In a couple of minutes, Alvie's eyes fluttered and then he opened them. This time he did not appear to be suffering from confusion, although the first words out of his mouth seemed to contradict that.

He glanced at Stella and said, "There have been some difficulties with accounting matters that I have been experiencing lately at the showroom." If he expected any of us to be able to interpret his somewhat obtuse statement, he was sadly misguided.

"We can discuss accounting later, Alvie," Stella Conroy said to him, sounding annoyed. "Right now, just show us where you store your cars."

The map that Dodge had pulled up was color coded. Alvie Weather wheeled his chair over close and looked at it. "See where they indicate transit sheds?" he asked. Everybody nodded. "My space is in the middle section of the shed on the far right. It's about 4,000 square feet, give or take. The office's just a cubby really. We threw it up ourselves to gain a little privacy. Maybe three hundred feet in the back left corner of the space. Y'all get to it off Burnett Avenue, not Shipyard Boulevard."

"How do they control access?" Jefferson asked him.

"The security system there is top of the line. After 9/11, North Carolina didn't mess around," Alvie said. "If y'all are comin' off a boat, they give you a badge. Land access is controlled by smart cards. Their command center is real high tech, and it's redundant with the Port of Morehead City. Can't just anybody wander around those grounds without they get stopped and interrogated. The whole place is live-videoed twenty-four hours a day."

"There must be a way for visitors to gain access," I said. "It's not as though it's a prison."

"Well," Alvie said to me, "I've got a certain number of badges I can devote to visitors. The gate's got the corresponding numbers and whenever I send somebody over who wants to look at a car, that person shows the badge and they let him in."

"But you and certain members of your staff are regulars," Mickey Huntley said. "The guards all know you, you don't set off any alarm bells, and you just run a smart card through a reader and drive right through and go about your business. Right?"

"Yes," Alvie said. He was whispering.

"And that is why you mentioned some accounting difficulties," the lawyer said.

"Yes," he whispered again.

"Whom do you suspect, Alvie?" Mickey Huntley said. I realized I was holding my breath and let it out.

"I don't know," he said. "I have to think on it."

"Well," Stella said in that no-nonsense voice of hers, "while y'all are thinkin', we might as well break down that funny soundin' voice on that Skype video."

"I wonder if there might be a little somethin' to drink," Alvie said to nobody in particular. He stood up and started to walk back to the front of the cottage.

"No," I said to him, which stopped him in his tracks. "You stay here with us. Jefferson will get you some water, or soda, but we need to see if you recognize the voice once we've cleaned it up."

"I'd welcome a soda," he said as Jeff Davis left the room.

Dodge had been switching software and now was playing with a bunch of sound waves that looked like different colored lines running across his computer screen. The altered voice said again, "I assume this satisfies your sophomoric requirement and that you will now proceed to gather the amount of money requested. You will be contacted tomorrow regarding the exchange."

Dodge did something that slowed the voice way down so that it sounded like an improbable basso profundo coming from the depths of a well. He fiddled some more and the words came out in a rush in a high pitch, as though whoever was speaking was overloaded on speed.

"It doesn't want to settle," he said. "I can't seem to get away from the exaggerations, the extremes. This is odd."

"Are there different parameters you'd use for a female voice?" I asked.

"Of course," he said, and he flipped a switch and another bunch of sound waves came up. After a bit of work, he hit a little arrow in the middle of the screen, and what we heard was high and lightweight, like the voice of a southern teenage girl. She sounded like an air head.

I looked at Alvie. "I have no idea at all who that is," he said. "I've never heard that voice before in my life."

I noticed Sarah. She was looking at copies of the emails we had received earlier from the kidnappers. "What's on your mind, Sarah?" I said to her.

"These emails both use the pronoun 'we'," she said. "The speaker on the Skype video doesn't. She says 'I'. And when the kidnappers first contacted Alvie, they said there would be no phone calls. They didn't want him to hear their voices."

"So, what's that mean?" Stella said. "They somehow entice a girl to record what they want her to say?"

"Think about it. Someone offers you twenty or fifty or even a hundred bucks and asks you to read a sentence or two into a microphone as a joke on someone, and you decide the message is harmless, what do you do if you're just a kid?" Sarah Ehrenson looked at each of us. "You do it, of course, and then you forget about it, go to the mall and shop."

"So we've got an unrelated voice," Cooper said.

"It certainly looks that way to me," Sarah said.

Jefferson finally came back to the room and handed Alvie a glass of something resembling ginger ale. I brought him up to speed.

"These are smart people," he said. "And if they are keeping her at the transit shed, y'all might want to consider askin' the port security force for help."

"Why don't you call your manager, Alvie," Stella said. "See if he's been over there these last couple days, noticed anything out of the ordinary."

"All right," Alvie said to her. "Do y'all know where my phone is?"

"Right now it's out of commission," I said. "It went in the ocean with you." I handed him my phone. I thought he looked embarrassed, remembering his dip in the Atlantic.

He dialed a number and then said, "Hello Margie." And he paused. "Yes, I'm takin' a couple days. Can y'all connect me with George?" Alvie paused. "Oh? Did he say why?" Another pause. "I see. Okay, then, Margie, y'all make sure you mind things, hear? We don't want anybody runnin' off with one of our little beauties." Alvie ended the call. "I am now goin' to call his home," he said to the room. "He called in sick today; said he had the flu. It might could be true."

Again he dialed a number. When no one answered, he ended the call and handed the phone back to me. "George is not at work," he said. "George is not at home. George is not a frivolous man. He lives alone, he does not have a wife, I am the only real friend he has, and he now appears to be missin'."

"Could George be our guy, Alvie?" Stella said to him.

"It's possible," he said, "maybe even probable, I consider it. He has been havin' a little problem with his income and expense reports these past few months."

"How little a problem, Alvie," Mickey Huntley asked him.

"Oh, maybe a few hundred thousand, half a million. That may sound like a lot, but it isn't really. Not in my business. I stumbled over it a week ago. But he's worked for me for years. All's he had to do was talk to me, if he's in some sort of trouble. He's no thief and it's a murky, tricky line of work, with car theft being what it is. Why in the world he would choose to kidnap my wife as a way out of whatever mess he may have gotten himself in, I just can't think. It makes no sense to me at all."

'Well," I said, "it may make no sense to anybody else in the entire world. But for some reason, it makes perfect sense to George."

CHAPTER NINE

Stella Conroy and I were a few hundred feet from the Burnett Street entrance to the Port of Wilmington. I was driving the big Mercedes van that Sarah had bought to get us from Ithaca to Carolina Beach, and Stella was holding the smart card that Alvie had given her, which would grant us access to the docks. It was seven o'clock in the evening and already pitch black. There was no moon, save a sliver on the horizon. But when we pulled up to the entrance to the docks, there were plenty of flood lights illuminating the open areas. Seeing where we were going would not be a problem.

Stella swiped the card through the reader, and we were in. I headed toward the river. The transit sheds where Alvie rented his space were next to it. As we drove into the interior of the port, darkness became the more prevalent condition. I could see cameras up on poles on either side of us, and I expected they were following our progress in the command center if every camera was live, which I assumed it was. We were now in a part of the port that was illuminated by spots rather than floods, and shadows danced around the various shapes of the buildings and trucks and cranes and cargo holds.

As we pulled alongside the shed where Alvie kept his cars, my cell phone vibrated. I took it out of my pocket and looked at it. Sarah was calling me.

I hit speaker phone so Stella could hear. "We're in position," I said to her, "outside the transit shed. Is there a problem?"

"Probably," she said. "Alvie just got another email on his computer. All it said was there'd been a change of plans and that they would be in touch. What do you make of it?"

Stella and I looked at each other and then she shrugged. "We can't make anythin' out of it," she said to Sarah. "So we're goin' in to see if this is where she is or was and if she's gone, there's a fuckin' clue left for us to follow. We'll get back to you soon as we know somethin'."

We got out of the van and walked up to the front of the transit shed. There was a wide door on sliders that was padlocked. "It's a Master Lock," I said. "Maybe we should have taken the time to get the key from Alvie's house. I don't want to shoot the damn thing off. I didn't bring my silencer."

Stella Conroy had taken a set of instruments from her coat pocket. She removed a tension wrench, stuck it into the keyhole and held it where she wanted it. Then she inserted the lock pick and began feeling her way through the tumblers. In a few minutes, I heard a click and she swung the hoop of the padlock to the side and removed it from the hasp. We both stood back a bit and drew our guns. She nodded to me and I moved to the door and slowly drew it open. The interior was totally silent and dark, although when I glanced I thought I could decipher shapes that were probably cars.

"I'm goin' in," she whispered to me. I nodded.

I looked again into the interior dark space and then I saw it: a thin silver wire she was about to breech. I moved so quickly to catch her, I stumbled, landed on my knees, and fell on my face. She looked back at me in exasperation.

"Stella," I hissed. "Stop." It was too late.

The moment her foot tripped the wire, the explosion that rocked the shed was deafening, throwing her up and out of the structure like a rag doll. She landed on her back, twenty feet beyond the Mercedes. It would have struck me full front, but I was low to the ground, and it knocked the wind out of me and shoved me face down, halfway in and halfway out of the now-destroyed shed. Sirens began blasting immediately.

I struggled to my feet and staggered over to Stella Conroy. She was unconscious and her coat had disintegrated. It lay in shreds around her. There was a deep and bleeding slash on her forehead that some flying piece of debris had caused. Her left leg was bent at an unusual angle. I dropped to her and put my finger on her neck to seek a pulse. I thought I found one, but I could not be sure. A security van pulled up next to me as I tried to assess the damage that had been done to her. Two men walked over to me and picked me up and looked at me.

"My partner needs an ambulance," I managed to say. I was seeing double. My voice sounded like a croak. "She may be badly injured. You've got to help her." I had no idea where either of our guns had got to.

Another guard was on the ground, looking at Stella. "She's right about that," he said. "This one's in pretty bad shape, her pulse is weak. We ain't got time for an ambulance, we want her to survive. We gotta get her in the van and go right now. Call ahead to New Hanover," he said. "We'll sort the particulars later."

Ten minutes later, sirens still blaring, and with a crew of nurses and doctors standing at the emergency entrance to New Hanover Regional Hospital, the security cops from the Port of Wilmington handed an unconscious Stella Conroy over to a gurney manned by orderlies. People started doing things to her like attaching tubes and monitoring devices, and somebody opened one of Stella's eyes and said, "She may be hemorrhaging. Check the vitals again. Prep her for an exploratory. We may have to go in if we can't stabilize. There could be serious internal organ damage."

I was numb. The dock security forces had me surrounded in the emergency ward waiting room, and I felt as though I might pass out myself.

A nurse walked up to us. "This woman needs attention," she said to the port police.

"We've got to question her," said the guy who'd told the others to call an ambulance. "She blew up a building at the Port. It could be terrorism."

"That will have to wait," the nurse said, "unless you want to be hit with charges, or worse, have her death on your hands. Can't you see she's in shock? She may be bleeding in her brain. Do you know your name?" she said to me. I thought about that for a moment and realized it was in my best interest to say that I did not. I needed to get away from these cops. I had things that I had to do. And blow up a building? Terrorism? What the hell. These guys and their imaginations were nothing I could deal with right now.

"No," I said shakily. "I'm in a hospital?"

"Yes," the nurse said. She gave the security cops a disapproving look. "You can hang around here," she said to them, "or you can come back tomorrow. We are dealing with traumatic injury here. She isn't going anywhere."

When the nurse had installed me in a semi-private room without a roommate, she took my temperature and vitals and ordered a CAT scan and gave me a pitcher of water. Then she inquired if I wanted anything else. I looked at the phone on the bedside table. "Is it live?" I said to her hopefully.

"Yes," she said, and looked at me. "But I have to ask. Did you blow up a building? Are you a terrorist? Do I need to call our own security to stand outside your door? You don't look particularly dangerous to me." I had forgotten, since last year when Tallahassee Bodine had been brought here because of significant injuries, how kind these nurses were.

"No," I said. "We were there looking for someone who is in trouble. We were trying to locate her. Stella accidently tripped a wire that exploded the bomb. I need to know about how she is. I need to see her." I realized I was about to cry. I bit my tongue.

She studied me for a few moments. "So you do know who you are. Well, you're only a small distance from where they're treating your friend. She's in one of our evaluation rooms down the hall to your left. But she looks to be seriously injured and is still unconscious. And your blood pressure is way too high and that concerns me. We need to monitor it. The doctor will be along shortly."

When she'd gone I grabbed the phone and dialed an outside line. After five rings, Sarah said, "Hello?"

"It's me," I said. "Just listen. Stella tripped a wire in the transit shed that blew it to smithereens and threw her across the ground twenty feet or so. She's hurt. No one is certain, right now, just how serious her injuries are. We're at New Hanover Hospital and I don't know what they're doing to her at the moment, but they may have to operate. I'm scraped and bruised and I have a headache that could level an elephant, but I'm basically okay. They put me in room 211 and the security cops from the dock think that Stella and I exploded the bomb and that we're terrorists. I don't know whether they are still here waiting to talk to me or whether they have left but I do not have the patience or the stamina to deal with them in any case.

You have got to somehow keep Cooper from going haywire about Stella, so I leave it to you how much you want to tell him. The best choice may just be to say you don't know and let him talk to the doctors. Initial vagueness is often kind. I am wearing one of those ridiculous hospital gowns where my rear end is exposed, so when you come, bring me suitable clothes, including underwear. Everything I had on was ruined. Just tell Jefferson that I am fine and to please stay there with the kid and have Mickey drive you over here."

Sarah had listened to this in silence. When I stopped talking, she said pleasantly to me, "Of course, Cash. I'll get right on it. Shall I bring Alvie along? It might be helpful. He could probably straighten out that confusing issue you mentioned."

"That's a good idea, especially if the cops are still camped here. He'll be able to explain to them whatever the hell he wants them to know. But for Christ's sake, don't let him descend into hysteria."

"Okay, then, I'll make sure that doesn't happen. We'll see you in a bit."

As I hung up the phone, a handsome man who looked like a doctor walked in and said to me, "I hear you encountered an explosion tonight. That can be dangerous. How do you feel?"

I thought if I told him the truth, that I felt like a sack of shit, he might admit me, so I lied and said I was just fine and eager to know how my friend was doing.

"I believe they just prepped her for surgery," he said, as he began to probe my abdomen. "I don't know the details. The next time the nurse visits you, she should be able to give you more information. Does this hurt?" he asked, as he sunk his fingers into my lower belly. It hurt like hell.

"No," is what I said to him.

CHAPTER TEN

Sarah Ehrenson hung up the phone, glanced at everyone, and said, "May I see you for a minute in my study, Mickey?"

"What's goin' on," Jeff Davis asked.

"Nothing to be concerned about. I just need to check on something. We'll be right back," Sarah said, and headed quickly for the back of the cottage. When she and Mickey were in the room, she closed the door and said to the lawyer, "Stella tripped a bomb inside the transit shed. She's seriously, perhaps critically, injured. Cash is in a room in the hospital with what sounds to me like a concussion but she did not tell me that. We need to get over there with Alvie, because the port police think they planted the bomb and that they are terrorists.

We can't tell Cooper the extent of Stella's injuries or he will go ballistic, so say something palliative to him and we'll let the doctors tell him. I've got to grab some clothes for Cash. She says to leave Jefferson here with the kid. So can you round up Cooper and Alvie, and I'll be right out to join you. We may as well take Cooper's car; he'll be easier to handle if he's got to concentrate on driving. Thank God Dodge already left. He'd be seriously considering our hold on sanity if he was still here."

Mickey Huntley took in this information without comment, nodded and walked back to the great room. She went over to Cooper Grey and said to him, "There's been a bit of trouble, Coop. We have to go over to the hospital. I don't have details so we need to get a move on. Alvie, we want you to come along. Cash has told Sarah to tell you that she's okay, Jefferson, and that you should stay here with Jesse. We'll be back as soon possible."

"I can't just sit here," Jefferson Davis said, "and twiddle my thumbs."

"Please," Mickey said and looked hard at him. "Cash specifically asked that you stay with the child. I'll call with news. I promise."

Cooper Grey was frowning when he said to Mickey Huntley, "What is it you're not saying, Mickey?"

"Obviously, I'm not speculating about what I don't know, Cooper," the lawyer said. "And it's foolish for us to stand around here wondering when we should be heading over to the hospital to fill in the blanks."

Sarah Ehrenson hurried into the room with a small suitcase in her hand. "Everyone all set?" she said easily. "Let's take your car, Coop. It's a lot more comfortable than Mickey's." She took Alvie Weather by the elbow and walked him to the cottage door.

"Make damn sure y'all call me," Jeff Davis said. "Better still, have Katherine call me. Or I'll be drivin' over there to see for myself what's really goin' on."

The kid hadn't made a peep as the situation unfolded. Now, he said to Sarah, "Tell Miss Stella and Miss Cash we're thinkin' on 'em. I know they're fine. But still, y'all tell 'em. Thinkin' on friends always helps."

The Port of Wilmington Security Force had called the FBI, and by the time that Sarah Ehrenson and company walked into the hospital's emergency room entrance, they were getting ready to converge on room 211 and question their terrorist suspect, Cash Delaney.

"What the fuck," Cooper Grey said. "Are those guys here because of Cash and Stella?"

"Yes," Sarah said. "I didn't say earlier, but Stella tripped a bomb that exploded and blew up the transit shed. Consequently, the port cops and the feds think they're terrorists. That's why Alvie is here. He's going to explain it to them. Would you like your lawyer to go with you, Alvie? Mickey can probably cut through the bullshit faster than you can."

Alvie Weather looked at Mickey Huntley and said, "I can't be tellin' them about Mallory without they'd make it worse. They'd put her at even more risk."

"I'll handle it, Alvie. Give me five dollars," Mickey Huntley said. "That hires me and ensures that privilege applies. You say as little as possible, but agree with whatever I say. All right?"

Alvie Weather nodded, and he and Mickey Huntley walked over to the cops.

"Evening, gentlemen," Mickey Huntley said to the group of law enforcement officers. "I expect you're here to inquire about the circumstances surrounding the detonation of a bomb earlier tonight at the Port of Wilmington. I am Attorney Michael Huntley and this is my client, Alvie Weather. Mr. Weather is the lessee of the transit shed in question. How may we help you with questions you must have?"

"Two women blew that shed to hell and back," said an FBI agent whose name tag identified him as David Keating. "We investigate all potential terrorist acts, and we're about to question one of the perps about this one."

"You are not in possession of all the facts," Mickey Huntley said. "Mr. Weather hired the women to go to that shed, and he gave them his smart card to assure their access to the port. He suspected that one of his employees was stealing from him. Mr. Weather is in the antique car business, and several costly autos have gone missing over this past month. The wire that caused the explosion was accidently tripped when one of the two women failed to notice it and breeched it. So these individuals, both of whom are licensed private investigators, are victims rather than perpetrators. But you are right about one thing: someone rigged that shed to explode, and whoever it was is still at large."

The FBI guy didn't say anything. He cleared his throat, looked over his shoulder at the other men standing behind him, then turned back and said to Alvie Weather, "Is what she just said true?"

"It is absolutely true, sir," Alvie said. "I am the owner of Port City Antique and Collectible Autos and I lease that space for cars I need to store. I am most distressed that these investigators, who are also my friends, have walked into harm's way on my behalf. And unless you choose to hold me for some reason, I would like to go to inquire as to how they both are doin'."

"Is it the whole truth?" asked Agent Keating.

"Sir?" Alvie Weather said.

"It is what we know right now," Mickey Huntley interjected. "I expect there will be more to learn once the crime scene is investigated. But we leave that to you. Here's my card," she said, handing one to Agent Keating. "We will be happy to go over any more questions that might arise as things progress. We are as anxious as you to learn what really happened at that shed. But right now, we are going to see to the welfare of these injured women."

Agent David Keating nodded. He said to Alvie Weather, "We'll be seeing more of you, Mr. Weather. I'll be in touch." Half a minute later, all of the law enforcers had left the hospital building.

"You do have a concussion, Ms. Delaney," the handsome doctor said to me. "It's not life-threatening but it shows clearly on the scan. You will most likely be living with a decent-sized headache for a week." Sarah was sitting in a chair next to the window. She was watching me very carefully as if there was something I might do or say to make his pronouncement obvious to everyone. So I just sat there on the bed and kept quiet. It seemed the wisest choice.

"Are you admitting her, doctor?" Sarah asked him.

"I could," he said to her, "if I had a reason to believe she would ignore the instructions she needs to follow at home. Do you think there might be a reason?" He was looking at Sarah appreciatively, the way men do, and paying no attention to me at all, so I gave her the fish eye. I did not want to be admitted. I am not happy in hospitals. Nobody knows this better than Sarah. But I knew what she was thinking, which was something along the lines of "better safe than sorry." Finally, I thought I saw her relent.

"I don't think so," she said. "Cash is fairly diligent when it comes to matters of health. She'll be fine. And I'll make doubly sure of that."

"My own Nurse Jackie," I muttered. Sarah looked at me and stood up. She opened the suitcase she'd brought and laid out my clothes on the bed.

"If you'll have her discharge papers ready, doctor, we'll get out of here when she's changed her clothes," she said to the sadly unsuspecting man who was still gazing openly at her, angling for a physical encounter. I hoped to hell he didn't start to drool.

This sort of attention is not always something that Sarah handles tactfully, so I mentally crossed my fingers until she said, "And thank you for your kindness and your courtesy. If you'll just excuse us now, I'll get her dressed."

That shook him out of his romantic fantasy. "Oh," he said, "of course. And it's been my pleasure. Just stop at the nurse's station when you leave. Everything will be waiting for you. I'll include some high-strength ibuprofen. It'll temper the headache pain. Just be sure she doesn't overdose."

When he'd left, I grinned and said to her, "If you ever need another doctor in a New York minute, he's your man."

"Shut up and get dressed," she said. I stood up and started to grab my clothes just as Cooper Grey walked in.

"Stella's out of surgery," he said in a rush. "They had to repair two ribs that cracked in the explosion. That stopped the internal bleeding they were worried about. They said it was a miracle she didn't suffer what they called a coup contrecoup head injury that apparently could have killed her. One of the nurses said it was most likely because she was a good distance from the point of the explosion.

The surgeon told me everything went fine and they think she'll wake up in a little while, and that she can probably go home in a day or two. He told me she'd be disagreeable for a while because the healing ribs will be painful. But hell, when isn't she pissed off about something? The rest of the stuff is mostly cosmetic, although there's a chance she'll have a sizable scar on her forehead and maybe on her left leg. Jesus, if I ever lost that woman, I don't know what I'd do."

I felt as relieved as Cooper looked. I had not known whether Stella Conroy would live or die. Knowing she'd live made everything else, including sizable scars and irascibility, entirely incidental.

CHAPTER ELEVEN

The morning after the explosion, Agent David Keating of the FBI was standing just outside what had once been a transit shed at the Port of Wilmington. He had two other agents with him along with the head guy from the port security force. To Keating's left, was the shell that had once been a big Mercedes van. Keating decided it was the two private investigators' automobile. The windows had all been blown out and it was missing two of its doors. Whatever color it had once been was gone and it was now just a miserable dull gray. All the tires were flat. It had burned for a while after the blast and anyway, he thought to himself, the whole place stinks as bad as a crematorium. He had on a big pair of rubber boots over old pants, and a windbreaker, an outfit he might have worn for trout fishing; he kicked idly at a piece of metal that had been blown out of the shed. It looked like part of a car's front bumper.

"Okay," he said to the others, "let's do it. We know we've got the skeletons of cars in there. Let's hope we don't have human remains as well."

The four men walked slowly into the mess and looked around. There were dozens of metal mounds that had once been cars. Keating threaded his way through them. He carried a large beam flashlight that he scanned over the husks of the automobiles and the floor of the shed as he walked.

"We need to find what's left of the bomb," he said to the others. The men fanned out. It was a large area to search. "It may not be much, especially if it was something improvised, like a pipe bomb. But we've got to try. Bombs have signatures, although God knows if this was amateur night at the port, we may learn nothing regardless of what we find." He was approaching the far perimeter of the shed, when he tripped over something he had not noticed. He looked down and focused his flashlight beam. It was a human leg that had been separated from the body where it belonged.

"Over here," he said to the others. "This may be close to the origination site. I've got a severed leg." The others walked over. The security guy gagged and Keating said, "Don't lose it in here. Go outside if you have to vomit. You don't have to come back. This scene is contaminated enough as it is." The man hurried to the door and ran outside.

"Let's see how much of this body we can locate," Keating said to his men. "Be real diligent now, boys. There have got to be at least a few fragments of the bomb material somewhere around here too. If I had to bet money, I'd say it was a pipe bomb because they're easy and any imbecile can build one, although he stands a good chance of blowing himself up before he gets to plant the damned thing."

One of his men laughed at this and then said, "Here's the head and half a torso, Dave. It's male, at least it looks like it was. There's no breasts I can see. No face either."

"Go get a couple body bags out of the van," Keating said to the other guy. "We'll take these parts to the county coroner. Any teeth left in the skull?"

"Yeah, there's plenty."

"Okay," Keating said, "so that guy, what's his name, Alvie something, should be able to give us a list of who had access here and who had reason to be stealing from him. That's the place to start. Let's finish up."

An hour later, they had found most of the body parts and another corpse that was intact, but badly burned, along with a piece of steel and debris fragments they figured was what was left of the pipe bomb. Two hours after they had started, Agent David Keating had changed his mind about the place to start his investigation. He said to one of his men, "Give the regional office in Raleigh a call. A double homicide? Give me a fucking break. There's more going on here than just some lunatic stealing cars."

Darius Millar, Mickey Huntley's handsome, black, multi-talented, and gay assistant, was sitting at his computer reading the New York Times when his boss walked into the office. She was wearing one of her usual Donna Karan pantsuits in a shade of rose that complemented her light brown skin and cream sling-back heels, and she was trailed by a thin, unhealthy looking white man, shorter than she was, who was somewhere between forty and death. He was clean shave,n and his lank brown hair was professionally cut. He was dressed in a pale blue custom-tailored suit and a heavily starched navy blue dress shirt. His tie was a solid repp in yellow. Darius Millar thought the man's black leather shoes were Armani. The man is gay as pink ink, Darius thought to himself. He's a closeted gay conservative Republican and Mickey must be feelin' a terrible sorrow for the poor bastard, because she really loathes Republicans, especially gay ones.

"Join us in my office, Darius. Bring a standard contract," Mickey Huntley said. "And some coffee. I am running on absolute empty."

When he joined them in the office, the first thing Darius Millar did was hand Mickey Huntley a large cup of French roast coffee, black, and a bialy with cream cheese which he had toasted in the little kitchen in the suite, because whenever Mickey said "absolute" just before she said "empty" it meant she hadn't had either coffee or food. Sarah must be on strike.

"Would y'all like coffee? Tea? Anything?" he said to the man in blue.

"No, thank you, I'm fine," Alvie Weather said.

Mickey Huntley waved her hand around. "Darius Millar, this is Alvie Weather." The two men shook hands. "Alvie's our latest client, and we need to execute a contract. Date it a month ago, Darius," she said between bites of bialy and swigs of coffee. "The usual boilerplate and then specifically regarding possible criminal activity suspected at his transit shed at the Port of Wilmington."

Darius stopped writing and looked at the lawyer. "Y'all referrin' to the one blew up last night, boss?"

"I am," Mickey Huntley said

"It's all over the news this morning," said Darius. "It's the first thing I heard after my alarm went off. That blast tore that shed apart. They said the local FBI was callin' for reinforcements out of Raleigh. Two dead people. One in parts, the other burned so bad he or she melted into a great big blob."

Mickey Huntley was glaring at Darius Millar while her client had broken out in such a sudden, heavy sweat, she knew what was coming. Alvie Weather fainted, toppled out of the office chair, and fell in a heap to the floor.

"God damn it, Darius," said the lawyer. "Did it ever occur to you that this man might not be prepared to listen to such a gruesome narrative? Can you pick him up and lay him on the sofa? Get a warm cloth for his forehead. He'll come around shortly."

While they waited for Alvie to regain consciousness, Mickey said, "This aforementioned criminal activity at the transit shed is a beard, Darius. Alvie's wife Mallory has been kidnapped, but we do not want the FBI involved in that. They would take it over and completely muck it up. And anyway, whoever has her has threatened to kill her if we call authorities. Stella and Cash were at that shed last night because we had some indication they might be holding her there. It was Stella who tripped the wire that blew the bomb. Cash has a concussion and Stella has two cracked ribs and a couple of serious lacerations. And we are all scared to death because that blob, as you so indecorously explained, is unidentified and may be Mallory."

"I apologize, boss," Darius said sheepishly. Mickey's private phone rang.

"Mickey Huntley." There was quite a pause before she said, "Do not let them see her without me. They do not have an automatic right to interrogate her without benefit of counsel. Lock the door if you have to; I'll be over there within the hour. With luck, I'll get there before they do." She looked at Darius Millar. "We've got to wake him up. Take the contract with you, have him sign it, and get him to my car. When you drop me off at the cottage, take him to Jefferson's boat. The FBI is on its way sometime this morning to interview Cash. So far, they have not seen the need to get a warrant. I want to make sure they don't change their minds about that."

Stella Conroy was sitting up in her hospital bed, drinking warm sweet lemon juice, and talking with her father on the phone.

"I am just fine, Daddy," she said. "I cracked two ribs. I couldda broken my damned neck, the blast tossed me such a distance. Cash said it musta been twenty feet. There's no good reason for y'all to drive all the way over here. I'm goin' home either this afternoon or tomorrow mornin', and Cooper is like a fussy mother hen, which means he is all over me every minute of the day. I am exhausted by his concern."

"Why were y'all there anyway?" Sheriff Billy Conroy asked his daughter.

"I can't discuss that on a phone, Daddy," Stella said to him.

"Ridiculous," her father said with resignation. "Mandy called me this mornin' from Raleigh. I guess she's forgiven me for last year's trouble with the Governor. She says the local G-men are callin' in the troops. These local guys ain't takin' y'all's word that it's a car theft thing, not with two dead bodies in that shed. Just so you're aware."

"I am aware," Stella Conroy said. "But they will do whatever they get in their heads to do. We have just got to keep doin' what we know needs to be done. So far, they haven't bothered me, although I expect they will. Mickey Huntley's runnin' interference, and nobody does that better."

"And y'all can't even tell me who the client is?" her father said.

Stella Conroy fiddled with her glass for a minute. "Alvie Weather," she said.

"Well, holy mother of Christ, Stella," said Sheriff Billy Conroy. "That nitwit's crazier than a shit house rat. What's he gone and done now?"

CHAPTER TWELVE

"Listen, Jesse," I said to the kid. "We're going to try to help you with whatever your issues are, but you've got to do what we ask right now. There are people who are going to complicate our lives for a while. So Jefferson says to tell anyone who inquires that you're his nephew. That's all. If anyone wants to know more, they can ask him." We were sitting in two chairs in my study. There was still a tennis match in full swing in my head, and all I really wanted to do was sleep.

"Are y'all really his girlfriend?" he asked.

This kid had cornered the market on non sequiturs. "What's that got to do with what I just said to you?"

"It's just y'all are different from girls," he said and looked away from me.

"Nope," I said, "I've got all the requisite equipment."

"It ain't that," the kid said. "It's more you're harder'n boss is. I bet, it come to that, you'd lick him good. It ain't right a man has a woman tougher'n him."

I wanted to laugh, but I knew that would be a mistake because he was so obviously earnest in his concern for Jeff's psychological, and apparently physical, well-being. So I smiled at him instead.

"I'm not always tough," I said. "Jefferson knows how to handle me. He's a very smart guy, Jesse. You don't have to worry about him."

I watched the kid digest this information and wondered just how he'd process it to make it fit his formula.

"Well," he finally said, "ain't nothin' wrong with equals."

Sarah walked in the room.

"The Feds are here," she said, "and so is Mickey. We don't want them coming back this way; they might get curious and wander into my study. You know how Feds get whenever they see computers. So you've got to go out there. Mickey says to try to appear scattered."

"Appear scattered?" I said to her. "I am scattered. Serena Williams just served an ace in my head and I've been debating the metaphysics of romantic relationships with the kid." I turned to him. "You stay back here and keep quiet. Read a book or something. There's a whole bookshelf of interesting stuff."

"Just let Mickey do the talking unless they force you to say something," Sarah said. I nodded. The kid watched us go.

Sarah breezed ahead of me, and Jefferson Davis came to my side and helped me into one of the more comfortable wicker chairs in the living area of the great room. I wondered how wise it might be to cross my eyes, decided unwise, and instead frowned at a guy whose name tag labeled him David Keating. Mickey Huntley was looking unconcerned. She was sitting on a bar stool at the kitchen counter, drinking a cup of coffee. I didn't know where Alvie was. The man cleared his throat. He was the only agent in the room so he must have left his associates outside.

"Thanks for seeing me," he said. "I just have a couple questions." I didn't say anything. After waiting a moment in case I did want to respond, he continued. "Why'd you go to the transit shed last night," he asked.

"She and her partner acted on instructions from their client, Alvie

Weather," Mickey Huntley said.

The agent turned and looked at her. "I'd just like to hear it from Ms. Delaney," he said evenly.

"Hearing it from me is the same as hearing it from Ms. Delaney," Mickey Huntley said to him.

"No," he said, "it isn't."

"It is as far as the law is concerned," the lawyer said, "which is all you should be concerning yourself with right now."

I figured that this pissing contest could go on all day and my headache was getting worse, so I said, "What Mickey told you is all there is to it. Alvie wanted to see if there was any evidence at the shed that someone was stealing cars. I have an awful headache," I added. "How long will this have to go on?"

Sarah got up from the sofa and went into the kitchen. She opened a bottle of water and took one of the humongous ibuprofen pills the doctor had prescribed and handed them to me. I swallowed the pill, laid my head back on the chair, and closed my eyes.

"I cannot in good conscience allow this to continue," Mickey Huntley said. "My client is suffering from a serious concussion and should be in bed, not out here answering questions that have already been answered."

"I'm only asking why they went last night. What was the predicate?" Agent Keating was both persistent and literate, and I thought this question was a very good test of just how fast Mickey Huntley thought on her feet.

"The action was predicated on the client's concern," she said to him. "The man whom he suspected of malfeasance had called in sick yesterday, and when Alvie checked, he could not locate him. A red flag went up, and he called Cash and Stella, thinking they might catch the man in an act of thievery. When they arrived at the shed, they caught, as you know, a bomb instead."

Faster than a speeding bullet was a good way to describe how swiftly she thought.

"Okay," Agent David Keating said. "What's this man's name?"

"George something," Mickey Huntley said. "I'll have to ask Alvie Weather what his last name is."

"I might help with that," the agent said and looked at her. "The body that was in parts when we found it has been identified as George Cunningham. He'd been fingerprinted due to the nature of his work. He was the manager at Port City Antique and Collectible Automobiles owned by your client, Alvie Weather."

"And the other body?" Mickey Huntley asked.

"We've no idea, yet," he said. "We're working on it."

Minerva had been sleeping on the sofa in between Jefferson and Sarah. She woke up suddenly and stretched to nearly twice her length. She instantly realized there was someone in her world she did not know and this has always been a major concern to her. She jumped off the sofa and ran across to where the agent stood. He looked down at her and bent to scratch her head.

"Don't do," Sarah said, too late. Minerva sat back on her haunches and swiped at him with her right claw. Bright lines of blood appeared and beaded on the back of his hand. He never lost his equanimity. He simply walked into the kitchen and ran cold water on his hand until the bleeding stopped. Minerva had returned to the sofa and gone back to sleep.

"Predators come in all shapes and sizes, don't they, counselor," he said to Mickey Huntley. "Pity the mice of this world. Thanks for your time. I'll be in touch."

When he'd gone, Mickey Huntley said, "He knows there's more to this than we've told him. He's smart. And he strikes me as dogged. We'd better hope that other corpse isn't Mallory and that we find her before this whole thing blows up in our faces, because there are good cases to be made for obstruction and conspiracy. I am content, so far, that you are all covered by deniability, and the contract I drew for

Alvie is predated a month ago. And, of course, Alvie is under no compulsion to tell the FBI, or any law enforcement officer for that matter, anything about the kidnapping."

"At least he didn't wander into the back and find Sarah's computers or, for that matter, Jesse," Jefferson said. "That's an unrelated complication we don't need right now. Did y'all tell him to say he's my nephew if anybody asks?"

"Yes," I said. "He was more concerned with my suitability to be your girlfriend."

"Say what?" he said in astonishment.

"I am, in his eyes, harder and tougher than you, and a man shouldn't have a woman who can lick him in a fight."

Mickey Huntley laughed out loud. "What did you tell him?"

"Oh, I allowed that Jefferson knew how to handle me and that I wasn't always tough. And then Jesse finally allowed that there was nothing wrong with equals."

"So he's a feminist of sorts," Sarah said.

"Yes," I said. "It's a trait worth encouraging."

"What's he doing back there besides arguing with you about the status of the human condition," Jefferson said. "Playing computer games?"

"No," I said. "I told him to keep quiet and read a book."

Jefferson Davis looked at me. "That would have been a grand idea," he said. "if Jesse could read."

CHAPTER THIRTEEN

The guy driving the 1974 white BMW 2002 tii with the temporary plates was obeying the speed limit on his way to the outskirts of Supply, North Carolina, an unincorporated township in Brunswick County about an hour northwest of Wilmington, where his best friend from childhood lived close to, nearly in, the Green Swamp. The driver's name was Riley Satterfield, and he was the only kidnapper of Mallory Weather who was still alive. He had stashed her in the backseat of the car when he'd left the transit shed where his partner Dutch and the crazy mother fucker who'd hired them to snatch her were lying dead. She'd been asleep the entire time he'd been driving because he'd spiked some orange juice with liquid Xanax, and she'd been real thirsty and then unconscious.

When he got to the crossroads near his friend's place, he turned right. A few minutes later, he pulled off the road and followed what was little more than a path a horse and rider might take. When he was so far in he wasn't visible from the road where he'd turned, he saw the house, an unpainted shack on cinder blocks, and the four outbuildings where his friend lived. Then he saw him, pushing a wheelbarrow full of chopped wood.

He cut the car's engine, stepped out and locked the doors, and turned to holler at his friend whom he hadn't seen in nearly a year. "Hey dude," he yelled and walked over and fist bumped the guy everybody called Tommy Too. It was a name the cops tagged him with a long time ago. Whenever there was petty trouble, their reports dutifully identified the juvenile delinquents responsible, and they always ended this way: Tommy, too.

"Long fuckin' time, Riley," said Tommy Too, conferring a gap-toothed grin on him. "You and Dutch still pushin' weed? I sure as hell ain't sayin' no you got a little."

"I gotta bag a trainwreck in the trunk," Satterfield said, "for later. Right now, I gotta serious mess I'm fixin' to have y'all help me figure out."

"Anybody chasin' you?" TT said. "Cause if there is, we gotta move. I ain't want the law on my land. I got a shed now, deep in the swamp I wanna go frog giggin' and stuff."

"No one's after me," said Riley Satterfield. "Nobody knows nothin' about me. But I am tangled up in a situation of some other fool's devisin' and I need to see can I figure out a way to make it pay off."

"Talk to me," TT said, heading for the weathered gallery that fronted his home.

"Three weeks ago," said Satterfield, pulling up a chair and sitting, "one of our best ganja clients, rich guy sells cars, asked did we want to make an easy ten grand. We listened. What it amounted to, we hadda knock some broad out, take her to the port, keep her there in a shed full of cars, send emails the guy wrote that we kidnapped the broad and wanted money, then the guy'd step in, save her so's he'd be a hero. Course, he'd also pocket the money. But we'd escape ten thousand easy dollars richer. Everybody's happy."

Tommy Too stared at Riley Satterfield. "Where's Dutch," he said uneasily.

"Well, that's part a the problem," Satterfield said. "He's dead. The guy shot him, was lookin' to shoot me. I clipped him first. We'd just about finished wirin' the whole place to blow. Somethin' about the car count he said he needed to lose. I think it was he wanted us dead so's the cops' interest would end. Probably both things was on his mind as cover, the cars and us in a blown-up shed. So there I was, with this broad, Dutch and the other guy dead, and a building that would blow the second somebody tripped the wire."

"Uh huh," TT said skeptically. "And I can help y'all how?"

"The guy was askin' two million, get the broad delivered safe," Riley Satterfield said and stared at his friend. "And even though it was a made-up story, I kept the laptop he was usin'. I know who's the guy he was askin' to pay up, how to reach him."

"Two million?" an unbelieving Tommy Too exclaimed.

"What I said," Satterfield answered. "I'm thinkin' we at least deserve somethin' now that Dutch's dead. He ain't never hurt nobody. But it'll take two of us to pull it off. You in, dude?"

"Did y'all blow the shed?" asked TT.

"Not me. I picked that old basic car out there, grabbed the bastard's gun, loaded the woman in the back seat, closed the circuit on the wiring and drove to a turn offa River Road, figurin' what to do next. I'm sittin' there and blam, I hear the explosion. Sounded like the fuckin' end of the world. Wouldn't surprise me none if they conclude the broad's dead, they can't identify Dutch. That's why I'm thinkin' we might find the guy all eager as a pup to deal right quick, he hears from us."

———————————

Billy Conroy was still concerned about his daughter Stella after that unfortunate accident at the Port of Wilmington, so he took the afternoon off from his job as Sheriff of Brunswick County and drove to her house in the neighboring New Hanover County town of

84

Carolina Beach. It particularly concerned him that her current client, Alvie Weather, was a man he didn't trust as far as he could throw him. He was fey and unpredictable in Billy Conroy's opinion, and however he made his money was definitely a matter of speculation among certain members of the law enforcement community.

And he also knew that as independent and tough as his daughter always appeared to be, she nevertheless harbored a sometimes unhealthy loyalty to people she had known most of her life. And Alvie met that criterion. He wondered what Stella's partner, Cash Delaney, thought of Alvie, because Delaney had absolutely no emotional ties to anything or anyone southern. She was a Yankee through and through. So far, Sheriff Billy Conroy didn't hold it against her. Quite the contrary, he thought to himself, she's a fine counter balance to Stella's impetuous nature.

When he pulled up outside his daughter's house, there were three other cars already there. He recognized only one: his daughter's gold Mustang. When he opened the front door, he saw Stella, lying on a sofa, and a man and Mickey Huntley, who was speaking in an angry tone of voice.

"This is harassment," the lawyer was saying to the man. "You are putting my client at unnecessary risk to prove the unprovable. Why you are intent on continuing to treat my clients as criminals, I do not know. What I do know is that you are putting this woman's health in jeopardy. She has said all that she is going to say to you today and the next time you decide to speak to anyone who's a client of mine without me in the room, I'll file charges. Are we clear, Agent Keating?"

David Keating nodded, said, "Ma'am," to Stella Conroy and walked out of the house, looking hard at Billy Conroy as he did so.

"Daddy," Stella Conroy said, "that guy Keating is turnin' out to be a whole mess of trouble. He's FBI."

"I know who he is, Stella," her father said. "I've known him for years. He's tough; you try to bamboozle him, it might come back to haunt you. And all to protect the likes of Alvie Weather?"

Mickey Huntley looked intently at Billy Conroy. "What is it I need to know about Alvie Weather," she said to the Sheriff, "besides the fact that he faints at the drop of a hat."

"I don't trust him," Billy Conroy said. "I never have. He figured out, years ago, how to get where he wanted to go, which was anywhere as far away from his roots as conniving and swindling could take him. But that's purely my opinion. He's never broken the law far as anybody knows and worse, Stella's always had a soft spot for him, don't ask me why. Y'all wanna keep in mind, though, counselor, Stella's also got a soft spot for big hungry dogs that hunt."

"This is not for Alvie, Daddy," Stella said. "He called because his wife's been kidnapped."

"Mallory?" said the Sheriff.

"Uh huh. Alvie called three nights ago. We've all been tryin' to figure it out ever since and right now we are more confused than ever, cause the guy who was most likely responsible is dead, along with somebody else who's unidentified and we got no earthly idea whether Mallory is the other corpse or, if she's not, where the hell she is."

They heard a car pull up outside and turned to see who was coming. Cooper Grey walked in with Jefferson Davis and the kid, Jesse Shine, who was carrying a big bunch of daisies.

"These here daisies are for y'all, Miss Stella," said the kid. "I chose 'em myself. Cooper said y'all are keen on daisies."

"Thank you, Jesse. Daddy," Stella said to Billy Conroy, "will you get a vase for these?"

"I'll see to it, Stella," said Cooper Grey, taking the flowers from his wife.

Jefferson Davis glanced uncomfortably around the room and said, "We've got to get movin', son. Will we expect y'all for lunch a little later? Good to see you, Billy."

"I don't bite, Jefferson," the Sheriff said. "Not even ex-sons-in-law."

"You was hooked up with Miss Stella, boss?" the kid exclaimed to Jefferson Davis. "And you lost her? Are y'all serious out of your mind?"

Everyone but Jeff Davis laughed. "I wasn't married to Stella, son," he said to the boy. "I was married to her sister. Now, let's take our leave and go. Okay?"

When they'd gone, Billy Conroy said, "Who's the youngster?"

"His name's Jesse Shine," Stella said. "That's about all we know. But he's a smart kid, and we're fixin' to see can we help him any."

Her father frowned. "Shine? We have a mess of Shines over around Varnamtown. Call themselves oystermen. What a joke. Bunch of troublemakin' drunks, the men were. I don't know how the women kept the children fed, if they did. Lotta children. Lotta neglect. I think we did an investigation once. As I recall, one of the kids died under odd circumstances. Nothin' came of it. We couldn't prove a crime had been committed. But I always thought, you take a look at the circumstances of those children's lives, the whole situation was a crime."

"Are they still there?" asked Mickey Huntley

"They were people without options, Mickey," Billy Conroy said. "So they are unless they're dead."

CHAPTER FOURTEEN

I was resting on the sofa in the front room of the cottage. I was wearing my favorite warm pajamas, and I had a hot cloth over my eyes. Sarah had chosen a classical mix of Chopin, Mozart, Debussy, and Pachelbel. She'd turned it low, and Minerva and I were both drifting on a placid river of sound. The occasional clink of utensils and murmurings of voices from her and Darius Millar as they cooked in the kitchen added to my sense of well-being. I did not want this perfect moment ever to end. It ended.

"Billy Conroy was at Stella's when we dropped off the flowers," Jefferson Davis walked into the cottage and said hurriedly to me. He sounded in a panic. I removed the cloth from my eyes and looked at him. The kid had wandered into the kitchen.

"Is that indicative of a disaster? He's her father for heaven's sake." I said to him. "Of course he was at her house." I was really annoyed that my idyllic moment had come to a screeching halt.

"It's, you know, Jesse," he said so quietly I could barely hear him. But I was in no mood to indulge his whimsies.

"What about Jesse?" I said in a normal voice. I was really truly annoyed at having lost my peace and tranquility. Minerva sensed my annoyance, glanced at me to gauge the depth of my unhappiness,

88

decided it was deep, and took off for parts unknown. Sarah heard me and turned to look at us. The kid was eating a piece of yesterday's pizza and watching both Jefferson and me. Darius Millar was ignoring the whole thing. He was busy whipping something that looked like mashed potatoes. I suddenly realized that I was starving. "I'm really hungry, Sarah," I said. It was the first time I'd been hungry since my encounter with concussion.

"The meatloaf is done," Sarah said to me. "Darius is finishing the mashed potatoes. We used both butter and sour cream, and we added parsley and chives. I made a Waldorf salad with walnuts and golden raisins. And there are hot sourdough rolls. How does that sound?"

"Like heaven," I said.

Jefferson was staring at me. "Sit down, Jeff," I said. "If you're concerned that Billy will complicate your intentions with Jesse, I don't think you need to worry about it. He's not a rigid man; what's more, he's Stella's father. But I do think it's time that you took a look at just what your intentions are. He is, after all, somebody else's child. Children aren't chattel."

Sarah walked over to me with a plate full of food. Darius was behind her with a TV tray. I swung around on the sofa and looked at them. "You guys are my heroes," I said. "You have saved a certain girl from disaster."

The food tasted glorious and I intended to enjoy it. But I was watching Jefferson Davis wrestle with himself. Finally, something in his face seemed to yield.

"Jesse," he said. The kid had finished his pizza and was drinking a glass of milk. He walked over and sat on the arm of the sofa, next to me.

"Boss," the kid said.

"You need to tell us who you are, where you're from, what's goin' on with you so we can help you. We can't continue in the dark anymore and pretend you're just a boy we hired to work for us. If you can't do that, we've got to call the authorities. It's up to you, Jesse. We can play it either way you choose."

"Y'all need to grow a pair, boss, the way you let her handle you." the kid said. I couldn't believe my ears. I looked at Jefferson Davis. His face drained to a dangerous white, and I had no idea what he would do when he stood up suddenly and moved towards the kid. I reached to stop him and the TV tray with my food fell over and splattered on one of the sisal rugs underneath it. Jesse was so startled he fell off the arm of the sofa where he'd been perched, and his glass of milk went flying over his head. It landed with a crash on one of the wicker chairs. Sarah walked over to him and helped him up; the kid looked terrified.

"Why don't you and Minnie go back to my study and play some games," she said calmly to him. He stared at her, openmouthed but speechless, while his eyes filled with tears. "Everything will be okay, Jesse. Darius will go with you and show you a game I bet you've never seen before." She smiled at him and turned him towards her study.

Then she glanced at Darius Millar, who nodded and walked to the boy and put his arm over his shoulders. When the two of them were out of sight, she said to Jeff, "He's an abused child, Jefferson. Which I think you probably suspected when you decided to help him. We may not know the why and how of it yet, but this much we do know. Children don't flee love." Jeff was sitting on his haunches with his head in his hands.

I was picking up the remains of my lunch. He moved to help me. "It was such an incongruent phrase," he said to me. "comin' from a child. Nevertheless, my reaction was deplorable. I am ashamed of myself. I need to go and make it right with him. He deserves an apology."

"Give him a little space," I said. "He just got under your skin for a second. But children are resilient. Darius will have him feeling better in no time."

"We do know a little bit about him," Sarah said. "He told me he had a sister who died. He called her a corker. He told me he'd never again have as many good times as he had with her. He really loved his sister. It's obvious he worships you, Jefferson. Cash appears to be threatening to take him away from you. So Jesse verbally attacked what he loved before he lost it. Children are often able to withstand losses that they think they can control."

Mickey Huntley walked into the cottage and looked around. Then she went over to Sarah and put her hand on the small of Sarah's back. "You feel rather tense," she said. "You're flushed. Has something happened?"

Sarah turned to face her. "It's nothing a cup of peppermint tea won't alleviate," she said. "We can brew it in the microwave in my bedroom."

"Right now?" Mickey Huntley said.

"Right this very minute," said Sarah Ehrenson.

"Tell Darius to check on Alvie," Mickey Huntley said to Jeff and me over her shoulder. "And if he asks, tell him I'm busy and not to be disturbed until further notice."

———————————————

Billy Conroy studied his daughter while Cooper Grey was in the kitchen of Stella's house making Columbian coffee, the only kind Stella drank.

"So the manager of Alvie's automart was behind the kidnappin'?" he said to her.

"Most likely," Stella said. "But since he's dead, it's tough to ask him."

"But why?" Billy said.

"We do not have a clue except he'd been stealin'," she said. "We don't even really know exactly what he'd been stealin'."

"Makes no sense, Stella," her father said. "You don't cover up a theft with a kidnappin'. It's like diggin' your own grave two feet deeper than six."

"Well," she said, lighting a cigarette, "we won't know until and if we're ever contacted about Mallory again. The last message said there'd been a change in plans. That was just before I tripped the wire that blew the bomb in the transit shed. It's an absolute disaster."

Cooper Grey walked into the room with a tray and three cups of coffee. "Tell me about this Alvie," he said to Stella.

"Don't go all 'Daddy' on me, Cooper. He's just a guy I grew up with who was smarter than his circumstances indicated. He crawled out of the ditch he was born in and now he's rich."

"He's a foolish man," Billy Conroy said. "A totally unreliable man."

"How can you and I be so far apart when it comes to our thinkin' on Alvie?" his daughter said to him.

"You have a soft spot for him," Billy Conroy said. "I don't. Although I will grant he raised himself way above the circumstances of his birth. And he was always polite, which did not necessarily indicate he was sincere. We sorta mastered insincere politeness below the Mason-Dixon line, Stella."

Stella Conroy nodded and eased herself into a careful stretch on the sofa and wondered how to get rid of her father. She'd just taken the time to enjoy a good long look at her husband, and he was tanned and lean and buff and gorgeous and if she could just figure out how to keep from screaming about her two cracked ribs, she thought she would surely enjoy an interlude with the man.

"Well," she said, "if y'all don't mind, I'm tired, Daddy. I need to try to sleep a while."

"All right. I'll check with you later," her father said. "But keep me posted, Stella. Hear?" Billy Conroy walked out of the house.

"I'll drive over to the cottage and see if they've heard anything about Mallory," Cooper Grey said. "You rest. I'll be back."

"Not what I had in mind at all, Cooper," Stella Conroy said, "y'all get my drift."

Her husband looked at her. "You said you were tired," he said to her. "What about your ribs?"

"I lied," she said. "We'll think of something."

CHAPTER FIFTEEN

"The boy is in serious need of professional help," Sarah Ehrenson said to Mickey Huntley. She was lying on the bed with her head on Mickey's lap and she was no longer tense. Bonnie Raitt was singing those famous lyrics of hers quietly in the background: 'Let's give them something to talk about. A little mystery to figure out.' Mickey Huntley was listening contentedly to both women.

"He'll be a challenge to whomever that falls to because he's intelligent and manipulative, and worse, he's uneducated," Sarah went on. "And had he been conscious of just what he said to Jefferson, he would have a streak of cruelty worthy of someone indifferent to cause and effect."

"Let's not label the boy a sociopath just yet, Sarah," said Mickey Huntley.

"I expressly didn't," Sarah said. "Because I don't believe for a minute that he is. But what he said to Jefferson was startling to say the least. Jeff went so pale it was frightening. And believe me when I say I saw how angry he became."

"Billy Conroy told a few of us that he knew of a family of Shines somewhere around Varnamtown," Mickey Huntley said. "His description of the lot of them was anything but stellar."

"What in the world is Varmintown?" Sarah said.

Mickey laughed. "Varnam, Sarah; not varmint. It's a pleasant fishing community on the Lockwood Folly River where they used to do a lot of oystering. But Brunswick County has a whole host of people living way below the poverty line, and Billy said these Shines lived somewhere around Varnamtown, not in it. That, in North Carolina, can mean you're a quarter mile from the middle class and you are so poor your life is always at risk from everything: pollution, starvation, disease, the weather, family violence. Billy did say a child died in that family and that they'd investigated but nothing came of it. There seemed to be no indication of a crime."

Sarah Ehrenson sat up and looked at Mickey Huntley. "Jesse told me about his sister. She died. He didn't elaborate. But it was clear he'd been strongly affected by her death. His brief recount to me was a perfect depiction of fatalism."

There was a discreet knock on Sarah's bedroom door.

"Yes?" Sarah said.

"It's Darius," said Mickey's assistant.

"Come on in," Sarah said.

"Alvie's in the living room," said Darius Millar. "He just checked his email. There's another message about Mallory, boss. It's kinda screwy and Alvie has started talkin' to himself."

"Has Cash seen it?" Mickey asked.

"She's not out there. There's nobody out there except for Alvie. I don't know where they are. So far, Alvie seems to be bearing up under pressure. Least he ain't fainted yet."

"Give him time," Mickey Huntley muttered as she and Sarah followed Darius to the living room where Alvie Weather was sitting on the sofa, holding his head in his hands and chattering unintelligibly. "And Darius, do not say ain't."

"Sorry, boss, I musta forgot myself in all the excitement," said Darius Millar, rolling his eyes.

"Let me see the email, Alvie," Mickey Huntley said. "It must be time stamped. When did it come in?"

"Somethin's wrong," Alvie said, which confused everyone who heard him. "Somethin's so wrong she must be dead."

Sarah sat down next to Alvie and fiddled with his keyboard and said to Mickey Huntley, "It came in two hours ago." She read it and frowned. Then she turned the screen so Mickey could see it. This was the message: "The womans fine. We are threw foolin'. Next time, we will say ware to drop the cash. Be reddy."

"Different actors," Mickey Huntley said. "That does not mean your wife is dead, Alvie. I don't suggest you leap to that conclusion."

"They're just rednecks bent on torturin' me," Alvie Weather said. "Mallory is dead. She's that other body in the transit shed. I feel it in my bones. I need to go home. I need a doctor. I need a priest."

"You need a drink," Mickey Huntley said. She looked at Sarah Ehrenson. "Why don't you see if you can reach either Cash or Stella," she said evenly. "Darius will fix Alvie a drink and we'll consider how best to proceed." Sarah walked outside and sat down on an Adirondack chair.

She dialed Cash Delaney's cell and heard it ring nearby. It was somewhere in the cottage. She then tried Jefferson Davis's cell. It went directly to voice mail, where she left a brief message asking Cash to get in touch with her. Then she dialed Stella Conroy. The phone was answered on the first ring.

"Sarah?" Cooper Grey said in a whisper.

"We've heard from the kidnappers, Coop," she said. "Is Stella there? Things have changed disconcertedly and Alvie is convinced that Mallory's no longer living. He's unraveling again."

"She's asleep," Cooper Grey whispered. "Let me get to the living room where we can talk. Okay, that's better," he said in his normal tone of voice. "What's changed?" he asked.

"Well, for one, the kidnappers," Sarah said. "At least the ones who have contacted us this time."

"I don't follow," Cooper said.

"We've gone from Henry Higgins to Huckleberry Finn," Sarah said. "From excruciatingly correct English to the parlance of hicks."

"And you're thinking this means what?" he asked.

"That's the point, Cooper," Sarah said with exasperation. "We don't know what to think. It's not terribly often that kidnappers engage in switcharoo among themselves. Wake Stella up for God's sake and put her on the phone."

"Okay," said Cooper Grey resignedly. "Just a minute." He turned and saw his wife standing in the doorway in her favorite silk scarlet chemise with a lazy smile on her face. "Sarah's on the phone," he said to her. He reluctantly handed her the cell and gently ran his hand back and forth over her stomach.

"What's goin' on," Stella Conroy said to Sarah Ehrenson.

"There's a new email about Mallory from people we haven't heard from before," Sarah said. "It's unusual, and Alvie is unsteady. I suggest you join the conversation as soon as possible. I can't reach Cash, but I have left a message."

"Give me thirty minutes," Stella said, ending the call. She looked at her husband.

"You look like a starvin' man," she said to him. "What's that all about?"

"You just look so," he ·said and tried to think of the word he wanted, "accessible, I guess. I hate to waste the opportunity."

"Nothin' got wasted, Cooper," Stella Conroy said to him. "Believe me, baby, nothin' got wasted at all. But that was then. And this is now. And if Alvie is losin' his marbles again, which Sarah says he is, I am seriously startin' to feel annoyed I ever agreed to help the sorry son of a bitch in the first place. Right now, I have got to take a very careful shower."

"I'm a very careful man," said Cooper Grey. "I'll help."

"I thought you might," she said.

CHAPTER SIXTEEN

The FBI forensics analyst from Raleigh was looking for local FBI agent David Keating and found him standing in front of the transit shed that a bomb had totally destroyed at the Port of Wilmington several nights ago.

"You still haven't released this scene? You must be driving the insurers and the reinsurers stark-raving crazy," the forensics specialist said to Keating. "What do you think it's possible you can decipher here that you don't already know? You can't read tea leaves in a holocaust. Gross destruction always trumps particulate analysis. We can't be totally certain of the automobile count. Somebody constructed one hellacious mother of a bomb."

Keating fiddled with his car keys. "I'd like to understand why," he said. "I've been given a crime scene with an unbelievable amount of circumstantial evidence. I hate circumstance. And I'd sure as hell like to know about that other body."

"I can tell you what the body isn't," said the specialist from Raleigh. "That's if you're interested in negatives." He smiled at his colleague. "The body's not female. I can't determine age more accurately than to say the male in question wasn't old. The few chances for DNA analysis from what was left of teeth weren't helpful. Apparently this fellow, whoever he was, didn't like dentists. Or didn't need them. And he's in nobody's data base so far.

He died of a gunshot wound to his upper left quadrant. The bullet blew apart his left lung and he bled to death, actually rather quickly because it also transected an artery. It was a thirty-eight, and if you could have recovered the gun we could have established provenance. But all of that melted steel made the task impossible. Things melted and merged. Still, it's not so different a cause of death from the other corpse, where a single bullet to the chest indicates that somebody shot George Cunningham at fairly close range and literally blew apart his heart. They look like incidents that simply cancel each other out."

"But why wire the shed? Or worse, did someone other than those two men wire the shed? And what about the guns we did recover?" David Keating asked.

"They're both licensed. The Beretta is the property of Stella Conroy. The Colt belongs to Katherine Delaney. Neither was involved in those two deaths. The port police returned the guns to their owners. One of your men explained to me that these women are private investigators. Is that information correct?"

"Yes, as far as it goes," Keating said.

"I don't know what you mean," the forensic analyst replied. "Are these women suspects? It was my understanding they were hired by somebody to look into possible chicanery at the shed and that one of them tripped the wire accidentally."

"I don't think either one of them, or the man who hired them, or, for that matter, the man's attorney, has ever told me the entire truth. And I can't find leverage to use on any of them to see if I'm right."

"Who's the attorney? Sometimes, there's a way to co-opt a lot of these guys. We've got interesting files on hundreds of them."

"It's Mickey Huntley," David Keating said. "I recognized her the minute she walked over to me to give me what is now the official story behind the incident. She doesn't know me from Adam, but I doubt there's a cop anywhere in North Carolina who doesn't know who Mickey Huntley is. And law enforcement tends not to mess with her. It never gets us anything but trouble."

"Well then, David," the analyst said, "take a look at the guy who hired her. Who is he, how does he make his money, what does he have to lose, and why would he choose to lie to you rather than accept your help. What's his name again?"

"Alvie Weather," David Keating said.

"What an odd name."

"Yeah, it is. And he's an odd sort of guy. But you've given me an idea," Keating said. "There's a cop who might be able to shed some light on what's really going on with these people. Thanks. Will you tell my guys I'm going to be gone for the rest of the day? I'll call them later on."

"Where'll you be in case they want to get a hold of you?"

"Over in Bolivia talking to Billy Conroy, the Sheriff of Brunswick County."

It was four o'clock in the afternoon, and Sheriff Billy Conroy was in his office finishing up a bunch of paperwork that he'd been avoiding for a week and considering stopping off at Chaser's for a drink or two before heading home. He was still thinking about his daughter Stella and the concern he harbored about the kind of work she did.

He knew very well that if that particular improvised exploding device had been just inside that transit shed door instead of way at its back side, his daughter would now, most likely, be dead, and he would be enmeshed in the unthinkable activity of making funeral arrangements for her. A man can't bury his children, he thought to himself. I'd be dead six months after they laid her in the ground.

He rested his forehead on his hands. It would do him no good to fuss about his daughter and her chosen occupation. It never did him any good to fuss about Stella at all.

She was a walking contradiction, and you either took her on her terms or let her go. Billy Conroy could not let his daughter go. So he did his best to stay out of her professional life while keeping as up to date as he possibly could about it.

He signed the last of the paperwork and heard a knock on his door. "Louise, that you?" he called. His secretary of ten years always knocked.

"It's me, Sheriff," said David Keating, walking into Billy's office and looking around. "Have you got a minute or two? I could really use a cup of coffee."

Billy Conroy sat back in his chair and stretched his sturdy six-foot-four-inch frame while he looked at the FBI agent standing in front of him. How the hell am I gonna play this, he thought to himself. I can't start lyin' to the fuckin' FBI. But I can't enlighten him about the situation with Alvie either. And that is what he is most assuredly here to ask me about. The Sheriff looked at the agent.

"Help yourself to a cup of my finest blend," Billy said. "I grind it myself. Deprives me of a fortune every month but the older I get, the less I begrudge the cost of things I love."

When David Keating had gotten himself a cup and sat down in one of the chairs that fronted the Sheriff's desk, he took a sip and said, "Jesus, Billy. This is damned good coffee." He took another sip, set the cup down on Billy's desk, and said, "What can you tell me about Alvie Weather?"

Billy Conroy crossed his arms over his chest and turned slightly to his left to stare out of his large picture window. He watched a male cardinal with his bright red breast flit from branch to branch of a scrub oak tree. The female was one tree over, watching her mate. This particular pair had graced his sight for the past year.

Finally, he looked back and said to Agent Keating, "Not my jurisdiction, Dave. He's New Hanover's problem, if there is one. You need to be talkin' with that Sheriff over there."

"That Sheriff over there? You and he don't get along?"

"We have our differences. But they've got nothin' to do with what y'all just asked me. What is the problem? Is Alvie in some sort of trouble?"

"Your daughter nearly died trying to answer that question," David Keating said.

"Stella?" Billy Conroy said and laughed. "Well, you talked with her earlier today. Fact is, somethin' had you so steamed, you didn't even say hello when you passed right by me and walked out her door. What can I tell you that she didn't? I don't take careful notice of all what Stella is doin'. And she don't see fit to share."

"It's Alvie Weather I'm interested in," Keating said.

"Look here, Dave" said Billy Conroy, "years ago, when I was a cop in Carolina Beach, Alvie's family lived in a trailer on River Road that was mostly sheets of aluminum welded together, and poverty would have been a step up for them. They called straw bales heat. As I recollect there was a mother, a father, and three or four children. And none of them were law breakers. The father made a hardscrabble livin' haulin' other people's trash.

Some way or another, Alvie got out from under that boot heel of destitution, and my understandin' is he made good for himself. He's always been different. Over the years he was a kid, I've heard him called everything from a faggot to a retard, neither one of which, by the way, is true. But he's no criminal as far as I know. And that's the sum total of what y'all can learn from me regardin' Alvie Weather."

"He's got Mickey Huntley for a lawyer," David Keating said.

"Uh huh," the Sheriff said. "I heard her this mornin' when I got to Stella's. What's that got to do with anything? Mickey Huntley's as good as it gets, Dave. If you can afford her, you can hire her. You

103

know that as well as I do."

"There's something about this that nobody is telling me," David Keating said. "And with Mickey Huntley standing in front of him, there's no way on earth I'll ever get to talk to Alvie Weather alone to find out what it is."

"I can't help you with that, Dave. Smart lawyers are a part of the legal fabric. You and I work in support of a system that says everybody on the face of this green earth is innocent of everything imaginable unless we can prove otherwise. But I will say, I can't hardly believe that Alvie'd be involved in blowin' up his own merchandise and sendin' my daughter into harm's way for his own nefarious reasons."

David Keating smiled at Billy Conroy and stood up. "Thanks for your time, Billy," he said. "If anything does strike you as pertinent, will you call me?"

"You're gonna pursue this?" Conroy said.

"Just until I'm convinced there's nothing to pursue," the FBI agent said. "Somebody wired that shed for one reason or another."

"Well, we'll wait and see which comes first," Billy Conroy said. "You droppin' the investigation or hell freezin' over."

CHAPTER SEVENTEEN

Jesse Shine was walking carefully over Snow's Cut Bridge, paying attention to where he put his feet. The walkway was narrow and the traffic was steady. And he was uncomfortable, being as visible as he was, worried that he'd be seen and stopped and returned to his miserable family, his dump of a home. But he couldn't risk staying where he'd been and have the authorities called to pick him up. When he finally crossed and headed down to flat land, he turned and looked behind him. But nothing he saw caused him concern, so he hustled on. At the first stop light in the road that he came to, he turned again to look behind him and thought he saw Jefferson Davis's truck cresting the peak of the bridge. He was standing at a crossroads. He quickly turned right and hurried down a narrow two-lane road.

As he walked along the road, Jesse looked around. There wasn't much to see except junk and half-dead trees and squirrels and sand. A few houses were scattered here and there. The further in he walked, the emptier the area became. Midway down the road, he saw a big barn a ways in on his right. It was in serious need of help to keep it from collapsing on itself. But he didn't figure that'd be anytime soon. He thought it might be a fine place to spend the night and gather his thoughts. He'd taken two pieces of pizza and a bottle of water from that cottage where the boss's woman lived. So he had his dinner taken care of, and he was warm enough in his new clothes.

He looked around carefully and saw nothing or no one. There was a sign saying something. He looked at it. But he couldn't read, and anyhow the whole place was deserted. He walked slowly up to the barn, pushed aside the hanging door, and looked inside. Empty. He walked in and scared a bunch of sparrows that'd been nesting on one of the ceiling beams. They scattered and flew away in all directions. Jesse Shine grinned to himself. He'd almost peed his pants.

He saw a small roll of burlap in the corner of the barn and walked over to it. It looked clean, so he smelled it. It was okay, so he laid it out like a rug and took a few pieces of wood he found and fastened it down and made a square. My living room, he thought to himself. Maybe I could stay here, make myself a home. Ain't no need to bother nobody, and there's gotta be lots of fishermen around these parts in need of deck hands. I could make out fine, long as Jefferson and that woman don't find me.

He knew she didn't like him. Well, he hated her. She was a foreigner, and no way she belonged down here. But if anybody found him and turned him in, it'd be her. He glanced outside and realized the sun was going down. He wondered if he could quick see about some wild berries to go with his pizz,a so he went back outside and wandered further into the land behind the barn. Pretty soon, he stumbled on a garden of sorts. He quickly looked every which way but again he saw nothing.

He dropped to his knees and examined the fare in front of him. There were onions and a few tomatoes and some of what he thought could be potatoes. He looked to his left and saw fruit trees. His mouth started to water. I been eatin' good these last few days and my appetite's all growed up, he thought. And I've fallen on a harvest.

"I planted all this my own self," said Tallahassee Bodine, who had walked up behind the child. "Y'all are welcome to help yourself, boy, though you are mostly observin' leftovers meant for the compost heap. Or you can join me in my home and help me fix a proper meal. I got some big fat shrimp need eatin'."

"Y'all live here?" The boy had jumped up and was startled. He was looking at the blackest man he'd ever seen but he wasn't scared. The man was bald and skinny and dressed in so many colors Jesse couldn't keep track, but he felt like comfort. And Jesse liked comfort.

"Back a ways," Tallahassee said. "I got me a fine old house takes care of me with heat and everythin'. Nights are chilly now. I'm goin' in. You can come or not. Suit your own self."

Jesse Shine thought about his patch of burlap in the barn and his cold pizza and his bottle of water, and he decided to go with heat and cooked food. So he followed the black man and thought on eating good stuff, especially tomatoes and potatoes and shrimp. He could hardly believe his luck. He'd never had help from a nigger before, but he guessed there was a first time for everything. Jesse wasn't old enough to scorn whatever good was offered to him.

Stella Conroy was trying to calm Alvie Weather, who by now had consumed four solid fingers of my best bourbon, while Cooper and Sarah and I sat around in the living room and wondered just what the hell we had gotten ourselves mixed up in.

"She's dead," Alvie wailed.

"No one except you believes that, Alvie," Stella said. She was preternaturally calm in her handling of him. "And I am wondering why."

I glanced at Cooper Grey who gave me a surreptitious thumbs up.

Alvie Weather stared at her. "What do you mean? What are y'all implyin'?" he said to her.

"You tell me," my partner said.

Alvie Weather shifted, by which I mean he dropped the hysteria, assumed the cloak of maturity, and thought about what he said to Stella Conroy until he uttered, "You think I am involved with my own wife's disappearance?"

"You have been acting like a complete horse's ass from the beginning, Alvie, and now you insist Mallory is dead. What would keep me from a conclusion that you have somehow engineered this whole entire episode and that y'all don't care if your wife is dead or alive. Or worse, you know her current status. Two people are dead already, one known, one unidentified, your transit shed and all of its expensive contents have been destroyed, your wife is three days missing, and all you are goin' on about it is you want your money back and you want to go home and y'all need a doctor and a priest."

Alvie Weather stared at Stella Conroy until tears started falling down his face. He made no move to stop them. Instead, he said, "I am, as you say, a horse's ass, Stella. I am a man good with numbers, a man good with butt-kissin', a man bright enough to cut a million corners to get rich. Which I got. But I am not a man who betrays his core, as weak as y'all think that might be. I had no hand in the takin' of my wife."

"Then you need to leave it to us to decide whether or not she's dead," Stella said. "We are better equipped to look at that than you are. These creeps contact us the next time, we'll be more than ready. Hell, we may be able to locate them before the next contact. Sarah is thinkin' she can zero in on their location like she couldn't do last time. Sometimes when the players change, so does the brain power. If your manager was drivin' this scenario, he's gone and the players that are left at the margins aren't nearly up to the likes of Cash Delaney and me."

As my phone rang, I sincerely hoped she was right. "Yes," I said.

"Delaney."

"He's nowhere," Jefferson Davis answered.

"You've got to give it time, Jeff. He may come back to you on his own. You're important to him."

"No, Katherine. It was me who spooked him. I'm gonna go to the boat," he said. He sounded distant and sad. "This whole mess is my fault. I'll see y'all tomorrow."

It's not in my nature to coddle men any more than it's in my nature to want to be coddled by them. But he sounded so forlorn, I felt his anguish even though I doubted I could do much to relieve it.

"Do you want me to come over for a while?" I asked.

"Yes," was all he said to me before he hung up his phone and ended the call.

I left Stella and Sarah and Cooper to deal with Alvie Weather and walked over to Jefferson's boat. It was in darkness when I got there. I felt my way on board and looked around the deck. He wasn't there. I took the few stairs down into the galley and saw him. He was sitting on a bench at the dining table drinking what looked like bourbon straight.

There was a bottle from the Sawtelle still sitting on the table. I got myself a glass and poured a couple of fingers in it. Then I sat down opposite him and took a sip.

"I was growin' attached to that boy," he said quietly to me. I chose not to respond. Instead, I took another sip of bourbon. This was going to be his story, and he needed to tell it. Anyhow, I was quite certain I had heard it all three years before in Ithaca, New York. And I knew how that had ended.

"There are things I want," he said, and he looked at me. I looked back and waited. He drained his drink and poured himself another. "I allowed myself to dream," he said.

I sipped the bourbon from the still of two black men who had been slaughtered for no reason other than happenstance and corruption and greed. It was the best bourbon I had ever tasted.

"What are the things you want," I finally said to him. It all seemed so insignificant, next to remembering the massacre of those two men. I wondered whether or not this constituted a deficit in me.

"I want to marry," he said in a rush. "I want to have children. I want a family and a place and a reason to get up in the morning because they are there and they need me. I want it to be with you."

I felt so weary I thought I might just lay my head down on the little galley table and go to sleep. But he was worth fighting for. So instead, I drank the last bit of bourbon in my glass and said, "Do you remember the first serious conversation we had after we got together, Jeff?"

"Say what?" he said, nearly knocking over the half full bottle of bourbon.

"The first time we talked about ourselves to one another. Remember? We were on the deck in the dark."

He looked at me as though I'd asked him to explain the theory of relativity. Well, in a metaphorical kind of way, maybe I had.

"No," he finally said. "Not really."

I nodded. I often wondered just how much men listened to women when their hormones were running rampant. Or, for that matter, vice versa.

"Because I wanted to be absolutely clear with you," I said, "before we committed to a relationship, I told you a few things about myself that were non-negotiable."

"Uh huh," he said. He poured himself another drink and slammed it back.

"I told you that I have known for a long time that I didn't want children. Does this mean I dislike them? No. It just means I don't want to mother them. There are other things that interest me more. And children, raised right, are very time-consuming, and generally it falls to women to provide that time. I also told you that I had very little interest in marriage; it's a contract that I've never thought benefits me much, if at all. Again, it's a personal decision every woman makes for herself. I like to have to answer to myself, I like my independence, I like to work a lot at things that I believe make a difference in some small ways. And I like my own name."

"I guess I thought you might change your mind, you loved me enough." he said barely above a whisper.

"But I do love you enough. Just not for this particular scenario."

"Well, then," he said; and that was all he said.

"I'm really sorry that I'm not the woman to help you realize your dreams, Jefferson," I said with some regret. "And I'm not particularly happy about that, even though it's the truth. Because I do love you. I'll probably always love you." Then I turned and walked off the boat and started the long trek home, having traded headache for heartache. It seemed an impossible distance, but I'd make it.

I suppose I'm a feminist. Certainly, I know a lot of people who would adamantly drape that mantle on my shoulders and then make a personal judgment about it. But it's too small a word for me and for many other strong women I have known. It's a label and labels are naturally reductive. And anyhow, I'd prefer to think that men, rather than women, are feminists. However, that's a fantasy I tend to keep to myself, mainly because the only man I ever said it to looked at me with such incomprehension on his face that it frightened me. So I'm content to say I am just the kaleidoscope of me, full of passions and contradictions.

And I have a mother who is a real political force in the county where I was born, and a father who is an artist who barely makes a living selling what I think of as portraits and still lifes in Abstract Expressionism. But my mother is not just a politician. And my father is not just an artist. They are two individuals whose interests are multi-dimensional. They are addicted to opera. They love to play poker for rather substantial sums of money in Atlantic City. They are avid baseball fans and constant readers. And each is an amateur gourmet chef in the kitchen. We ate well and eclectically when I was growing up.

But they have never tried to invest any of their own ambitions or passions in either me or my brother Daniel. I suppose they are, in a way, parents who practice benevolent neglect; as a result they raised two healthy, independent children. Danny is a studio musician in Manhattan. And, as I said, I'm just me. My head started to hurt from all of this introspection.

I was crossing the dune in front of the cottage when my phone rang again. I wasn't planning to answer it, thinking it would be Jefferson, but I looked at the name and changed my mind.

"How are you, Tally?" I said. "I haven't heard from you in a couple of months of Sundays."

"I've been meanin' to get over there, my own self," said Tallahassee Bodine. "Things just get ahead of me and my intentions. But at the moment, I got a little situation probably relates to y'all."

"What might that be?"

"A skinny white kid in new clothes and a full belly is asleep in one of my big chairs in front of the fire. He won't say nothin' about who he is except to let slip he's a deckhand for a man grows oysters he calls boss who owns a great big boat over in the marina in Carolina Beach."

"Jesse Shine," I said. "Is he going to be staying there with you for a while?"

"I can't say," Tally said. "I ain't gonna restrain the boy and he's highly agitated about some woman he says don't like him who he hates and who hunts people for a livin'. He don't wanna be hassled by her." I listened to him chuckle. "He is surely full of his cantankerous opinions for such a young'un. But right now, he is soundly sleepin'. Be my guess he'll stay that way through the night, though I ain't wanta guarantee it, Cash. Young boys is mostly unpredictable."

"Well, someone will be over there in a little while, Tally, probably Jefferson, and thanks for calling. Let's have dinner one of these days; Sarah has been hoping for some of your fresh fish," I said.

"I'm goin' out for spots this week end," said Tallahassee Bodine. "I will see what I can do to get Miss Sarah what she's hopin' after. Y'all take care now, hear?" he said as he ended the call.

CHAPTER EIGHTEEN

I woke up the following morning and enjoyed a moment of not remembering the events of the previous night. That moment was short-lived. I am not naturally moody, but today you'd have had a tough time proving it. When I wandered into the kitchen, Sarah was already there, drinking tomato juice and fixing coffee.

"Why did you go to bed last night without saying a word to anyone," was the first thing she said to me. She was wearing one of several stunning full-length caftans she owned. I was always struck by how much it resembled a famous Mark Rothko painting, "Rust in Blue." "You're not a discourteous person."

"Jefferson wants a wife and children, and all the trimmings," I said to her and poured myself a glass of the juice. "I'm his choice for wife." I looked at her and shrugged my shoulders, but my eyes were quickly filling with tears.

"Jesus Christ," she said. "Not again." I had ended a ten-year relationship with Allen Church last fall in Ithaca, over much the same issues. She put her arms around me and held me while I cried. When I'd gathered myself enough to stop the waterworks, she stepped away and studied me. "So many men," she said. "So many male imperatives." I laughed in spite of myself. I still felt heartsick.

We heard a car pull up outside, and Sarah went to the door. Her caftan rustled pleasantly along the old oak floor as she walked. I was wearing sweats because I intended to tire myself out later at the community gym.

"Hello, Sheriff," Sarah said. "Come on in, the coffee's fresh."

Billy Conroy strode into the cottage like a man on a mission, which I had to admit he usually was. "Stella says you've all but nailed the kidnappers to a five-square-mile section of Brunswick County," he said to us. I had not known this due to my retreat from civilization last night in favor of solitude. I looked at Sarah.

"That's true," she said. "But the problem we face is that most of the area seems to be in a place called the Green Swamp. I'm going to see if they send me another email today and hope that I can get closer to them. Stella and Cash will need to make a decision about whether or not to contact them again and ask for proof of life again for Mallory."

"Let me take a look at the designated site, Sarah," the Sheriff said. "That swamp is a bitch for people to access what with gators and snakes and spiders and the occasional black bear. Of course, the crazies who live all through there are the worst predators of all. They'd as soon shoot you as look at you. What disappearances we have had around here in the past are mostly credited to the humans who inhabit that Swamp. I don't recommend anybody venture in there if it can possibly be avoided."

I had poured him a cup of coffee and handed it to him. He and Sarah walked back to her study. I walked outside with my own steaming cup.

It was one of those early winter days in southeastern North Carolina you could believe was really spring. The sun was hot and bright and there wasn't any wind roiling the ocean. Yesterday's quarter moon was a ghost of itself on the horizon. It was a primary colors morning. I walked a ways south along the beach, away from the pier. I did not want to risk seeing any sign of Jefferson today. It had been all I could do to call him last night to tell him about Jesse. I noticed the distance I'd put between myself and the cottage and turned around. Stella Conroy was heading toward me, looking stalwart and serious and mad as hell.

"Is it Mallory?" I said to her, fearing the worst.

Stella grabbed the empty coffee cup out of my hand and flung it a good distance into the ocean, where it sank like a stone. "What in this fucking world is wrong with men," she said to me. "Can y'all please enlighten me?"

"What's happened," I said anxiously. I could imagine Alvie Weather slitting his wrists or hanging himself.

"What's happened?" she exclaimed. "What's happened is Jefferson's over at my house makin' himself sick and Cooper cannot figure one simple thing to suggest he might do to fix whatever mess he's made and that damned kid's just sittin' around takin' up space and they are all of them drivin' me crazy. I told Daddy to find out where the hell the boy's family is and we'd take him home. Meantime, Jefferson's havin' a serious nervous breakdown and Cooper's as useless as an ashtray on a motorcycle. What the hell went on last night?"

I tried to take in all of what she'd said. There were times when Stella simply overwhelmed me, she was such a force of nature.

"Jeff put me in an awkward position," I finally said.

"I'm in no mood for understatements, Cash," she said. Then she looked closely at me. "You've been cryin'." It wasn't a question.

"He said he wanted to marry me, Stella," I said. "He said he wanted children, and the whole nine yards. It came from so far out of left field I was flabbergasted, and it struck me a good solid blow right in the solar plexus. I told him no, I wasn't the woman who would make his dreams come true."

Stella Conroy sucked in a huge bunch of air and let it out slowly.

"Well of course y'all told the silly twit no. What in the world did he think you'd say? Doesn't he know you at all? I swear, men in love are the most ridiculous things on earth. Look here," she said to me, "Jefferson will come to his senses. He probably got all wound up with thoughts of a wife and children because of that runaway kid. Right now, though, he's just pathetic. And he's in my house. And that means my husband is also in my house. And that damned kid. I am allergic to squatters. I'd welcome any small relief you can bring to the current situation.

"I'm sorry, Stella, but it's not my move to make," I said. "And I just can't put myself anywhere near that runaway child because he misinterprets my intentions for him. However much he's in need of help, it can't be my responsibility to provide it."

"It's not any of our business to provide that boy with anything," Stella said irritably. "Do we look like nuns from Catholic Charities? Somehow or other Jefferson got a romantic fixation in his head, and at the moment he imagines he's hell bent on livin' it. I feel like I'm sloggin' through a short story by Carson McCullers."

"Well," I said, surprised that Stella had ever bothered to read McCullers, "whether you like her writing or not, she was right about one thing: the heart is a lonely hunter."

"Come on, Cash," she said to me, reaching for my arm. "We'll forget about the men while they sort themselves out. I expect Coop will eventually think of something to yank Jefferson out of his self-inflicted delusion. Most likely, all it would take is a walk down memory lane for when Jefferson was married to my useless sister.

We've got a pretty good idea where Mallory Weather is, if she's still alive. Daddy's workin' with Sarah, cause the Green Swamp's harder than a preacher's dick to navigate. Sarah wants to know if we want to send another email. I vote yes. How 'bout y'all? Let's nail these bastards."

"Did you just say Green Swamp and preacher's dick in the same sentence?" I said to her.

"Uh huh," she said. "Why? Did I offend you?"

"You are a constant source of wonder to me, Stella," I said and fell in beside her.

"Well, you gotta be true southern born and bred to really appreciate my drift on that particular description," she said and grinned at me. "But trust me, it is apt."

CHAPTER NINETEEN

"How much shit did you give her?" Tommy Too asked Riley Satterfield. They had carried Mallory Weather from the car to the house and she was still out cold on a narrow vinyl sofa in what passed for a living room. "Y'all maybe overdosed her, dude."

Riley Satterfield considered this while he stared at the woman motionless on the couch. "I don't remember exactly, TT. I was in a massive hurry to split that scene. I guess I coulda been a little heavy handed. But I've done the stuff for years. It's safe enough."

"Ain't no drug total safe," TT said. "Is she breathin'?"

"Well if she ain't she's dead, and there's nothin' to do about that. Go over there and check."

"I ain't gonna go near her," Tommy said quickly. "She's your business."

"If y'all want part of the money, she's our business," Satterfield said to his friend. "Grab your shavin' mirror and stick it by her mouth. You don't gotta touch her."

Little puffs of breath blurred the mirror. Mallory Weather was alive and still asleep. "We gotta get her out of here," Tommy said quickly. "She'll be okay for a few hours in that shed of mine in the swamp, after we figure out when and where we want the money dropped. That'll give us time, grab the money, tell whoever where to find her, and get the hell out of here." He looked at his friend.

"We can't hardly carry her through that fuckin' swamp," Riley Satterfield said in response.

Tommy Too grinned widely. "I got Daddy's old airboat when he died last year," he said. "We ain't gotta carry nothin' but the clothes we got on."

"Well all right, dude," Satterfield said. "We are cookin' now. Quick find a pillowcase to slip over her head. I don't want she should get a look at either one of us and it's for sure she's gonna wake up soon."

"You'd best hide that car y'all stole, too," said Tommy Too. "Be a shame to have a piece of junk like that old BMW get us caught. Pull it into that last little shed of mine, the one with a roof."

Alvie Weather had called a taxicab to drive him to his home. He needed to get away from the situation that'd been forced on him with the kidnapping of his wife, and he needed to be alone to think. So he'd agreed to let Stella Conroy and her associate Cash Delaney continue with the case until and unless they deemed it necessary to bring in law enforcement. He continued to believe, as he had told Stella, that his wife was dead. But he understood that this was not only an unpopular but also dangerous belief for him to hold. It put him in a bad light.

But however this played out, he knew he was in a bad light regardless. This last shipment of automobiles had been going to be his last foray into the world of high-end smuggling, something he'd been carefully succeeding at for the last four years, ever since he had married a woman who lived a larger-than-life existence and whom he adored. In Mallory's world, money was fantasy, and she spent it with a reckless abandon that had at first terrified Alvie and then had thrilled him. She lived as though life held no consequences. He'd never known anyone like her, and the liberation she'd brought to his soul was the most intoxicating thing he had ever encountered. He had known from the beginning that he'd do anything necessary to keep her with him.

At first, it had taken just a few hundred thousand dollars a year along with what his legitimate business brought him. He'd managed this with less than a half-dozen stolen cars that he'd been able to supply with the necessary papers of lading. But over time, her monetary needs increased, and for the last two years, she'd been what he ordinarily would have called totally absolutely out of control. This last book, the one with the portrait of that woman he'd touched in his living room a few days ago, Mallory had researched to the tune of nine hundred thousand dollars. Trips to Paris, Budapest, Cairo, Florence. Two weeks at a time. And then the dénouement in Monte Carlo. He had found himself dipping into capital.

So he'd upped the ante and agreed to launder a European associate's money through his company in exchange for a thirty-carat flawless diamond which would be smuggled in the wheel well of an unglamorous but still valuable automobile: a 1974, white BMW 2002 tii. He had estimated that he would realize approximately ten million dollars from the eventual cutting of the stone. He'd had no illusions of selling the rock outright. But the ten million, along with what he'd already amassed, he expected would keep him from dipping into capital when invested properly.

Now, it was all in ruin. His wife was gone. His manager had somehow been involved in something he knew nothing about and could not begin to fathom. And the diamond was somewhere in the middle of a massive fire where no one was exactly sure what was there and what had burned and who was dead.

"I am as poor a man as I was on the day I was born," Alvie Weather said out loud to his empty living room. "God help me, poorer." Now, he needed to decide whether or not to tell Stella Conroy the truth. The question was, if he did decide to confide in her, what would Stella Conroy choose to do about it?

Cooper Grey was quietly running out of patience with his best friend, Jeff Davis. "Did you honestly think she'd fall all over herself and swoon 'yes' when you dumped your dream on her?" he said. "Who the hell did you think you were talking to? Rhoda or Mary or Mrs. Huxtable? Think about it, Jefferson. It'd be like me telling Stella to shut up and lie down and be still and take it. She'd shoot me, for Christ's sake."

"I know," said Jefferson Davis. He was a mess, his clothes wrinkled, his face covered in stubble, his eyes bloodshot red. "I know all that. I was half drunk, wasn't thinking clearly. But Jesus, Coop, what's wrong with wanting to marry the woman I love."

"Nothing. My best suggestion is find a more pliable woman to love or get over your fantasy with this one. I seriously doubt you'll ever get her to walk down any aisle. I really thought the two of you were happy with the way things were. God knows, you got your chops and your wallet busted once before, marrying that silly southern belle Stella calls a sister."

"Stella married you," Davis said bitterly. "Twice, in fact."

"And what's it mean, Jefferson? We don't have kids, we don't live together. We don't even share the same last name. It's the same damned arrangement you have with Katherine, save a piece of paper that says Stella's my wife and will inherit my life insurance money if I die before she does—and the way she's going, that seems unlikely. I tell you we are tested men, living with these women. But the heart goes where it goes; it's as simple as that. I wouldn't want to be without Stella in my life—ever."

Jesse Shine had been listening to this conversation. Now he stood up from his chair in Stella Conroy's living room, walked over to where the two men were sitting and put his hand lightly on Jefferson Davis's shoulder.

"It's my fault, boss," he said. "Miss Cash don't like me and I got between y'all. I'm sorry. I can be on my way soon's I eat a little."

Momentarily startled, Jeff Davis turned and focused on the boy. Finally, he said, "What do you mean, she doesn't like you. What would cause y'all to say such a thing? She likes you fine."

Jesse Shine was flabbergasted. "She told you to call the authorities," he said, his voice rising with the indignity he felt. "She wanted to get rid of me." He was shouting now.

Jefferson Davis stared at Jesse Shine. But it was Cooper Grey who spoke next. "Cash Delaney and I are northerners, Jesse," he said. "Something you adamantly pointed out to each of us. We are used to relying on the authorities when children wander into our midst. Can you understand that? Cash wanted to help you, not harm you. You have to learn to open your mind a bit, boy, and see the other person's point of view. She was concerned about you and about where you came from and what there might be to do about it."

Jesse Shine felt himself shift, felt a weight he could not bear land on him. He had not understood until now what concern looked like, sounded like, where it would take him, how it might help his meager life. He sat down on Stella Conroy's living room floor and cried his heart out.

A man from Bob King Automotive delivered a new Mercedes SUV to the cottage on Beach House Lane just as Sarah was inside finishing up her favorite breakfast of Eggs Benedict. Stella and I were outside in lounge chairs, composing an email that we thought would get a response we wanted from whoever was left of the kidnappers.

"Sarah," I hollered. "The new car's here." My voice hurt my head.

The man was about six-feet-six and skinny as a rail; all I could think of was Ichabod Crane. Except that his head was intact. "You the owner?" he said to Stella. "I need a signature."

"No," she said to him. "The owner's inside. She'll be right out."

In a couple of seconds, Sarah walked through the front door and stopped cold. "Jesus Christ," she said to nobody. "It's bright blue."

"It was an expedited order," the guy said to her. "This is what they had, Ma'am."

"I can't possibly drive a bright blue car," Sarah said emphatically.

"Ma'am?" the guy said, staring wide-eyed at her.

"I'm allergic to blue," Sarah said, looking unhappily at me.

"You are not allergic to colors, Sarah," I said patiently. "Sign for the car."

"Worst thing happens," said Stella, "we'll paint the damn thing."

"Can we do that before I have to drive it," Sarah said to Stella.

Stella Conroy sighed a deep sigh and said to me, "Is she serious?"

I grinned. "Absolutely, totally, without a shadow of a doubt." I said.

"Uh huh. Okay. Well then," Conroy said to Sarah, "I'll call Buddy in a minute. We'll have this sucker repainted immediately. Sign the man's paper, Sarah." So she did.

CHAPTER TWENTY

I parked the SUV in one of the spaces dedicated to cars at the side of the cottage. As I was returning to my chair, I saw Tallahassee Bodine and Junior Fisk walking down the lane. These men are particular friends of ours due to their connection to a past case that involved the murder of two black men, Jellicoe and Jerry Joe Sawtelle, in Sea Breeze, an old mostly abandoned town just over Snow's Cut Bridge. We had managed, thanks to Mickey Huntley, to preserve the twenty-four acres of Sawtelle land for public use, and Tally was the resident caretaker. Junior was his closest friend.

"Y'all got a minute or two," Junior said to Sarah and Stella and me. He still looked like the broad side of a barn, and the pale white skin of his face was beet red.

"You look like perfect heart attack material, Junior," Stella Conroy said to him. "You'd best sit down before you fall down."

"We walked from Sea Breeze," is what he said. "I admit to bein' a bit fat, Stella, my family runs to fat, but I am on a most constricted diet." If four hundred pounds at five-feet-six was a bit fat, then that's what he was.

"When he desires to be on that diet, his own self, he is," said Tallahassee Bodine solemnly. "Truth is it ain't that often. Last night, he ate for three at least, and that don't even count the five beers." Junior Fisk glared at him.

"What's on your mind, Junior," I said, not wanting to continue an exploration of his dietary habits.

"That boy Jefferson picked up from Tally's yesterday evenin'," he said. "He don't know me, but I sure as hell know him."

"Elaborate, please," Sarah said to him, sitting down on her designated Adirondack chair.

"He's a Shine from over around Varnamtown," said Junior Fisk, swinging his legs up on his lounge chair. "Don't anybody know exactly how many children there are in that family, but there's a passel, that's for certain. The father's a drunk who calls himself an oysterman, and the mother's as good a definition of a zombie y'all will ever meet. Rumor has it she is seriously accident prone."

"Are you implying abuse, Junior?" I asked.

"Tell them the gist of it, Junior," Tally said.

"Gist of it is, last summer either she tripped over a blade of grass and fell down an empty well, or some son of a bitch helped her. Bruised or cracked most every bone she had. The woman is still a walkin' advertisement for pain. Was no way to prove it wasn't an accident, though, so they patched her up and that was that. I expect your daddy knows about it, Stella, bein' as how it woulda fallen to his jurisdiction," he said to her.

"He did tell me a child died in that family," said Stella Conroy, "but he didn't mention anything about the mother. And it's not like Daddy to overlook somethin' like spousal abuse. He said they'd investigated the circumstances of the child's death but nothin' seemed to indicate a crime had been committed."

"Little girl name of Sara," Junior Fisk said to the three of us. "And that child's death depends entirely on how y'all define crime."

"What exactly are you tryin' to tell us, Junior," Stella said impatiently to him. "Is it possible y'all are not aware we're not mind readers?"

Tallahassee Bodine laughed out loud. Junior Fisk scowled at him before he said to Sarah, "I am thirsty enough to drink from the Atlantic, Miss Sarah. And I am startin' to feel a bit chilly out here."

So we went back inside and fixed hot chocolate, which brought Minerva out from under the sofa with her nose twitching and her tail straight up in the air. She's fond of the smell of chocolate. She doesn't, however, get to taste it. It would probably kill her, a fact I never mention to Stella.

Once settled, Junior Fisk continued his story. "My oldest brother's son, Truck, is a fisherman over in Varnamtown," Junior said. "Off and on over the years, the Shines have helped him. Well, the children have, anyways. Especially little Jesse. He's hung around Truck since he could barely walk. And Truck's always been good to him. But now he's got his own sons to help him. He sorta don't need Jesse anymore. He ain't got money to waste. Y'all follow?"

"Is the implication that this is the reason Jesse left home?" Sarah said to him.

"It ain't an implication, Miss Sarah," Junior said. "It is the exact reason. Those children have had to fend for themselves all their young lives; the ones that lived."

"And Sara," I said, "the one who didn't?"

"You might could say she died tryin'," Junior said to me. "Hollis Shine, their daddy, has a brother in Kinston. That's tobacco country, what's left of it. I expect he's got about twenty acres he plants to the leaf every year. It's a life lived by the margins, mostly. So two summers ago, Hollis sent him Sara to help pick the crop. If my memory ain't playin' games with me, she'da been about ten."

"Well," I said, "what happened?"

"She died, is what happened," Tallahassee Bodine interjected with some vehemence. Junior Fisk cleared his throat.

"According to Hollis, the child had always been sickly," Junior said. "Thin as a toothpick, yes. But she was full of energy. I remember her as a cheerful girl, always smiling, always letting her younger brother Jesse tag along wherever she was off to."

"Jesse said they were close," Sarah said.

"Joined at the hip," Junior said. "Mid-August that summer she took sudden sick, according to Hollis. Vomiting, diarrhea, sweats. The brother sent her home. Later that night, she died of a massive seizure."

"Jesus Christ, Junior" Sarah said. We all looked at her.

Tallahassee Bodine turned to her with a sad smile. "You know, don't you, Miss Sarah?"

"Was there an autopsy?" Sarah asked. She was staring at the floor; her voice had gone quiet.

"Of course not," Junior said. "Children die every day of the week. Most especially poor children. And if there's one huge sinful thing this state's known for bein' first in the country over, it's the hoards of poor children who live here."

"Green tobacco sickness," Sarah said, as though she had not heard him; her eyes filled with tears. "The substance penetrates the skin."

"What in the world are you talking about, Sarah," Stella Conroy said. "Have you lost your mind? This is America, not Africa." I put a hand on Stella's arm to quiet her.

"Nicotine poisoning happens in America, Stella," Sarah said. "Children picking tobacco are at serious risk; most of them in this country are migrants, usually Mexicans." Sarah stood up and walked out the front door.

I followed her. "Sarah," I said, "are you all right?"

She didn't answer right away. Instead, she walked over the small dune in front of the cottage. I went after her. "Sarah?" I said again.

Finally, she turned and looked at me. "It's getting to the point where I'm unable to bear the sickening hypocrisy of this country," she said quietly. "And it's becoming clear as a picture. The political and societal fabric of America is being ripped to shreds. Every time that outrageous, activist, and conservative bloc on the Roberts High Court renders a decision, I wonder what part of our fragile construct they have torn asunder. Look at their unconscionable opinion in Citizens United that opened the political process to nothing but the corruption of big money. Look at their callous decision on the Voting Rights Act, where they have the gall to suggest that minorities no longer need federal protection in places like Texas or Florida or even Ohio; or worse, to me, right here in North Carolina where we are standing, for God's sake. And now a child is dead, most likely from nicotine poisoning, and the North Carolina Tobacco Growers' Association officially asserts that no child under the age of sixteen works in any tobacco field in this state. We are being overrun by self-deluded liars with cash registers for souls."

I could not conjure a countervailing response to this scathing description of the current state of America. So instead, I simply said, "Let's see if we can save one small soul, Sarah. Jesse needs our help whether he knows it or not. And if we don't do it, who will?"

Sarah still did not look at me and did not choose to answer me. Instead she walked down to the edge of the ocean and sat on the sand. She kept her back to me, something that was rare in Sarah's world. She was watching a large schooner tilting in the wind. The ship was running at a good clip and was nearly horizontal to the sea. The men and women working the lines were silhouettes against the winter sun. I could hear laughter coming from them as they tensed against the strength of the afternoon breezes.

At that moment, a highly agitated Minerva ran up and over the dune, landed in Sarah's lap, stood up straight and licked her face as though in a frenzy; then she yowled so loudly it could have waked the dead. I swear some of the people on that schooner heard her. Sarah reached for her and held the little cat and rested her cheek against

Minerva's soft fur. "Yes, yes, you know I love you, baby," she murmured. "But right now, you will have to exercise some restraint. We have got a lot of important work to do, so you'll just have to wait awhile for whatever it is you want."

I breathed a sigh of relief. Sarah was back, at least for the moment.

CHAPTER TWENTY ONE

When Darius Millar put through the call to Mickey Huntley, he said to her, "Cop of some sort, boss," and hung up. The lawyer thought about that cryptic message for a moment before she picked up her phone.

"Mickey Huntley," she said perfunctorily.

"This is David Keating," the FBI agent said. "I'm calling as a courtesy to your client, Mr. Weather."

"Yes?" the lawyer said.

"We still haven't identified the second body in that shed, but we have learned some things. The body was that of a young male, and what was left of the teeth can't be traced in our database. We're going to look through the home of Mr. Weather's deceased manager, George Cunningham, to see what, if anything, we can uncover. You and your client are welcome to come along. In fact, Mr. Weather might be able to help us interpret items or information that otherwise could escape our attention."

I'm dealing with the only articulate, bright, intuitive and persistent FBI agent in the entire state of North Carolina, Mickey Huntley thought to herself. A few seconds later, she said, "I'm in court in an hour, Agent Keating. Could I substitute one of Mr. Weather's other associates to accompany him?"

"If you're talking about those two private investigators, you can send them both. We're going in at eleven o'clock." And, he thought, I'll finally have a go at all of them without your interference, counselor. So stick that up your fucking obstructionist ass.

As though she had heard his thoughts loud and clear, Mickey Huntley said, "That's fine, Agent Keating. Just do not plan on interrogating any of them, especially Mr. Weather. Because if you do, I will hear about it and you will have a lawsuit on your hands. Do I make myself clear?" With that, the lawyer hung up her phone and smiled. Then she dialed another phone. When it was answered, she said, "Call me on your private line at my private number," and again she hung up.

A few minutes later, using her prepaid phone, Sarah did what she'd been told to do. "I just got a call from Agent Keating," Mickey Huntley said, when she answered. "He's going to search George Cunningham's house at eleven o'clock and has invited Alvie to go along. I can't accompany him; I've got court. Stella and Cash can go in my stead. Have them pick him up and be sure they are there by eleven. And there is good news of a kind. The second body in the shed was a young male. That's all they know right now, but it should keep Alvie on the safe side of hysteria. And Sarah, if they see something that helps us locate Mallory, tell them to try to keep it out of the hands of the FBI. Okay? Otherwise we'll have a real mess on our hands."

"We've already got a mess," Sarah said softly.

"You sound subdued. Has something broken about Mallory?" the lawyer said to her.

"No." Sarah said.

"Well, then, what for God's sake,' Mickey Huntley said with some small exasperation.

"It's about Jesse's sister Sara, the one who died," said Sarah.

"Junior Fisk came to talk with us about it. It's distressed me quite a bit, Mickey. I can't stop thinking about it."

Mickey Huntley didn't answer right away because as a defense attorney she had the kind of imagination that went a bit awry whenever the circumstances of a death entered any situation.

Finally, she said, "Tell me."

"She'd been sent two summers ago in June to her uncle's tobacco farm to help pick the crop," was what Sarah said. "She was ten years old at the time."

It took the lawyer about thirty seconds to put this emerging picture into perspective. "First, that's illegal. Even in this state. Second, you are saying the child probably died of complications from nicotine poisoning. Is that right?"

"Yes," was all Sarah said.

Mickey Huntley looked at her watch and realized she had to hustle if she was to get to court on time. "I have to run now, Sarah. But I want you to listen to me for a minute. I know you. I love you and you are fully aware of that fact. You have the finest sensibilities of anyone I have ever encountered. And we will deal with this. There's nothing we can do for the child who died, but we can do something for the brother she left. I'll be at the cottage after court. We'll talk about it then."

"I'll be here," said Sarah as she ended the call.

George Cunningham had lived in a spacious brick ranch home a couple blocks past the Independence Mall on Oleander Drive in Wilmington. When Stella and Alvie and I pulled into the driveway, the FBI was already there, going through the open double-car garage

"George kept nothin' in that garage that wasn't related to cars," Alvie said to me.

He had calmed considerably ever since we'd told him that the other body in the port shed wasn't his wife.

"Where should we be tryin' to look ahead of the cops, Alvie," Stella Conroy said to him.

"He had a hidey hole," Alvie said. "There's a false floor in his bedroom. He kept most everything he cared about in a strong box in there. You'd never see it, you didn't know where to look."

"I'll let Agent Keating know we'll wait for him and his men in the house," I said to the two of them.

"We can't get to it with the FBI around," Alvie said.

"Why," said Stella. "Where is it?"

"Under a monster four-poster bed. And chances are good," Alvie said, "that even if they moved that sucker, they still wouldn't see it. George put multi-colored parquet flooring in that room. You stare at that close, you get dizzy as hell."

We all climbed out of the Mustang. Stella and Alvie walked up to the front door, and I walked into the garage. David Keating turned and glanced at me. "I see you're feeling a bit better," he said and held out his hand. I shook it. Minerva's claw marks were very slightly visible.

"There's still an elf or two running around in my head," I said. "But I am feeling better." Two of his men were tearing through a large cardboard box that looked to contain nothing but cans of motor oil. "Anything, so far?"

He shook his head. "Nothing yet."

"Well." I said, "Alvie's still suffering a hangover of shock from all that's transpired. We'll sit in the living room and wait for you. Are you going to be long in here?"

Agent Keating looked at me and gave me a tolerant smile. "I'll go with you," he said. "My men can finish up here." So the two of us walked through the door in the garage that led to the interior of the house. I hoped to hell we didn't encounter Stella or Alvie snooping around. It would bring any cordiality we might have established to a screeching halt. The door led directly to the kitchen. Nobody was in sight.

"Stella," I said as loudly as I could without screaming, "Agent Keating and I are in the kitchen." Alvie walked in with a sorrowful look on his face. I thought he might have missed his calling as an actor, he looked so sad. He was also starting to shake.

"He was my friend," is all he said at first. Stella Conroy hustled up behind him and put a hand on his shoulder. She looked scattered, but I don't think David Keating even noticed. He was staring at Alvie Weather who looked as though he might be getting ready to faint again. "I trusted him like a brother. Whatever his part is in this calamity, I cannot imagine." With that, Alvie slumped down on a barstool next to a kitchen counter and put his head in his hands.

"That's what we're trying to find out, Mr. Weather," Agent Keating said solicitously. "Maybe you should just rest and let us do the job. If there's something you can help us with, we'll come and ask you. Okay?"

"That's a fine idea," Stella said. "Why don't you go and rest in the car, Alvie." She gave me a quick look that said, "Get him out of here" so I walked over and helped him to his feet and the two of us started back to the car.

"How'd I do," he whispered to me as we were leaving the house.

"Just keep walking," I said.

When we got to the car, he said, "I'll get in the back seat and sort of lie down." When that had been accomplished, he pulled a legal-sized yellow envelope out of his suit coat and handed it to me. I glanced at it.

"What is it?" I said.

"A pile of money and a few names and a bunch of little cellophane things that Stella says is dope. She says probably cocaine. It was just lyin' there on the little table George always kept in his foyer." He sounded hopeful for the first time since I'd met him, as though finally we'd stumbled over a clue of some sort. And maybe we had.

This clue, however, didn't strike me as particularly good news, although I didn't share that with Alvie. Coke and money often lead to the kind of people psychiatrists label 'psychopathic.' You know. The guy who smiles at you when he slits your throat for no good reason whatsoever except it's Monday and he's bored. Where did Mallory Weather fit into this bleak equation? Or was this information something entirely unrelated to the kidnapping of his wife?

CHAPTER TWENTY TWO

Mallory Weather had been awake for an hour or so while she pretended to still be asleep on what felt like a dangerously narrow plastic-covered thing of some kind. Her back was flat against one side of the thing, and her manacled hands were hanging off it slightly. She was listening intently to two men who either were drunk or stoned or mentally ill. Possibly, she thought, a combination of all three. And both of them, to her ears, sounded dumb as a box of rocks. But that, she knew, could simply be the result of poor grammar and limited education.

"Don't fuckin' bogart that roach, dude," Riley Satterfield said to Tommy too. "Give it here."

"Hold your water, man," TT said, handing him the reefer and watching him suck in a huge lungful of the pot.

"This trainwreck is a fuckin' rocket," Satterfield said, as he exhaled the smoke with a whoop and a holler. "I am goin' to the moon. I am goin' over the moon, beyond the moon; I am jumpin' over the fuckin' moon. Dude. I am happy, happy, happy."

"I ain't never had better," TT agreed. "I am mellow as a cat in clover and giddy as a clam at high tide."

Mallory Weather had no idea what the word 'trainwreck' could possibly mean, but she knew enough to realize it was some sort of powerful intoxicant, and she also knew it smelled like pine and wet earth and vaguely like skunk; and the smoke was starting to creep inside the pillowcase that was covering her head. She closed her eyes. Then she heard a sharp dinging sound. She knew exactly what that was. These two had a computer somewhere in the room.

Dude," TT said. "The machine's talkin' at y'all. Maybe it's about the bread for the broad." Then he started a giggling jag and couldn't stop. Riley Satterfield didn't answer. He started chanting over and over something that sounded ridiculous to Mallory Weather.

You see Deacon Jones
He rattled his bones
Old parson Brown
Jumpin' round like a clown
Aunt Jemima she is feelin' ok
Bouncin' round full a pep
Watch her step
Watch her step
One legged ho
Dancin' round on her toe
Throws away her crutches
Hollers let it go
Oh baby hail hail
The gang is here
For a Carolina jubilee.

After what seemed like forever, the repetitive singsong stopped, while the intermittent dinging sound continued. "It's that mail thing," the guy who had been chanting said. Then he started to laugh, and this induced the other guy to join right in. In a matter of seconds, they were both hysterical. Mallory Weather amended her earlier assessment of grammar and education. These two nincompoops can't be the ones who kidnapped me, she now decided. Both of them would photosynthesize in sunlight.

When David Keating and his men were finished going through the house of the late George Cunningham, they had discovered absolutely nothing that would help to further explain why the man had been found dead and in pieces in the bombed out shed at the Port of Wilmington. The agent shook hands with Stella Conroy and Cash Delaney and thanked them for their assistance.

"Are y'all keepin' this a crime scene," Stella Conroy asked him. "Alvie is George's executor and he'd sorta' like to get started on dispensing things. He says there's a bunch of cousins he's obliged to get in touch with."

David Keating shook his head. "I can't justify it," he said reluctantly. "I'm going to have to conclude that Mr. Cunningham was killed trying to defend the merchandise at the shed and that he and the thief shot and killed each other. It bothers me, though. As private investigators, you can understand that."

"I'm sure we could, if we knew just what it is that bothers you, Agent Keating," Cash Delaney said.

David Keating considered for a moment whether or not he should trust these women any farther than he could throw them and finally concluded it really didn't matter one way or another. So he decided to show part of the hand he was holding. "I'd like to know why someone took the time to wire that shed," he said to her. "To me, that says there's at least another player running around out there, and I want to find him." He'd also concluded that if either Delaney or Conroy tried to allay his concerns with a plausible explanation, they were hiding something. Neither woman said anything.

"You don't agree?" he said.

"Well," Stella Conroy said, "we can most certainly agree the damn place was wired. I've got the taped ribs and Cash's got the headache to prove it. But that's about all we can agree on. Alvie wanted us to look into some thefts he was experiencing at that shed. That's what we did, and you know what happened. Can we hope y'all will inform us regarding your continuing investigation?"

"I'll inform Mr. Weather's attorney of any new developments," the agent said rather formally. The three of them shook hands again, and two minutes later, he and his men were gone.

Dressed in a pair of old comfortable Levi's and a plaid wool long-sleeved shirt, Sheriff Billy Conroy was driving his own car along Crusoe Island Road, headed for what the state now calls the small community of Riverview and what the locals still, and probably always will, call Crusoe Island. It wasn't really an island. It was bordered on three sides by the Waccamaw River and on one side by the Green Swamp, an enormous tract of land, part of which is now protected by the National Conservancy, and which is known for the vast array of wild orchids and Venus flytraps that grow abundantly in the longleaf pine savannas that are found throughout the Preserve. He had no jurisdiction in Riverview because it was located in neighboring Columbus County, but he had no legal business to attend to; he just wanted to talk with a man he had known for thirty years who lived there. That man's name was Lydell Duvall. His friends called him Bug.

After he'd slowed his car and parked it on a dirt driveway that ran beside a long doublewide trailer, Billy Conroy got out, hitched up his jeans, grabbed a bag that was resting on the back seat, and walked slowly toward the place. Two hunting dogs ran toward him barking their heads off. Behind one of the drawn shades on the porch addition, he could see the outline of a man holding what he knew was a rifle. Visitors to Crusoe Island were few and far between and often bringing trouble.

"You home, Bug," he hollered, while he bent to let the dogs smell his left hand. The inspection began and the barking stopped. They knew him. The dogs fell happily in step beside him as he continued toward the trailer. Conroy watched the screen door open, and a man about fifty years old walked out to look at him. He was shorter than the Sheriff, and he was dressed in a pair of overalls with a long-sleeved black sweater underneath and a pair of thick tan work boots on his feet. His hair was pure white, and his eyes were a shocking shade of navy blue. He was still holding the rifle down at his side.

"What brings y'all out here, Billy, without I asked you to stop on by?" said Bug Duvall evenly. "Somebody sideways with you again? It ain't any of my business if there is."

"I'm looking to pick your brain," Billy Conroy said good-naturedly. "Whatever's left of it. So either shoot me or put away that gun."

"Well," said Duvall, dropping the rifle carefully on a picnic table, "that depends entirely on just what you got in that bag."

Conroy set the bag down on the table next to the rifle, and the two men shook hands. Duvall walked over to a square open storage shed next to his trailer and reached for two small jelly jars. Billy Conroy took a bottle of Mount Gay rum out of the bag. Duvall nodded and set the glasses on the table. After they'd each taken a couple fingers of the rum, they sat at the table and looked at each other.

"What's it been, Bug," Billy said. "Six months?"

"More like a year since we got that last hankerin' for frog's legs."

"That's right. Man that was some fine feed," Billy Conroy said and smiled. "We musta come back with a hundred fat ones. Seems like I remember we fed the entire neighborhood. Susanna was one delighted lady that day."

"She's still delighted," Bug said without inflection. "Not always regardin' frog's legs, though."

"You lucked out with that woman, Bug," Billy said, taking a good swig of the rum. The smooth hot liquor was not one of his favorites, but it was the only thing Lydell Duvall drank.

"So they tell me, Billy. So they tell me. But seein' as she ain't here right now, y'all wanna give me an insight what's really on your mind."

Billy Conroy fidgeted with his jelly jar. "Stella's got a case," he said. "Discretion's essential. And I am emphasizin' truly essential. There is not the smallest margin for error with this."

"Okay," was all Bug Duvall said.

"A woman's been kidnapped. What we know so far indicates she's bein' held somewhere near or in the Green Swamp. Brunswick County, not Columbus. Anybody new been poachin' that you heard of? Anybody building anything might be suitable to stash a human's been kidnapped?"

Lydell Duvall shifted slightly to his left and looked at the empty stretch of road leading to his home. After a half minute, he saw two cars coming slowly down that road. Then he stood, picked up the nearly full bottle of rum, along with his rifle, and said to his friend, "Grab the glasses, Billy. We'd best repair to the living room. I don't want to talk about this out here. Some of these trees have ears, y'all get my meanin'."

CHAPTER TWENTY THREE

Stella and Alvie and I were sitting at the bar in Elijah's Restaurant on Chandler's Wharf, eating a bucket of steamed oysters dipped in melted butter, a hot loaf of garlic bread, and drinking ice cold Dos Equis with slices of lime. We were looking at three names on the piece of paper that was part of the stuff we found at George Cunningham's house. The names were all male, and two of them were most likely nicknames: Floyd Betters, Rowdy Gaines, and Big Daddy Washington.

"Big Daddy works out of a storefront on Marsteller Street, sells antiques," Alvie said, slathering another oyster with lemon and butter and popping it into his mouth. "Boy," he said, "these oysters are excellent. I've been forgettin' to eat since Mallory's been gone. Let's get another bucket." Neither Stella nor I objected to this suggestion, so he raised his arm and gave his hand a little twist. The bartender nodded and went to place the order. "The other two, I've never heard of."

"What's your business with Big Daddy?" Stella said. She was dipping a crust of the garlic bread into a dish of Calabash hot sauce she'd ordered. "It's not like the two of you move in the same social circles."

"He buys his cars from me," Alvie said, burping softly. The waiter set the second bucket of oysters down in front of us and asked if we wanted anything else. "Three more beers, please," Alvie said and smiled at him. "Gets a Classic Lincoln Continental every two years. The man's as regular as clockwork."

"He haul his money over in a wheelbarrow?" Stella said.

"Oops," I said, draining the last of my beer just as the guy put down the second one.

"Yeah," Stella said. "Oops is exactly right. Big Daddy's been runnin' a faction of the Bloods on Wilmington's north side for the last ten years. Their economic development plan is heavily invested in drug labs in boarded-up houses and bags of cocaine that've been hit so hard they might as well be talcum powder. That stuff's for their customers who haven't hit puberty yet. It's a recruitment tool for finding new runners. The serious customers are treated to a high grade of skag. Gets 'em hooked good and fast. Nothin' like a customer for life, even if the life span's a tad short."

"Skag?" Alvie said.

"Heroin," I said to him. "Probably from Mexico."

"I see," Alvie said. "Well, I don't ask the man his business, Stella," he said, covering another oyster, this time with the hot sauce. "Far as I'm concerned, he sells expensive antiques. And his money spends, just like everybody else's. If I was required to do background checks on the people who buy my cars, I would be out of business right quick."

"Is he safe to talk with?" I asked Stella.

"Is he likely to shoot us on sight, you mean," she said to me.

"Why would y'all say such a thing," Alvie said to her, his voice registering alarm. "I've known the man for years. He would never shoot me or any of my friends. He wouldn't harm me at all."

Stella studied him like a mother protecting an innocent child. "Have another oyster, Alvie," she said. "Keep your strength up."

"Well then," I said to the two of them. "We need to talk with him to see what he can tell us about George Cunningham and this envelope of money and cocaine. We might even be wise to tell him about Mallory to see if he knows anything. He certainly isn't likely to notify the cops."

"I can call him," said Alvie, sounding somewhat mollified. "In fact, he's about due to be callin' me. He orders in December. His last one was a hot pink number with dark grey leather interior. I get them special. Takes me months to find and restore them. That's mostly because he always wants suicide doors, and they are becoming harder and harder to find. The last one shipped from Yemen. Cost a fortune."

Stella Conroy looked at me. I nodded. Alvie was totally oblivious to what he'd just said. The same couldn't be said for the two of us. We were both, at that moment, wondering how much trash of a certain kind had been slipped unnoticed through those doors at one time or another over the years. We didn't communicate that thought with Alvie; he was enjoying a meal and a good mood for the first time since this whole nightmare began.

Sarah Ehrenson was sitting in the midday sun drinking a cup of red zinger tea when Buddy Hoyt showed up driving her new and newly painted Mercedes SUV. He climbed out of the car and walked over to her and smiled. She smiled back. They were comfortable with each other, this older southern man from the hardscrabble hills of West Virginia and this young Jewish woman from the west side of Manhattan.

"Here you go, Miss Sarah," he said to her, handing her the keys. The car was beautiful. She'd decided on copper for the color this time rather than black; mainly because she was no longer feeling funereal. "You like it?"

"I love it," she said to him. "It's perfect, Buddy. How about a cup of coffee."

"Sounds good," he said, following her into the cottage. "Man, that blue was a bitch to cover. It put up one monster of a fight. Y'all got one of those scone things you're always bakin'? I worked right straight through lunch."

"I don't know," she said. "Cash may have eaten the last one. How about a roast beef sandwich on rye with some of my German potato salad. That's more like lunch anyway."

"I would be one very happy man," he said, taking a seat on the couch. "Speakin' of Cash, where is she? I thought I might run into her."

"Somewhere with Stella," Sarah said. "Working, as usual. Why?"

"She stopped by the other day, asked could I get her Jaguar shipped to here from Ithaca. I told her I'd look into it, get back to her."

"And?" Sarah said, putting a plate and a cup and saucer down on the coffee table in front of Buddy

"Might cost a bit, but it's easy enough to do," he said, taking an enormous bite out of the sandwich. He smacked his lips, gave her a thumbs up, and started in on the potato salad. Minerva walked in from the back laundry room and looked at him. "Hey, cat," he said to her. He always called her 'cat.' Minerva went over to him and wound herself around his ankles before moving to the front door and emitting a raucous yowl.

"Why not put a cat door in," Buddy said. "Save a bit on earplugs."

"She's too much of a hunter," Sarah said, opening the door for Minerva. "She would go out at all hours of the night and drag home a menagerie of dead things that would distress me when I got up in the morning." Just then, one of her computers sounded. "Excuse me, Buddy," she said. "I'll be right back."

As she walked back to her study, Sarah Ehrenson was hoping it was a message from the kidnappers. It had been nearly twenty-four hours since she'd sent the last message asking for proof of life for Mallory.

She quickly opened the email program and saw that indeed it was a reply from them. There was one attachment and a message. The message said: "No more krap. Look at the pix." She clicked on the attachment. What she saw was some sort of rough-hewn rectangular shelter, quite large, and a few old dusty carpenter tools and pieces of furniture. She also saw an ancient tractor and several things that looked like plows you could attach to it. There were narrow slits of sunshine playing on the room from a couple of horizontal windows high up one of the walls. In the forefront, she saw two men with black masks covering their faces. In the middle, a rather small woman with deep green eyes and straight brown hair was sitting on a chair, staring into the camera. Sarah recognized Mallory Weather. She looked unwell and exhausted, and she was holding a sign. It said, "If you don't want to find this woman lying in an unmarked shallow grave, be ready at ten o'clock tomorrow night to follow our instructions for where to drop the money." Sarah knew they'd made Mallory write that message herself. She started to feel sick, grabbed a small wastepaper basket and vomited most of the red zinger tea she'd recently enjoyed.

Cooper Grey and Jesse Shine were polishing the brass on the Portofino, Jeff Davis's 50-foot Sea Ray that was moored at the town pier in Carolina Beach. It was at least a good day's work, probably two. An hour earlier, Davis himself had gone shopping for food and drink at Trader Joe's in Wilmington.

The man and the kid were companionable and intent on the job.

Then, out of nowhere, Jesse Shine said, "My daddy hurts things."

Cooper Grey leaned back on his heels and put his polishing cloth down on the boat's teakwood deck. He'd been waiting for an opening like this and didn't want to blow it by frightening Jesse back into silence. Then he turned to the kid and said matter of factly, "Tell me a little bit about your daddy, son. What's his name?"

"Hollis," said the kid.

"And what kinds of things does he hurt?"

"Any kind goes against his way," the kid said. "Once, I had a cat like Minnie. One day, she talked back to my daddy, just like Minnie does with y'all, so he broke her neck. Me and my sister Sara buried her down by the river."

Just then, Jeff Davis hollered, "Hello the boat. I could use some help here, guys."

"Then," the kid said, getting up to go help Davis, "another time, my mother told him there weren't no more beer, so he threw her down a dry well. Took my older brothers and me hours to haul her out of there."

Cooper Grey, who had seen more than his share of familial abuse over the years he'd worked as a bail bondsman, felt his forehead bead with sweat. Then he stood up and went to help his friend Jefferson Davis with the provisions. He knew he'd soon have to take a ride over to Varnamtown. He just wasn't looking forward to it.

CHAPTER TWENTY FOUR

Billy Conroy was standing in front of the half-wall that separated the kitchen from the sunken living room in Bug Duvall's spacious mobile home. He was admiring a series of gorgeous photographs of wild orchids that Duvall had been commissioned to shoot for an issue of National Geographic. There were dozens of 16 by 20 portraits, including several of his favorites: yellow-fringed, fringeless, as well as white-fringed orchids. They were all native to the Green Swamp. So was Bug Duvall.

"You work a lot for the Geographic these days, Bug?" Billy asked.

"As much as I can," Duvall said. He was in the kitchen searing a couple of catfish fillets. He'd landed the big eight-pounder yesterday in the Waccamaw River. "They pay good and they're steady. I did a shoot for them last year—spiders. That was one hellacious job. Hadda do it in August. You can't hardly breathe in the swamp in August, Billy."

He walked back to join his friend and handed him a plate with a fresh fish sandwich topped with coleslaw and tartar sauce. "Let's sit over here by the window," he said.

When they'd eaten, Duvall took a pipe out of his side pocket, filled it, tamped it, and lit it. Billy Conroy always wished, at times like this, he still smoked.

"You remember the Dauterive clan?" Duvall said, sipping on his glass of rum.

Billy Conroy glanced out the picture window that overlooked the extensive vegetable garden in the big backyard. It was the sole province of Susanna Duvall, Bug's wife and the mother of his six children. "Those Louisiana transplants?" he said. "Some of them live in my county. A few of them have slept in my jail over the years."

"The head of the clan died awhile back." Bug said. "It has unsettled the parameters of the older boys' ambitions a bit. Old man Dauterive pretty much kept them in line, save the occasional stuff like bar fights and such. He was a flower poacher, you know. Wasn't a whole lot of return in it, but he was good at it. He kept his family fed."

"Nobody ever caught him at it in my county," Billy said. He was wondering where in hell this thing was going, but it wouldn't do him any good to try to hasten the story. Bug moved at his own pace.

"Two of his older boys, Pete and Ray Ray, are rumored to be haulin' handguns to points north. I say rumored because nobody's actually seen them. Myself, I believe it's likely true. Those boys have been whinin' about poverty under the old man's iron fist for years."

"They buyin' local, you think?" Billy said.

"I doubt it," Bug said. "More likely, they've gone back to their roots in Iberia Parish; my guess, Jeanerette. Or over in St. Mary's— Morgan City. Black market stuff you couldn't hardly find around here." He poured himself another drink. Billy Conroy put his hand over his glass. He'd had enough of the rum.

"The youngest one, Tommy, got the old man's airboat after he died," Duvall said, finally getting to it. "He's built a sort of lean-to in the swamp, sits on cinderblock, and he's poachin' protected species: American alligators, fox squirrels, black bears, and bobcats, not to mention the birds he kills for his own amusement. This ain't a rumor.

This I've seen, though he's unaware of it; I've photographed the bait and the traps. And I've got one sadly beautiful photo of a line of Henslow's sparrows and cockaded woodpeckers hanging upside down dead on a wire runnin' from a longleaf pine to that lean-to of his. He probably sells them for taxidermy. I knew I'd have to do something about it one of these days. I just couldn't figure what. The young man's a natural born predator and he's voracious."

Billy Conroy felt his pulse quicken. This was the information he'd been looking for. "You're speakin' of Tommy Too." he said. "That boy's been trouble bound since birth. I don't know how many times we picked him up on some minor charge or other. He's not been around much lately, though. Might could be you have just informed me why. But he's still got a two-acre plot of dirt with a bunch of fallin' down shacks on the outskirts of Supply." Duvall nodded and relit his pipe. "Where's the lean-to," Billy said, standing up.

"You'd never find it, Billy," Bug said. "I'll have to show y'all. And it can't be today. Our youngest is in a Thanksgiving show over at the school later this afternoon. She's a pumpkin. I gotta go. I promised Susanna. And I never break a promise to my wife."

Alvie had called Big Daddy Washington, who told him he would meet him at his shop on Marsteller Street at three o'clock. We had an hour to wait, so we drove back to George Cunningham's house to take a look inside the hidey hole, as Alvie called it. The three of us managed to shove the bed away from its intended place, and Alvie walked over to what looked like nothing except parquet tile and put his weight down on a corner of one of the squares. Up popped a piece of the floor. Inside, what looked to be a hole the size of a piece of typing paper was a strong box that was a tight fit. I reached for the handle and yanked it up and out.

"I don't have a key," Alvie said.

"We don't need a key," Stella said. "Give it here," she said to me. I handed it over and Stella dropped it hard on one of its corners. The box sprang open and stuff spilled out. There were legal papers from a few banks and one lawyer and two passports and a wallet. There was no name attached to two of the bank statements, just a number; both of them were based in Luxembourg, and both were simply letters of instruction. We looked in the wallet. It held ten thousand dollar bills, and one five-thousand-dollar bill. Both of the passports contained pictures of George Cunningham. Only one of them contained his name. The other one was in the name of Floyd Betters. There was also one small piece of paper with just a name: Riley Satterfield.

"It appears that your best friend George was plannin' a long vacation, Alvie, likely as someone else." Stella said to him.

"Yes," was all he said in reply.

"Do you know a Riley Satterfield," I said to him.

"No," Alvie said. He looked like someone had just hit him over the head with a frying pan. His eyes were unfocused. He was definitely on information overload. Stella and I exchanged a look, and I nodded and dialed my cell phone. When it was answered, I said, "We need anything you can find about a Riley Satterfield. Also, a Floyd Betters. Get back to me as quickly as you can."

"We've heard from the kidnappers," Sarah said, as though I hadn't spoken. "They want the exchange to take place tomorrow night at ten o'clock."

"We'll listen to it when we get back," I said. "Right now, this other information is vital."

Fifteen minutes later, as we were walking back to the Mustang to head over to Big Daddy Washington's store, my phone rang. It was Sarah. "Talk to me," I said, hitting speaker phone.

"There's a Riley Satterfield who used to live in Supply. He's got a juvenile sheet a mile long, mostly petty theft. He spent two years in a detention center for what they label 'wayward juvenile offenders.' He's twenty-six years old now. I am sending you the photo from his driver's license. It was taken last year. The address on it is no longer viable. Right now, he's off the radar. There are unconfirmed reports that he makes a pretty good living selling marijuana. The Wilmington police have him on their watch list."

The photo of Satterfield filled my cell phone screen. I glanced at it. He looked like every other skinny white guy with long greasy hair and a ribbon mustache I'd passed on the street for the last five years. There was nothing particular about him, not even his eyes. They were empty, as though he hadn't had an idea his entire life. "Okay," I said to her. "What about Floyd Betters."

"He was easy," Sarah said.

"What's that mean?" Stella said to her.

"It means he's dead. Has been for the last six months," Sarah said. "He died in an automobile accident over in Pender County that the authorities called suspicious; but nothing ever came of it. I would guess they called it suspicious because the car just blew up with him in it."

"Pender County," Stella said. "Lotta things happen in Pender County that never get explained. For all we know, they probably called it spontaneous combustion. It's like North Carolina's version of the wild wild west over there."

"Do we know how he made a living?" I asked Sarah.

"We do," she said and stopped talking.

"Well?" I said.

"How to put this," Sarah said, "so that what's important receives the proper emphasis." She was playing with my patience, something she often did.

"Try, please," I said.

"He was a currency and commodities trader," she said. "That he was unlicensed to ply that trade is of interest, mainly because the currency part of his business is thought to have involved counterfeiting. It's never been proven."

"No kidding," I said.

"No kidding," she answered. "And not always United States currency. Apparently he was also fond of our neighbors' monetary designs in Mexico and Canada. I've got to go. Minerva is tearing up the kitchen looking for something to eat." I listened to a dial tone.

As we piled into the Mustang, I realized I was starting to get a headache and not from the concussion. Every time I turned around, this damned case presented more and more questions and fewer and fewer answers. And Mallory Weather was still out there, somewhere, presumably in the middle of it all.

CHAPTER TWENTY FIVE

Mickey Huntley was back in her office after a depressing afternoon in criminal court. Her client, a defeated middle-aged woman named Isobel Bring, who'd been arrested and charged with attempted murder for trying to mow her husband down with his new Cadillac CTS, had been on the stand for three straight hours testifying to the most revolting litany of spousal abuse Mickey Huntley had ever elicited from anyone. Yet, at the end of the three hours of testimony, the Prosecutor for New Hanover County, Assistant District Attorney Byron Jessup, had actually stood up and asked her if she had any regrets about her actions.

"Yes," Isobel Bring had said quietly. "I regret I failed to kill him." You could have heard a pin drop in the courtroom, while Byron Jessup looked sternly at Mrs. Bring and then switched his gaze as though to chasten the twelve people on the jury.

Darius Millar knocked softly and walked into Mickey's office. "Boss," he said, and took a chair in front of her desk. She was sitting behind it with her head in her hands. "Boss," he said again. Mickey Huntley raised her head and looked at him.

"This fucking justice system," she said to him. "That fucking Byron Jessup."

"Don't call it before the jury does, boss," Darius Millar said to her. "You know how y'all fuss when you do that."

Mickey Huntley looked wanly at him. "You think I fuss?" she said.

"Least inflammatory word I could think of right this minute," he said. "Bleed might have been more accurate."

"What's caused this cheerleading effort from you?" she said to him.

"I heard your summation," he said, and walked over to a sideboard behind her desk. He took a couple of glasses out and poured a drink for both of them. When he handed Mickey Huntley hers, he said, "There are six women on that jury, boss. And at least three of them were head down, trying to disguise the heartache on their faces. It ain't rocket science to think that one or more of them will hang this jury, at a minimum. I swear you've never been better."

"I didn't see you in the courtroom," she said.

"I was up in the balcony," he said and clicked glasses with her.

"Well," Mickey Huntley said, "let's hope your admittedly biased assessment is correct. And Darius, do not say ain't."

"Boss," he said and smiled, knowing now that she'd corrected him Mickey Huntley was feeling better, and knowing he'd once again done his job.

Sheriff Billy Conroy was back on the road, this time in Brunswick County, this time driving his official car. He had arranged to meet with Bug Duvall tomorrow morning at a designated spot on the Waccamaw River to take a look at Tommy Dauterive's lean-to in the Green Swamp. If nothing else, he thought, I'll get him on poaching protected species, put him out of business, and scare the living shit right out of his foolish ass.

At the moment, though, he was going over to the young man's home, if you could call it that, outside Supply. He'd been there once before, when Tommy'd taken a shot at what he called an intruder. Turned out to be his neighbor, looking for his dog. Nobody'd been hurt. Nobody'd filed any charges.

Conroy drove slowly along the rutted dirt road leading to the place and finally pulled up in front of the shack where Tommy Too lived. He didn't hear a sound. He got out of his car slowly and unhooked the holster holding his gun. "Tommy Dauterive," he hollered. "Show yourself, boy. It's Sheriff Conroy." Nothing but silence followed.

Billy Conroy looked around and saw nothing. He went over to the structure that Tommy called a house and climbed the few steps to the sagging gallery, where two chairs and six empty beer cans were scattered around. He went to the front door and quietly opened it. His nostrils were immediately assaulted by an acrid smell he knew only too well. Marijuana, and recently. He walked into the shack. It was empty. After five minutes of looking around the sparsely furnished place, he had found nothing to suggest that Tommy Dauterive was involved in the kidnapping of Mallory Weather.

As he was about to get back into his car and drive away, he noticed that one of the many outbuildings scattered around the property had its doors closed and locked. It was the only one with a roof, and this made him curious about what this boy had that would require the protection of shut and padlocked doors. Maybe he's got a mess of animal skins in there, he thought. If so, it's evidence.

Billy Conroy walked to the small shed, took out his gun, and shot the lock open. He slid the doors apart and looked inside. Someone had backed or pushed an old car into the shed. It looked like a bucket of rust to Billy Conroy. Maybe the boy is going to try to restore it, he thought. After a cursory glance, he realized it was an old BMW. Well, at least the kid has some taste, he said to himself, and went back to his car and drove away.

When Stella Conroy parked the Mustang right in front of Big Daddy's place on Marsteller Street, there were two black men who could have passed for sumo wrestlers sitting in a couple of wrought iron love seats on either side of the store's front door. I think I stared. They barely fit.

"Those are two of his nephews," Alvie said. He still sounded subdued; his good mood had been replaced once again by fear and uncertainty.

"Sure they are," Stella Conroy said. "Most likely known as Frick and Frack. You could shoot a clip into either one of them; they'd swat you like a fly. Well, let's go. We sure as hell don't want to keep his majesty waiting."

"Stella," I said, with a slight edge to my voice. The last thing I wanted was for her to try out her assessment of these men.

"I know, I know," she said to me. "I will attempt to be on my best behavior with these disgustin' bloated dirt bags."

Alvie Weather blanched. I sent a silent prayer to whatever goddess watches over delicate situations like this. Probably Concordia.

As we approached the front door, nephew number one, on the left, stood up. He nodded at Alvie, who by now had started to falter. I braced him at his elbow for support.

"I gotta take a look," the guy said.

"At what," Stella said. "My curriculum vitae?"

The guy frowned. "Say what?" he said to her.

"We're here to see Mr. Washington," I said hurriedly before this devolved into the gunfight at the O. K. Corral. "We have an appointment and we're running a bit late."

The guy didn't seem to hear me at all. "What did y'all just say to me," he said again to Stella. His neck was sweaty.

"Nothin' you'd understand, you moron," she said to him. Clearly, she wasn't trying hard enough at manifesting good behavior. I let go of Alvie Weather and stepped up in case I needed a better angle for a warning shot.

Alvie said, "Oh no—oh no, please," and sat down hard on his butt, as the guy took a step toward Stella with his left arm raised to backhand her across the face. His hand was the size of a shovel. He'd knock her halfway across the street if he connected. She didn't even blink.

"Think twice," I said loudly to him with my colt leveled at his forehead. By now, the other guy was also on his feet. "Sit back down," I said to him, "and relax. This is just a misunderstanding. Tell Mr. Washington his three o'clock is here. Do it now." He dialed his phone while Stella and nephew number one continued to glare at each other.

"You called me a moron," he said to her. "Women don't say things like that to me, they like the way they look. I ain't stupid."

"My mistake," Stella Conroy said. Then, unbelievably, she added, "But you surely could have fooled me, fat boy." The look on the man's face said she was dead where she stood. Nothing I could say was going to stop him now. He went right up to her and put both his hands hard on her shoulders as though to pick her up and toss her like a mannequin, after which he'd no doubt stomp and beat her to death. I slid the safety off my gun.

A second later, Stella did a deep knee bend to lose his hold on her, stepped back a bit, rose back up and kicked him between his legs with such velocity and force I thought his baby-making potential was probably a thing of the past. The primal scream that came out of him brought a bunch of people running from surrounding stores and apartments; and when the guy toppled over like a huge stone statue, he barely missed poor Alvie, who would have been crushed flat by his weight.

At that moment, the front door opened and Big Daddy Washington looked out at the strange tableau in front of him. "What the hell," he said.

"Hello, Maurice," my partner said, "Long time no see. I expect what we have here is a simple failure to communicate."

"Stella Conroy," he said, as though her name alone could make him nauseous. "You did this?"

"Did what, Maurice?" she said. "Oh, you mean King Kong there kissing the concrete? Yeah, I helped him remember his manners." Big Daddy Washington nodded. I was helping Alvie to his feet.

"You should have told me who your friends were, Alvie," Big Daddy said. The fallen fat man was moaning softly and holding his crotch and trying and failing to get back to a standing position. "Help him out, for Christ's sake, Moses," Big Daddy said to the second nephew.

By now, Alvie was showing all the signs that announce his intention to faint. I gripped him hard by his arm and held him up. But miraculously, he didn't faint. Instead, he said, "I'm sorry, Mr. Washington. I didn't realize there was such hostility between you and Ms. Conroy; but nevertheless, she is my friend and she and her partner here, Cash Delaney, are helping me. You see, my wife Mallory's been kidnapped and there's somethin' we found that gives us hope y'all could aid us in our quest to find and rescue her. I am a desperate man, sir, without my wife. And after all our years of beneficial interaction, I count on your kindness and good will."

You've got to give it to Southerners. When they decide to work it, their rhetoric soars. I was impressed, and not the least by Alvie's obvious sincerity.

So was Big Daddy Washington. "Stella and I do have our antagonisms, Alvie," he said. "But they don't amount to an ant hill next to your trouble. Come on in. Let's see if I can help you locate your wife."

CHAPTER TWENTY SIX

Jefferson Davis and Cooper Grey were putting the groceries that Davis had bought at Trader Joe's in the various places aboard the boat where they belonged. Jesse Shine was up on deck continuing to polish the boat's brass.

"I got all the things I need to whip up one of Katherine's favorite dinners," Davis said. "Mussels in white wine, garlic, and butter; a real Caesar salad, thick loin lamb chops, and Anjou pears with Stilton. I found a 2000 vintage BV merlot last night in the wine cellar I forgot I had."

"Bribery will get you everywhere," Cooper said, putting a package of scones and a loaf of sourdough bread in a tin-lined drawer next to the refrigerator. "Of course, you first have to persuade her to get on the boat before you can feed her."

"I am working on that, Cooper," Davis said. "Are y'all really of the opinion she's irreparably angry with me?"

"I don't know. I only know Stella would be madder than a hornet defending its nest if I'd performed the way you did with Katherine."

Jeff Davis put the last of the perishables in the refrigerator. "Well," he said. "Katherine isn't Stella. I can hope she's more distressed than angry and that she'll be willing to accept my explanation."

"Boss," Jesse Shine called out. "Miss Sarah's on the dock, she's wantin' to come on board." Jefferson Davis looked at Cooper Grey; the two men hustled topside.

"Permission to board," Sarah said to the two men.

"Why would you even ask," Cooper Grey said, going over to assist her.

"It seemed wise to learn whether or not we were all still friends," she said. She wasn't smiling.

Jeff Davis looked balefully at her. "Katherine told you," he said.

"She did," Sarah said.

"Just how angry is she," he said softly. He was rubbing his hands up and down his pant legs. His nerves were clearly on edge.

"This isn't my business to talk about, Jeff," she said.

"Give the man a break, Sarah," Cooper Grey said. "Right now, he's in hell. Even purgatory's better than that."

"Well," Sarah said, after taking a moment to consider whether she should say any more than she already had, "The truth is, Jefferson, I saw no anger at all. Just a bone-weary sadness. It seems you wanted more from Cash than she was willing to give. I believe she thought you'd actually listened to her when she told you what she could bring to a relationship. Cash likes to believe that people who are important to her really do listen to what she has to say. And if you have the audacity to tell her any of what I've just said, then shame on you, Jefferson Davis."

———————————————

Big Daddy Washington didn't look like any drug dealer I had ever encountered. He looked like what Alvie said he was: a dealer in expensive antiques. He was wearing a black and gray pinstripe three-piece suit. There was a rose-gold watch fob spanning the suit vest.

His shoes were soft dark grey leather. His cuff links were onyx. Although he was tall, probably six-foot-two or so, there didn't appear to be an ounce of fat on him. His skin was the color of milk chocolate. He was probably in his middle forties. All in all, he was a striking individual.

"Let's take this discussion to my private quarters," he said. "If you'll follow me, it's at the back of the store." You might have thought he'd graduated from Cornell. For all I knew, maybe he had.

As we wended our way to his office, we passed room after room of gorgeous and unusual antiques. There was one billed "The Oak Room," another billed "Before 1800," another that was filled with what looked to me like a wide variety of maple antiquities, including one bird's-eye maple lowboy that I wanted to walk over and just admire; one room was filled with paintings, another with sculpture. I realized his establishment ran from Marsteller Street to the next street over. It was huge. It wasn't any wonder that Alvie had believed Big Daddy when he said he made his money selling antiques.

"You've expanded, Maurice," Stella said. "The last time I was over this way, y'all had a room full of junk you'd hauled from the dump, called it collectibles."

"The last time you were here was regrettable, Stella," Big Daddy said, as he opened his office door. "Do you want to rehash?"

"No," she said.

I had no clue what they were talking about, but I knew it couldn't be good. I was grateful for her restraint. Alvie hurried through the door and took a seat in front of Big Daddy's partner's desk. Stella and I sat on either side of him.

"Now then," Big Daddy said. "Enlighten me."

"Mallory was kidnapped four days ago," I said. "What we have learned to date tells us that Alvie's manager, George Cunningham, was involved. He's now dead, along with another still unidentified man. It appears that they shot each other in Alvie's shed at the Port of Wilmington, where we think they were holding Mallory. That shed was wired and subsequently exploded when the trip wire was breached. At this point, we are dealing with person or persons unknown who continue to reach us via email. Our last communication from them sets tomorrow night at ten o'clock for the exchange of two million dollars for Mallory Weather."

"I heard about the bomb at the Port," Big Daddy said. "It's got a number of associates of mine all fired up because the FBI's got Raleigh involved, and nobody's saying anything about what's really going on."

"The FBI has no information to put out," Stella said. "They don't know about the kidnapping, and subsequently they are scratchin' their heads tryin' to understand why two guys would shoot each other over a bunch of cars in a shed at the port. The lead investigator thinks there's somebody out there who can explain it all to him because the shed blew up after the two of them were dead. So he's not willing to close the case and move on. The man wants his questions answered."

"As you know very well, Stella," said Big Daddy, "those boys are overly suspicious by nature. They see a happy man, he's too happy. Must be something's wrong. Check it out until you make the poor bastard miserable. But Alvie, how do I fit into the situation? I don't know a damned thing about it."

Alvie reached into his suit jacket and pulled out the envelope we'd found. "This was on a table in George's foyer," he said, handing it to Big Daddy. "We got to it before the FBI did."

Maurice Washington took the envelope and removed the money and cellophane bags and the slip of paper with three names, laid them all on his desk and studied them.

"My my my my my," he said after a minute or so. "What in this wide wicked world was George planning to unleash?"

"That's the trouble," I said. "We don't know. But you do know

George?" Big Daddy looked at me as though he was trying to decide if I was bright enough to understand left from right. I must have passed the test.

"George is, was, a wannabe player," he said. "He called me must be six, seven days ago; was I interested in some information that would take down a major competitor of mine. Competition's what keeps me on my toes. I told him no. That's the last time I heard from him. I don't know what he was peddling, although these bags of cocaine, if it is cocaine, put an idea in my head. They're probably from whatever competitor he was speaking about."

"What about the other two names," Stella said. We could both feel Alvie's disappointment. He was sitting with his head down, staring at the floor.

"Floyd Betters is dead," Big Daddy said. "His car blew up somewhere in rural Pender County with him in it. Called himself a commodities trader. To Floyd, that meant counterfeit money and crystal meth. Street chatter is his fifth wife hired the hit due to Floyd's nasty habit of chasing after any woman he happened to run across in the course of an afternoon or evening. First rule of marriage: understand your woman. Floyd never managed to master that. Rowdy Gaines is another story entirely. Moses," he hollered. "We need some refreshments in here."

Refreshments turned out to be finger sandwiches of lox and chives and cream cheese and a glass of sweet iced tea. Big Daddy's phone rang. "Tell me," he said. Then he looked up at the ceiling and rolled his eyes. "Not now Violet," he said. "Why? Because I am busy doing God's work. That is why." He hung up and grinned at us. His teeth were very white and straight in his mouth. He could have done toothpaste commercials had he needed the money. "My wife is testy," he said. "She thought we were destined for Myrtle Beach when you called. For some reason, she likes it down there in winter."

"Rowdy Gaines," I said to get him back on track. He nodded.

"Rowdy's out of Durham," Big Daddy said. "He owns one of the biggest books in North Carolina. He'd take a bet on whether or not you woke up tomorrow if the price was right. Then he'd see to it you lost the bet, one way or another. This name can't mean but one thing: George must have owed him a bundle."

"What's a bundle," Stella said, sitting forward in her chair. I felt her excitement. Maybe we were finally getting to it.

"At least half a million, probably more. Most likely George had dug himself a hole he couldn't get out of. He was a hopeless, inveterate gambler; his true weakness was college sports, although he dabbled in just about everything, including politics." he said. "That give you an idea of the heavy hitters in Rowdy's little black book?"

"We've got one other name," I said. "Riley Satterfield." Big Daddy laughed.

"Well," he said, "he's a kid who's a train wreck, sells trainwreck. George probably bought from him or his partner, Dutch Boutelle."

"What is trainwreck," Alvie said, with a frown on his face.

"Pot," Big Daddy said. "Riley's got a few steady customers. I heard he and Dutch grow the stuff themselves. I like to keep track of them, make sure they don't cross lines. The two of them live over in Brunswick County, somewhere near Supply, close to the Green Swamp."

Stella Conroy and I stood up so quickly, it startled Alvie Weather. "What's wrong?" he asked anxiously.

"Nothing," Stella said. "We've got to go, is all. Thank the man, Alvie. We have got some serious work to do.

CHAPTER TWENTY SEVEN

Sheriff Billy Conroy was sitting in his office in Bolivia, North Carolina, wondering if he should call his daughter and decided it was better to let her pursue her own investigation of the kidnapping. He'd meet Bug Duvall tomorrow, take a look at Tommy Dauterive's lean-to and then decide if it was useful. His phone rang.

"Conroy," he said.

"We have some important information, Daddy," Stella Conroy said hurriedly into her hands-free phone. "We think we know about where the kidnappers are holdin' Mallory Weather." She was driving her normal bat-out-of-hell rate of eighty miles an hour, heading for Snow's Cut Bridge. She was occasionally brought to her senses by traffic lights.

"What?" he said, surprised. "Where, for God's sake?"

"You know a Riley Satterfield or a Dutch Boutelle?"

Billy Conroy felt a tingle run along his spine. "They are two juvenile delinquents I kept having to arrest back in the day," he said. What he didn't right that minute add was that they'd always been trailed after by a smaller boy named Tommy Dauterive. "Why?"

"We have it on good authority they grow pot somewhere near Supply, close to the Green Swamp, and Satterfield's name we found on a slip of paper in George Cunningham's hidey-hole lockbox," his daughter said. "Apparently, he and Dutch were Cunningham's regular suppliers. We think they could be Mallory's abductors, as well. Probably hired by Cunningham. Our source tells us George was in big-time debt to Rowdy Gaines."

Billy Conroy wondered how much more this case could possibly bring to his doorstep. "Rowdy Gaines runs a deadly serious high roller book out of Durham," he said to his daughter. "What in hell does he have to do with this?"

"Nothin' except our source tells us Cunningham likely owed him at least half a million dollars. We think he might have been fixin' to skip with the ransom, he pulled it off, because we also found a passport with his picture and somebody else's name."

Billy Conroy thought a bit before he said, "This source of yours? Reliable, you think?"

"Yes, Sheriff," Cash Delaney interjected. Stella shot her a look. "But not one you'd sanction. Big Daddy Washington."

"Well," said the Sheriff pragmatically, "it does us no good to shoot the messenger, although I wouldn't necessarily mind in this particular case. Where are y'all now?"

"We'll be crossing the bridge in ten minutes," his daughter said. "Sarah says we've got another message from the kidnappers. They want the exchange tomorrow night at ten o'clock."

"Okay. I'll meet you at the cottage. I have some new information of my own."

Alvie Weather, sitting in the back seat of the Mustang, allowed himself to hope once again that his wife would be found safe and unharmed. Then he knew he'd have to deal with his other dilemma. First things first, he told himself. If we get Mallory back alive, I can handle the rest.

Sarah Ehrenson had gone below deck to speak with Jeff Davis and Cooper Grey. The kid was up on the boat's flying bridge still polishing brass.

"Jesse seems to be feeling better," Sarah said to Jeff Davis.

"We had a talk," Davis said. "I explained to him what I thought he'd understand and then I apologized. I don't think he even knew what an apology was. Now, he does. Far as I can tell, right now, he's fine." He smiled at her. "And I must say I am also experiencin' a small sense of relief."

"Don't count your chickens, Jeff," she said. "I just drew the lines. You've still got to paint the picture. But that's not why I walked over to see you today. Junior Fisk shared some information about Jesse and his circumstances I thought you should know about. He implied that there's serious familial abuse in the Shine household. People feel that the father, for some unknown reason, threw the mother down a dry well; and Jesse's sister Sara probably died of nicotine poisoning after being lent to her uncle to help pick his tobacco crop two years ago when she was ten years old. There wasn't an autopsy, so it's not provable. It's a very ugly and disheartening situation."

"I can confirm the rumor about the mother," Cooper Grey said quietly. "Jesse opened up a bit to me today. His father, he told me, hurts things. And one of those things was a cat that Jesse had who annoyed the man: he broke its neck. The other was Jesse's mother. The man actually did toss her down a well because she told him they were out of beer. Jesse told me it took him and his brothers hours to get her out of there. I have to say, as often as I've run into abusive situations during the years I spent as a bail bondsman, this ranks right up with the worst of them."

Jefferson Davis sat down hard on a captain's chair, a stunned look on his face. "Good lord, good lord, good lord," he said, sounding both awed and dismayed. "No wonder the child said what he did to me so matter-of-factly. He has no sense of propriety. Worse, he's inured to violence."

"Probably," Sarah said. "But he does seem uninterested in hurting anything himself. He loves Minerva. He wants to be around you and your friends; he's a good little worker, and he's bright. Mickey says we can help him. Being the student of politics that I am, I have my doubts, especially given the current state of this State. But we'll see. She's coming over to the cottage after court this afternoon." Sarah looked at her watch. "In fact, she may be there now. I've got to run. See you later." And she was gone.

Sheriff Billy Conroy decided to drive to Dutch Boutelle's home to see if anyone was there before heading over to Carolina Beach to see his daughter. It was fifteen miles out of his way, so he took his cruiser and activated the flashing light. When he turned on Lula Trail, in Shallotte, the third trailer on the left, sitting on a half-acre of hard-packed sand fringed in back by a bunch of trees, was the one he was looking for. It was a Marlette single-wide, twelve by fifty six, about fifty years old. When it was new it had been bright white over turquoise; now, it was rusty ochre over a bluish brown. It was missing most of its skirting and two of its windows were boarded up. It was resting on a bunch of railroad ties. He pulled off the road, and put his hand on his gun before exiting the car. As he approached the door, he saw a small child hovering nearby. He smiled at the little girl.

"How y'all doin'?" he said to her. The child said nothing. She was about eight years old, and she was wearing pink tights with a pair of purple long shorts over them. Her wool shirt was black and a little too big for her, but it looked warm to Billy Conroy. She had a pair of green socks and new white sneakers on her feet, and she was a towhead. She reminded him of his daughter Stella at that age. "You live around here?" Still, nothing in reply. "Cat got your tongue?" he said, and walked over to her. The little girl stood her ground.

"Dutch isn't home," she said to him.

"Where's he at then," Billy Conroy asked her.

"Don't know," she said. "I haven't seen him in a while. He and Riley left to go somewhere."

"Riley Satterfield?" Billy Conroy said to her. "He lives here, too?"

"I guess. He didn't always. He moved in a year ago," she said.

"So they left a while ago," the Sheriff said. "How long is a while?"

The child considered this before she said, "Near a week. Dutch pays me a fiver to feed his parakeets. I been doin' it now since last Thursday. He owes me some." Billy Conroy nodded.

"The trailer open?" he asked her.

"Nope. But I got a key. Besides, I know who you are," she said seriously. "You've been on the TV a lot. Y'all want in?"

"That would be good," he said to her.

When she opened the door and walked in ahead of him, the odor that hit him in the face told him that this was where the boys most likely kept the weed they sold on the street. Billy Conroy wondered if the child even noticed it. He looked around the small space. There was an unmade sofa bed in the cramped living room, and a sink full of dishes in the tiny kitchen. A few water bugs scattered when he walked up to the kitchen cabinets to take a look inside, where he found nothing but more dishes and a few pots and pans. The little girl was sitting on a coffee table next to the sofa, talking to the birds.

Billy Conroy walked down the narrow hallway and looked in the first bedroom where he found a double bed and two dressers. There was a scattering of clothes lying on the bed, nothing of interest in either dresser, and more clothes hanging in the closet. He walked farther and passed an uninspiring bathroom. When he slid open the connecting door at the rear of the trailer, he found what he was looking for: marijuana drying out, marijuana in nickel and dime bags, and a cash box that was locked. He felt a tiny hand poking him in the back.

"What's your name, child," he said as he turned to the girl, blocking her view of the room.

"Queenie Abbott," she said to him, and squared her little shoulders as if preparing to defend against an unfavorable reaction from him.

"That's one fine name," he said to her. She grinned.

"It's my mimaw's," she said proudly. "I'm named after her. My daddy says I'm the most like her of anybody in our whole family."

"I just bet you are," said Billy Conroy. "Let's go see about those birds, Queenie. I think maybe y'all had better take them home with you for a little while. How would your daddy feel about that, you think."

Queenie Abbott shrugged. "Okay, I guess. But Dutch won't like it."

Billy Conroy thought about this. "Where's your daddy at now," he said to her.

"Work. He's the boss at the Subway in Supply."

"All right, then," he said to her. "Here's what we're gonna do. Y'all are taking the birds with you for safekeeping, and I'm gonna stop and chat with your daddy about it. Okay?"

"OK," she said. Then she added, "Has something happened to Dutch?"

"Nothin' that I know about right now, Queenie," he said to her. "But I'm the Sheriff around here so I like to be on the right side of things. Y'all understand?"

When the two of them left the trailer, Queenie Abbott was assuring the two parakeets that nothing was wrong; they were just going for a visit. Billy Conroy said to her, "You'd best leave the trailer key with me, Queenie. I might have to get back in sometime later on."

She looked quizzically at the Sheriff for a few moments. "Y'all are sayin' Dutch is never comin' home?"

The Sheriff sighed and put his hand on her left shoulder. "I don't exactly know right now," he said to her. "Maybe he is, maybe he isn't. But I will most assuredly be findin' out. You got my word on that."

"He taught me how to ride my bike," eight-year-old Queenie Abbott said. "Dutch's always been nice to me."

CHAPTER TWENTY EIGHT

"I don't know how it's going to go," Mickey Huntley said to Sarah Ehrenson. They were standing in the kitchen at the cottage on Beach House Lane, grilling shrimp in hot sauce and lemon-flavored olive oil and steaming rice in coconut milk for an early supper. Sarah was fixing a salad of avocado and red onion and Bibb lettuce.

"It's difficult enough to get a jury to acquit on battered woman syndrome in New York. But this is North Carolina, for God's sake, where too many men still see women as chattel, regardless of whether they will admit it or not. And I argued self-defense rather than temporary insanity. That always perplexes men, naturally. She hit him with a car, they say to themselves. Where's the imminent danger to her in that? And because men tend to dismiss charges of spousal abuse as hyperbolic, or worse, the fantasy of an hysterical woman, they often ignore it. But if these twelve people do convict her, she could get a prison sentence of what amounts to the rest of her active life. Darius insists there's at least one woman who will hang the jury. I have my doubts. Men find a way to bully women into submission around here, especially behind closed doors. And they often do it with an exaggerated use of manners."

"I don't want to sound like Pollyanna, Mickey," Sarah said.

"because I've never in my life been accused of that. But surely some sense of feminism has touched this State in the last fifty years. Women down here may joke about it as a way of deflecting attention away from it, but it must have taken root, especially in a somewhat enlightened city like Wilmington."

"We'll see," the lawyer said, just as her phone rang. "Will you get that, Sarah? I've got to turn these shrimp."

"Mickey Huntley's line," Sarah said. "I see," she said. "Of course," she said. "I'll tell her immediately." Sarah turned to the kitchen. "Your jury's back, Mickey," she said.

"Already?" the lawyer said in alarm. "It's only been a few hours. Hell, this can't be good. Will you call Darius and tell him to meet me at court? I may have to be restrained from clobbering Byron Jessup if the verdict goes against me." She hustled over to the door and slipped into her coat. "Save a little something for me," she said, kissing Sarah lightly on the lips.

"I always do," Sarah said, crossing her fingers behind her back for good luck.

We were quite a bit later than we had anticipated getting to the cottage because Stella had been stopped for speeding and hadn't been able to talk her way out of it. The State Trooper who had pulled her over was unimpressed with everything Stella threw at him. Finally, he had just written her the ticket, which amounted to a huge fine of over four-hundred dollars and most likely multiple points on her license, handed it to her, tipped his hat and told her to have a nice day. That gratuitous expression was more than Stella could bear.

"I detest cops," she said vehemently, lighting a cigarette and taking a deep drag and exhaling. The front seat filled with smoke. I opened my window and flapped my hands around to move it out.

"Stella," I said to her, "your father's a cop. You were a cop. A few of your friends are cops. You don't hate cops."

"Right now I do," she said crossly. "That particular self-righteous preening goddamned son of a bitch anyway."

Alvie Weather cleared his throat, and then he coughed. We were sitting at the side of the road across from a squat cinder block store that looked like a dump where you could rent, and maybe even watch, adult movies. "Girls, girls, girls," a handwritten sign screamed in bright orange on an unpainted two-by-four. The sagging neon sign above the door had run out of gas. The square front parking lot was gravel, and no automobiles were there. The place was sandwiched between two churches, whose denomination I had never heard of before. As odd as this juxtaposition was, I silently approved. I figured maybe the parishioners of those two establishments had prayed the sorry shack to death.

"It was most especially unnecessary, he said what he did at the end," Alvie Weather said primly. It dawned on me that he was trying to mollify Stella, and it did seem to catch her off guard.

I saw the beginning of a smile on her face, as she said, "You are exactly right, Alvie. Have a nice day, for Christ's sake. I should have told him to shove his nice day right up his tight white hidebound ass."

I turned and grinned at Alvie, who was looking rather pleased with himself. And so we proceeded at a rather sedate speed, at least for Stella, of sixty miles an hour until we came to the bridge. When finally we pulled up to the cottage, Cooper Grey was standing at the front of the house, knocking on the door.

"I wonder what's goin' on," Stella said, opening her car door. Alvie and I followed.

"Hey," he said to us.

"Hey yourself," I said. "Something happen?" The front door opened, and Sarah looked out.

"Oh, good," she said. "You're all here at once."

Alvie Weather had a frown on his face. "Where is the other gentleman who was so helpful the last time we were all together," he said. "I believe his name was Jefferson Davis. He very kindly fetched me a drink of soda when I desperately needed one." Leave it to Alvie, I thought to myself.

"He'll be along shortly," Sarah said blithely. "He's fixing a little supper for Jesse at the moment." I stopped in my tracks and stared wide-eyed at her. She stared right back, unfazed. So in an inadvertent way, I had answered my own question: yes, something had happened. I wasn't sure I wanted to know just what it was.

Mickey Huntley hurried into the courtroom where her client, Isobel Bring, was sitting at the defense table next to Darius Millar, who looked to be trying to calm her down. The woman's hands were shaking so badly she couldn't safely hold a glass of water to take a sip from it. This is what you do for a living, the lawyer said to herself. So put your stone face on, and go do it.

Mickey Huntley took her place on Isobel Bring's right, glanced at Byron Jessup, who was studiously ignoring her, and turned to her client, who was crying quietly. Mickey looked over Isobel's bowed head at Darius Millar.

"She threw up on the way over here, boss," he said softly.

"I'm very afraid," her client whispered. Sweat was beading on her upper lip, but when Mickey Huntley reached for her hand, it was icy cold.

The lawyer put her arm around her client's trembling shoulders and quietly said, "I promise you this will be all right, Isobel. Do you hear me? I promise. Even if I have to appeal it all the way to the Supreme Court."

"I don't know if I can stand up when I'm ordered to," the woman said, sounding totally hopeless. Tears were drawing wavy lines down her face.

"That's nothing to be worried about," Mickey Huntley told her. "You'll be fine. Darius and I will make sure of that. Can you try to wipe your face if Darius gives you a handkerchief?"

The woman nodded, just as the jury began to file into the room. Not one of them looked at the defense table. Mickey Huntley had decided years ago that this failure was a predictor of absolutely nothing. Nobody outside the legal profession was ever comfortable in a court of law, especially when a verdict was being announced.

A side door opened and the Right Honorable Alton Wallace of the Supreme Court of North Carolina from the Fifth District walked to the bench. Everybody stood, although the defendant stumbled a little.

The judge gaveled the people in the room back to their seats, and after a bit of ritual court proceedings, he turned to the jury and asked if there was a verdict. Told that there was, he ordered the defendant to rise and the verdict to be read. Isobel Bring tried to stand. Her legs wouldn't hold her.

"Your honor," Mickey Huntley said, "My client is unwell and under significant stress. I ask that she be allowed to remain seated while the verdict is read."

"So ordered," Judge Wallace answered, turning to the jury foreman and nodding his head. The jury foreman was, in this case, a forewoman, a fifty-four year old divorced bank teller named Dot Wills who was the mother of three grown daughters and the grandmother of seven little girls and boys. She had been the focal point of Mickey Huntley's closing argument in this case.

"In the case of the State of North Carolina versus Isobel Bring," she said very clearly, "on the charge of attempted murder in the first degree, we find the defendant Isobel Bring not guilty."

Mickey Huntley was stunned, although her face did not betray her. She had privately expected a guilty verdict with a possible lenient sentence from this judge, for whom she had a great deal of respect. Her client was sobbing, "What did she say? Tell me. What?" Darius Millar was grinning like the Cheshire cat, and patting Isobel Bring lightly on the back. Byron Jessup was openly scowling at the members of the jury, his jaw clenched, as though they had lost their minds. He looked unable to accept what he had just heard. As the judge was thanking the jury members for their service, Dot Wills glanced at Mickey Huntley, gave her a quick nod, and turned and walked away.

"You are not guilty of a crime, Isobel. You were, as you testified, defending yourself. You're free from this torment," the lawyer said to her client. "You are finally free at last." If Mickey Huntley heard an echo from an earlier time in those few, simple words, she kept it to herself.

Darius Millar was paving the way for his boss and her client to make the trek back to the law office while a bunch of reporters swarmed around them, waiting for a statement. Other than "no comment," none was forthcoming. As they reached the bottom of the courthouse stairs, Mickey Huntley saw the jury forewoman talking with a reporter from WSFX, a FOX News television affiliate in Wilmington. The lawyer paused as the reporter said,

"There seems to be quite a bit of consternation, not to say amazement, among some members of the legal community over your verdict today."

"Really?" said Dot Wills, sounding surprised. "I can't for the life of me imagine why."

"Well," the reporter said a bit smugly, "battered woman syndrome is most always unsuccessful in serious felony cases like this."

"I didn't know that," the forewoman said, "but it clearly shouldn't be. It's a darn sight better and more believable than that stand-your-ground thing, or whatever they call it, that's legal down in Florida, where a jury just found a man innocent of murdering an unarmed teenager in cold blood because he said he felt threatened.

This woman Isobel Bring didn't just feel threatened; she was threatened, for twelve long years. By the time that lawyer of hers got through letting us in on the real story, I wanted to kill the son of a bitch myself. And all that poor woman did was break his leg, because she actually swerved away from him at the last second. She didn't deserve to go to jail over something like that. Compared to what her husband did to her, what she did to him was just a tad short of nothing. Besides, she'd already served her time." Dot Wills smiled and looked hard at the reporter. "You get what I'm saying here, young man?"

If that laudably common-sense explanation of the not guilty verdict was what the Fox News reporter had been expecting to hear from Dot Wills, he unfortunately gave no indication of it. Instead, while she walked away, he remained silent for several seconds, staring after her, a big no-no in television land. Mickey Huntley and entourage hurried by, as the reporter finally recovered enough to say whatever his name was and for whom he was reporting.

CHAPTER TWENTY NINE

"I am chagrined," the note from Jeff said, "although I can't apologize and I know you would not expect me to; but you do need to know how much I love you and how much I do not want to lose you. Sarah has just called and said that both Cooper and I are going to have to help with this Mallory Weather kidnapping. Billy Conroy can't involve his force without involving the FBI. So can we put our private matters on hold while we work on rescuing this woman? You have no idea how bereft I am without you, Katherine." I was standing in my study with my back to the door.

"I see you read the note," Sarah said. I hastily wiped tears from my eyes. I had not been expecting anything like this to happen, given my previous history with Allen Church back in Ithaca. To say I was surprised would have been to understate it a little. I was flabbergasted.

"Can I let Jeff know that it's okay if he joins us?"

"Of course," I murmured

I listened to her dial her cell phone, and when it was answered all she said was "It's fine." I was still standing with my back to my friend. But Sarah wasn't going to put up with that. She walked over to me and turned me around and hugged me. "You got a keeper this time, Cash," she said to me.

I stepped back and smiled at her. "It looks to me as though we both did." I said. "And all we had to do was move to a place we'd never have chosen to go if it weren't for Laura's murder."

"Oh well," Sarah said, "that was just luck. Besides, living here keeps us sharp. Progressives like us can become complacent up north where a lot of people agree with us most of the time. A little controversy is good for the soul. What's more, the weather's wonderful and the seafood is always fresh. And eventually, the voting public comes to its senses and gets rid of the Republicans for a little while." I laughed and realized just how relieved I felt. Until now, I'd been unwilling to admit how unhappy I was about the situation with Jefferson.

Something iridescent caught the corner my eye, and when I looked I saw Minerva in the doorway with something scary in her mouth.

"Uh, Sarah," I said.

"What?"

"Turn around and look at our cat."

When she did, she said, "Jesus Christ, Minerva. Don't bring snakes into your home." Minerva preened, dropped the snake, and purred. The snake slithered right toward Sarah and me. It got about two or three inches away from the cat before she pounced and sank her teeth in the middle of its back.

"It's a rat snake," Sarah said, "They're not poisonous, and I think she wants to play with it." She walked over and took my New York Yankee's baseball bat off the wall. Then she went over to Minerva, who was making a funny clicking sound in her throat and swinging the snake back and forth, and said, "Drop it." The cat swung the snake a few more times and then she tossed it in the air. When it landed, about a foot from my toes, Sarah walloped its head with the baseball bat. Minerva registered her disapproval by swatting at the now dead snake and emitting a high-decibel yowl that brought everyone in from the living room to see what was going on.

"It's nothing," I said to the three of them.

"Nothin'?" Stella Conroy exclaimed. "That damn thing looks like a copperhead to me."

"Oh my," Alvie said. "They are poisonous."

"It would be if that's what it was," Sarah said. "But it's just a rat snake. Harmless, really.

"Let's get it out of here," Cooper said. "How'd it get in here, anyway?"

"Minerva wanted a playmate," I said.

"That cat," Stella Conroy muttered. I would have loved to hear what she might have added were she by herself.

Cooper picked up the rather pretty dead snake and walked to the front door. He was followed by Minerva, who was obviously interested in its final resting place.

"I want you to take a look at our last message from the kidnappers," Sarah said. "We need as many perspectives on the possible location as we can get."

"Do I want to see it?" Alvie Weather said rather timidly. "It hurts my heart to see Mallory in any kind of pain."

"I don't guess you'd be much help with the location, Alvie," Stella said. "You go on back to the living room and keep an eye out for Daddy and Jeff."

We were all walking out of my study: Alvie was going to the front of the cottage, the three of us were headed to the back, when I heard a voice say, "Where's everybody off to?" Jefferson Davis had arrived.

Sheriff Billy Conroy had driven to the Subway in Supply to speak with Queenie Abbott's father. He kept his conversation brief, but to the point, letting the man know about the situation with the parakeets, and telling him to keep his daughter away from the trailer where Dutch Boutelle and Riley Satterfield had lived and why.

After that, he had driven back to his office in Bolivia where he brought two of his deputies up to speed on the situation regarding the pot and cash box he'd found in the trailer, ordered them to set up a round-the-clock watch on the single-wide in case either man returned, and gave them the key to the place. But he did not expect that either Boutelle or Satterfield would be returning. He was fairly certain that one of them was dead, and the other one was still out there someplace holding Mallory Weather hostage for ransom. He did not share these thoughts with his men. He didn't want to compromise them in case there were problems with the Feds at a later date.

Then he'd climbed back into his cruiser and begun the thirty minute drive to Carolina Beach. On the way, he alerted Sarah Ehrenson that Cooper Grey and Jeff Davis would probably be needed to assist if and when they pinpointed Mallory's location. Then he turned on his siren and cut the drive down to twenty minutes. When he pulled up outside the cottage, he went to the front door and walked in. Alvie Weather was standing in the kitchen pouring himself a cup of coffee.

"Where's everyone?" the Sheriff asked.

"Back in Sarah's study," Alvie said. Billy Conroy tipped his hat and hurried down the hallway on the left. When he got to the room, Jeff Davis was saying,

"Zero in on that rear wall, Sarah, where that narrow window is." When she did, all they could see was a pile of stuff and some sunlight, although it was difficult to discern specific objects. Billy Conroy walked up to get a closer look.

"Is that the last photo you got," he said to Sarah.

"Yes," she said.

"I doubt that's where she'll be when they want to make the exchange," the Sheriff said. "That shed looks like one of any number of abandoned shacks that are found all over my county. Might even be one of old man Dauterive's, though I doubt it."

"Old man who?" Stella said to him.

"Dauterive," he said. "I have got to bring y'all up to speed." And in about five minutes, he did just that. "So now," he said, "I am goin' out tomorrow early with Bug Duvall to locate the lean-to that Tommy Too has built, and where I reckon they will eventually be taking Mallory Weather."

"If they haven't already," Cash Delaney said.

"Yeah," Stella said. "If you're right, Daddy, that the unidentified body in the bombed out shed at the Port is either Dutch Boutelle or Riley Satterfield, then whichever one is still alive is probably a killer. It's risky to alert whoever that is."

"I am not going to wander up and knock on the door, Stella," the Sheriff said. "And y'all would have to know Bug Duvall the way I do to know that we'll never be noticed when we check the place out. But if we're able to confirm that Mallory is there, all bets are off. We can't just walk away and leave her because they could decide to kill her regardless of any assurances to the contrary that they give us."

"Are you intimatin' they will kill my wife?" Alvie Weather said hysterically. He was standing in the doorway, and his eyes were the size of saucers. "I am payin' the ransom," he said. "I am doin' what they want. And still, they'll kill her?"

"We're just making sure that doesn't happen, Alvie," Stella Conroy said to him. "In fact, we're hoping to get to her before we even have to make the ransom drop."

Cooper Grey and Jefferson Davis walked over to the shaken man. "Let's go for a walk, Alvie," Jeff said. "It'll do us a bit of good to breathe some clean ocean air for a while. It's stuffy in here."

If anyone could think of a word or two to describe the atmosphere in Sarah's study at that particular moment in time, "stuffy" would not have been one of them.

CHAPTER THIRTY

Riley Satterfield and Tommy Dauterive were in Duffer's Bar and Grill on Main Street in Shallotte, eating two ten-ounce Black & Bleu burgers apiece, medium rare, with everything except the kitchen sink on top of them. Their side orders included fries, onion rings, baked beans, and coleslaw. They were drinking a pitcher of Fat Tire beer. Mallory Weather was stashed in the trunk of TT's brother Ray Ray's 1985 Chevrolet Impala. She was also unconscious again, because Satterfield had given her a sandwich and another glass of orange juice spiked with liquid Xanax.

It was seven o'clock in the evening, and the two of them were figuring out where to tell the woman's husband to drop off the two million dollars tomorrow night at ten o'clock. They had already decided to spend tonight in Ray Ray's place, where they had taken the last photo they sent as proof of life for Mallory Weather, because Ray Ray was down in Louisiana buying guns to transport and sell up north, and mainly because that was where Tommy kept his airboat.

"Daddy had two pocosins were his favorites for flower poachin'," TT said, swallowing a big gulp of beer. "One was in Columbus County, and we can't use it because it got cleaned out in the last controlled burn they did over there. But the other one is only about a mile from my lean-to: Brunswick County. And while my place is hard to get off of quick, daddy's small shelter in the pocosin ain't much more than a stone's throw from the Waccamaw River.

We could drop the broad off in my lean-to sometime before ten o'clock, email her location after we pick up the money, and ride my airboat right down the river into South Carolina; they'd never even see our wake, dude. And hell, Riley, once we're in South Carolina we're good as gone. That state's the real deal; nearly as good as Mississippi, Louisiana, even Texas."

"I do not know what the hell you are speakin' about," Riley said, "you say pocosin."

"That's where the swamp meets the longleaf pine savannah," TT said. "Pocosins are high ground wetlands. Daddy carved the belly out of a dead pine to give himself a bit of shelter, he needed to hide. So I'm thinkin' we could tell the husband to drop the money off in that tree."

Riley Satterfield considered this. "How would the man find it?" he said.

"Easy. It's a short straight line from daddy's old dock on the Waccamaw, just a few hundred feet from the Wildlife Ramp off 904 in New Britton. And daddy carved his initials on that dock and in the pine. I guess, we want to, we could hang a big bright sign on the tree says, 'Leave it here'. All's he'd need, besides a bag for the money, is a canoe, a pair of hip waders and a good flashlight. Are y'all really thinkin' he'll make the drop alone?"

"He'd best."

"What's he look like," Tommy said.

"No idea," Riley Satterfield told him. "But so far, he ain't fucked with us. I got no reason to think he's gonna start now that it's almost done. Say, listen TT, now that I'm thinkin' on this, why bother, take the woman to that lean-to of yours. We can just skip that part, dump her somewhere around Ray Ray's house, go directly to the money and split. Let whatever happens to her then just sort itself out."

"Yeah," TT said. "We can always point them at the shack, say we left her there. Nobody knows who built it anyway, 'cause there ain't nobody knows it's there."

The four of us were sitting in the great room in the cottage listening to the weather report for southeastern North Carolina for tomorrow when a car pulled up outside.

"That's probably Mickey," Sarah said, turning the television down. "Her jury was back a while ago. She may be in one hell of a bad mood, depending."

The lawyer walked in, grinned at everybody, and headed straight for the cabinet where we keep the liquor.

"I deserve a martini or two," Mickey Huntley said, grabbing a couple of bottles and a glass. "I got a not guilty verdict out of a North Carolina jury on self-defense in battered woman syndrome. It was absolutely warranted, but even Judge Wallace congratulated me."

"You got what?" Stella Conroy said.

"You heard me," Mickey said to her.

"What did y'all have," the Sheriff said to her. "An all-woman jury?"

"Naughty, naughty, Billy. No. Six and six," the lawyer said. She took a sip of her drink and smacked her lips. "But my foreman was a woman, and I knew she was a tested matriarch the minute I looked at her. I hoped she could and would carry the day. And she did just that."

"Well, it's not as though I begrudge the verdict, Mick," said Billy Conroy. "Hell, I know first-hand it's sometimes warranted. It's just rarely, if ever, successful. Maybe we are finally seeing a new day around here in balancing the scales of justice."

"Unlikely as that sounds, it's possible," Sarah said. "Your office phone will no doubt be ringing off the hook for the next few weeks."

"What's the latest from here," Mickey said. "I haven't heard anything since I told Sarah to have you two pick up Alvie and go check out George Cunningham's house."

After we filled her in, Stella said, "And Daddy thinks he knows where we'll find Mallory Weather. We're going tomorrow morning to check the place out, see if she's there."

"Maurice Washington," Mickey Huntley said musingly. "I never would have envisioned him as an ally. Where's Alvie? He must be feeling quite a bit better."

"Cooper and Jefferson took him for a walk," I said. "He overheard us discussing the possibility that the kidnappers might kill his wife regardless of what they say. He's worried."

Mickey was drinking her second martini when Sarah's private phone rang. When Sarah answered it, she said, "Hang on," and hit speaker phone. Darius Millar said, "Mickey, can you hear me?" He sounded tense.

"Yes," she said. "What's up?"

"I'm on my way to New Hanover Regional," he said in a rush. "Isobel Bring is in surgery."

"What," Mickey said. "Why?"

"She walked in her house; the husband was waiting on her. He broke in the back door. He shot her," Darius said. "My guy who called told me three times in the chest. Then the husband called the cops, told them what he'd done because, and I am quoting here, he was obligated to rectify a blasphemy, and then he split; nobody knows where he is. It's touch and go, boss. She flat-lined in the ambulance, but they brought her back."

I looked at Mickey Huntley. She was at an absolute loss for words, and who could blame her.

Sarah said, "She'll be right along, Darius. She's leaving now." She disconnected the phone and said to the lawyer, "Let's go, Mickey. I'll drive. You just concentrate on pulling yourself together."

Alvie Weather was feeling better about the successful recovery of his wife and had decided on a plan of action he needed to take in order to ease his mind. He and Cooper Grey and Jefferson Davis had walked along the beach as far as the boardwalk and gone into the Silver Dollar to get warmed up with a drink.

"I have been withholding a bit of information from Stella and Cash," Alvie said to the two men. They were sitting at a table, drinking Irish coffee. "Not that I think it's relevant to what's happened to my wife, but still, they have been so honest and good with me that I feel an obligation to confess what I have left unsaid."

Jefferson Davis looked at Cooper Grey, who said, "What's on your mind, Alvie?"

Alvie dithered with his coffee cup. "I have made a sort of deal with an associate of mine in Denmark to launder some of his money through my business in exchange for a rather large uncut diamond that was smuggled in the wheel well of an old BMW. I required only one thing: the money would not be the result of any illegal shenanigans. However, that car was among those in the shed when the bomb went off."

"Uh huh," Jeff Davis said. "Now why would you be doing something like that, Alvie, when you've got a fine successful business of your own."

"My wife is expensive," Alvie Weather said just above a whisper. "Her last book cost nearly a million dollars to research. We visited Egypt and France and Italy and I forget where all we went. She sells quite a few books, but nothin' close to what she needs."

"Has your wife ever heard of the internet?" Cooper asked.

"She says she has to experience the place to make it come alive on the page," Alvie said rather miserably. "And it is completely impossible for me to say no to Mallory. I adore her."

"What kinds of books does your wife write," Jeff Davis said to him.

"Romance novels," Alvie Weather said.

Cooper Grey considered this. "Are you asking us if you should give this information to Stella and Cash?" he said.

"Well, I guess I am," Alvie said. "I'm startin' to feel bad about withholdin' it from them; they've been so nice to me it makes me feel sorta rotten. And both of them were injured working on my behalf."

"That's one of the perils of their line of work," Cooper said. "And Stella's no strict moralist. By which I don't mean she has no standards. It's just that she doesn't try to impose her own code on other people. She wouldn't do what you did, but I doubt she'd lose any sleep over it."

"Katherine would probably have a similar reaction," Davis said. "Although she would most likely caution you against your actions by suggestin' you might not do well in prison. Y'all understand?"

Alvie Weather thought about that rather bleak possibility for a few moments. Finally, he nodded his head, finished his Irish coffee, and decided he'd confessed enough of his sins to quash his perturbation.

CHAPTER THIRTY ONE

Agent David Keating was monitoring a tapped line that belonged to Maurice Washington, who was not absolutely certain the line was safe to use because he had recently begun to suspect the authorities of harboring an excessive interest in some of his business dealings.

So Big Daddy was speaking rather pointedly albeit cryptically when he said to an associate of his, "Alvie Weather stopped by to see me today. Brought along a couple of his friends."

David Keating, who had practically fallen asleep in his chair, came fully awake at the mention of Alvie's name.

"Uh huh," the associate said. "He be tryin' to unload a lemon crate, some such shit, on you again?"

Big Daddy Washington laughed. "He's never shorted me on a deal, PopTop," he said. "If he does sell lemons, he must save them for the blue-haired set who would never notice anyway because they never drive. He did mention something that'll interest a few people, though. Might ease some consternation."

"Say what? Alvie?"

"He leased that shed blew up at the Port the other day."

"Whoa now. We meet a little later at the corner, you can finish."

"Nothing to finish. Somebody was stealing a few of his cars. He wanted to know who, so he hired a couple of PI's to find out. My guess, one of them tripped a wire and blew up the whole damned shed. He was just calling on me to assure me my car wasn't in that ruined shipment. Alvie's the man, it comes to personal service."

"I be sharin' this around here and there," PopTop said.

"By all means," Maurice Washington said, as he broke the connection. Maybe that will get you feds the fuck out of Dodge, he thought to himself as he was walking out of his store to pick up his wife and drive to Myrtle Beach for a week's vacation. He was already looking forward to the massages, the steam room, the fine food and wine, and the way his wife looked whenever she was as happy as he knew she would be just a few hours from now.

Listening to the dial tone on his phone, Agent David Keating wondered if it was worth his time to go and inquire about whatever else might have transpired when Alvie Weather and his friends paid a recent visit to Big Daddy Washington. After a few minutes had passed, he decided yes, it definitely was. But he had to be in Raleigh early tomorrow for a meeting with his boss. So visiting with Alvie and company would have to wait a couple of days.

Mickey Huntley was still in a state of shock when she and Sarah Ehrenson walked across the emergency room parking lot at New Hanover Regional Medical Center.

"Are you all right?" Sarah said to her. Mickey Huntley didn't answer. "Mickey," Sarah said sharply, grabbing her arm. "Stop walking and look at me."

"I never saw this coming," Mickey Huntley murmured. Her gaze wasn't really outwardly focused. She appeared to be having a conversation with herself. "But how could I have missed it? It was obvious from her testimony that the man was psychologically rabid."

Sarah shook her head. "How the hell could you, or anyone for that matter, have foreseen such a thing? Mickey! Look. At. Me. Right.

Now." The lawyer looked.

"You've got to stay in the moment, Mickey. There'll be cops in there who'll want to know things from you. Darius can't take care of this alone. Right now, you've still got work to do for your client who is fighting for her life. You can fall apart later."

"Yes," was all the response Sarah got, but she knew it was enough.

When the two women walked into the emergency ward's waiting room, Mickey Huntley's usual confident demeanor was in place. The first person to approach her was a middle-aged City of Wilmington Police Sergeant she'd known for many years. He looked very serious.

"Good to see you, counselor," Leonard Edwards said to her, offering her his hand. "Sorry about the circumstances, though."

"What's the word, Lenny?" Mickey said to him.

"Latest I heard, she's still in surgery. Your assistant's in one of the second-floor waiting rooms. I can take you up." Mickey Huntley nodded.

As the three of them entered the elevator, the Sergeant said, "Was there any indication he might seek some sort of crazy revenge if he didn't like the verdict?"

"Not a thing," the lawyer answered. "He didn't even attend the trial. I only know him from pictures. Do you have any idea where he might have gone?"

"No. But we've issued a bolo, and there'll be full coverage on the ten o'clock news. They're setting up a hotline now. I expect we'll get calls. He's pretty well-known in business circles. It won't be easy for him to hide in plain sight."

"If he's still in the area," Sarah said. "Is he a Wilmington native?"

"I don't know," the Sergeant said to her.

"Isobel told me they moved from Charleston to Wilmington eight years ago," Mickey Huntley said. She could see Darius Millar standing at the far end of the hallway she was walking down. His back was to her.

As the three of them approached him, Darius Millar turned around. He had tears in his eyes, and he was gripping his arms with his hands. His lips were pressed tightly together. He looked at Mickey Huntley and shook his head.

"She didn't make it, boss," he said. "The surgeon said those three bullets tore her up inside. Her heart just broke."

Mickey Huntley took a deep breath and went to him and put her arms around him. All she was thinking was, "What heart wouldn't?"

Sergeant Leonard Edwards had dialed his phone and was talking to his Chief. "He's from Charleston," he said. "We need to alert them to set up appropriate roadblocks."

Jesse Shine was teaching Tallahassee Bodine and Junior Fisk how to play Crazy Eights. The three of them were down in the galley of the Portofino. The two men were looking after the boy for the night.

"This game is stupid," said Junior Fisk, wiggling around on his butt. "I can't hardly hold all these cards with just one hand and my ass itches."

"You ain't supposed to be tryin' to hold the cards, Junior," Tally said to him. "The intention of the game is to lose them."

"And that is exactly what I am tryin' to do," Junior said with some annoyance. "The kid gives me nothin', that's what I can lose. Nothin'." He was holding eleven cards.

"You can drop an eight on the pile," Jesse said. "Change the suit to whatever y'all are holdin' most."

"Fine," Junior said. "Pass me an eight, I'll do just that." As he was drawing yet again from the pack, they all heard footsteps coming toward the boat. Tally and Jesse went to see who was doing the walking.

It was Alvie Weather.

"That's the guy lost his wife," Jesse whispered to Tallahassee. "Boss's girlfriend and Stella are lookin' for her. Boss and Coop are helpin' them out."

"Uh huh," Tallahassee Bodine said, having had no knowledge of this particular situation whatsoever, but suppressing his surprise. "Well, okay then, Jesse," he said quickly, "no need to rile the man's mind up about any of that unpleasantness. We'll just keep quiet on it. Y'all understand?"

"I got it," the kid said and winked at Tallahassee.

"Good evening," Alvie said to them. "Mr. Davis suggested I stay here tonight if that meets with your approval. I may be needed rather quickly early tomorrow."

"Plenty of room," Tally said, giving him a hand to help him board. "I am Tallahassee Bodine. My friend Junior Fisk is down below; and I believe y'all know Mr. Jesse."

"How you doin', Alvie," the kid said. "We're playin' cards in the kitchen."

"I'd enjoy a hand of cards," Alvie said. "What's the game?"

"Crazy Eights," Jesse said. "It's my most favorite."

Crazy Eights, Alvie Weather thought to himself. I detested that game as a child. I could never win. But then, I could never win much of anything when I was a child. To Jesse, he said, "I don't believe I know that game, son. You'll have to show me how it's played."

CHAPTER THIRTY TWO

Stella Conroy and I were standing in a huge field of high grass, and if we hadn't been wearing waders, our feet would've been soaked. Billy Conroy and his friend Lydell Duvall were a few yards in front of us, looking through night-vision goggles. It was five o'clock in the morning, and it was chilly and black as pitch, but for a few slices of moonlight that cut randomly into the landscape.

"Stay still," Duvall hissed at us. "I need to see has he moved the traps any." Neither Stella nor I moved the slightest inch. The thought of an animal trap breaking our bones had suddenly immobilized us both.

"OK, I got them in sight," Duvall whispered. "Follow me and Billy close. Don't stray."

We did as we were told.

All of a sudden a form was in front of us. "Stop," Billy Conroy said. We stopped. "Here," he said to us, handing us each a pair of goggles. "Take a look, see what y'all think."

What I saw was a square flimsy-looking structure made up of discarded materials. There was a heavy, thick cardboard roof that was held upright by four six-by-sixes, and it was lying on top of four walls of disparate products: two of wood, one of canvas, and one unidentified. The walls were attached up and down using staples and nails. A big wooden platform like you see in packing plants served as a floor. The whole thing sat on a bunch of cinder blocks. The wall that was facing us was canvas.

"If she's in there, and has been, for much more than two days, she's mostly likely dead," Lydell Duvall said. "It's been in the twenties these last few nights. If the cold didn't kill her, the diamondbacks would. They'd have been seeking shelter."

"She's not in there," I said to him.

"Cash is exactly right," Stella Conroy said. "That coyote by the door is looking for something to eat. If she was there, he'd be inside checkin' her out."

"They don't hunt humans," said Lydell Duvall.

"They don't have to hunt dead ones. And they are definitely eaters of carnivore garbage," Stella said.

"Let's just take a look," her father said. "We'll follow you, Bug."

As we approached the wood wall that served as the front of the structure, the coyote disappeared into the far grass. Bug Duvall looked at Billy Conroy.

"We'd be wise not to disturb this padlock, as useless as it is," he said to the Sheriff. "No sense givin' them a hint we know about this place."

Stella was walking around the corner where the unidentified wall was. She was carrying the pair of goggles. I was still wearing mine. "It's a sheet of heavy plastic passin' for a wall," she said. "And the room is empty." She'd cupped her hand on the plastic for a look. "Nothin's in it except a few dead squirrels, a couple birds, and a bunch of hungry maggots." I had drawn my gun and stepped wide of the two men.

"I'm going to shoot a snake that's primed for you, Stella," I said calmly. "Stay still. Nothing to be alarmed about." My shot blew the head off what I knew was a cottonmouth. I've seen a few of them over the years. The swamp seemed to swallow the sound of the gunshot.

Lydell Duvall looked curiously at me. "Who in this world taught you to shoot," he said.

"Annie Oakley," I said and grinned at him. The man actually smiled.

"Let's hightail it out of here," the Sheriff said, "while we're all still alive and kickin'.'"

We were climbing into Lydell Duvall's runabout when Stella Conroy looked at me and said, "I think I've told you 'nice shot' once or twice before. At the moment it most assuredly bears repeating."

"Something told me it wasn't a rat snake." I said. "Might have been telepathy from Minerva."

"That cat," she said and grinned at me.

––––––––––––––––––––

Riley Satterfield and Tommy Dauterive were startled by an echoing sound they both knew was a gunshot. They were standing next to the longleaf pine that Tommy's father had chosen for shelter. TT was holding a sign that said HEAR.

"What the fuck was that," Satterfield said to his friend. "It ain't nearly dawn. Who hunts this time of night? Cut that flashlight, quick."

Without the flashlight's beam, the two of them were in total darkness. "We can't just stand here, Riley," TT said. "That shot was way far off. Might even have been in Columbus County. Lotta crazies livin' off the grid over there. Time to time they shoot each other they get drunk enough."

Then they heard a motor start up. "What's that then," Satterfield said. "Somebody out for a boat ride?"

"You ain't a swamp man, Riley," Tommy said. "Swamp men get a jump on their table food. This instance? Likely catfish. The Waccamaw's heavy with sizable catfish. Men feed their families with that catch." He switched his flashlight on. "Here," he said. "nail this sucker up and let's go get breakfast. I got a real strong hankerin' for grits and eggs and sausage and biscuits."

Sarah Ehrenson was standing in the kitchen of the cottage on Beach House Lane making a pot of hazelnut coffee. It was six o'clock in the morning, and she'd been awake most of the night trying to reason with Mickey Huntley, which she had come to realize over the year that they had been together was a nearly impossible task whenever the lawyer truly believed she was responsible for failing to prevent something.

"I knew it was a remarkable verdict," Mickey had said at one point in the middle of the night. "I didn't expect it myself. Why I just let her walk off into the sunset I can't explain. At the very least, I should have had Darius drive her home."

"And Darius would have dropped her off and she'd still have walked into her home and been shot by her husband," Sarah had said reasonably.

"I should have taken her to dinner," the lawyer had countered stubbornly. "She deserved to celebrate."

"You're hell-bent on self-flagellation, Mickey," Sarah had said to her. "You've got to let it go. Otherwise you'll make yourself sick."

"I know you're right," Mickey Huntley had said. "But I need to do something, Sarah, anything, as impossible as that seems right now. I can't sit still. If Darius gets in touch, tell him I'm at the office. I'll call you later." And then she'd left the cottage and driven away.

Sarah was pouring herself a cup of coffee when her phone rang. "Yes," she said.

"It's me," said Cash Delaney. "The shed in the swamp is empty. They must still be holding her wherever she was in that last picture. Everything okay at your end?"

"Coop and Jeff are bringing the GPS tracker in a while. Mickey's penitent. I'm drinking coffee," Sarah said. She sounded exhausted.

"Mickey will work through this, Sarah. It's understandable that she feels terrible about what happened. Imagine how you'd feel."

"That's why I'm worried," Sarah said, as she heard a car pull up. "I've got to go. I think the boys just got here."

But when she walked to the door and opened it, it was Mickey Huntley walking towards her. "It's over," is what she said. "They killed the goddamned misogynistic prick on the outskirts of Charleston after he took a shot at a state trooper."

Sarah Ehrenson looked at Mickey Huntley. "Suicide by cop?" she said.

"I don't know and I don't care," the lawyer said. "He's dead, Sarah. That's what really matters."

CHAPTER THIRTY THREE

Alvie Weather was agitated. Both Tallahassee Bodine and Junior Fisk had been unable to calm him down. It was eight o'clock at night, and he had heard from Sarah that the rescue of his wife was under way. His imagination was in overdrive and would not let him rest. He created every scenario in which something could go wrong.

"See can you calm him," Tally said to Jesse Shine.

"Here," Junior said, "take him a small glass of bourbon. It'll help to settle his nerves."

"I ain't sure I know how to ease him any," the kid said.

"You ain't got to try to ease him." Tally said. "Just sit with him. Just talk with him. Sometimes, children can steady nerves."

Alvie was pacing on the deck when Jesse Shine walked up to him and handed him the glass of bourbon.

"Tally and Junior said to give y'all this," the kid said. He looked at the pacing man. Then he said, his hand on Alvie's elbow, "You don't got to fuss so, Alvie. Stella and Cash know exactly what they got to do. They are truly smart."

Alvie Weather stopped his pacing and looked at the child, whom he really hadn't noticed much before now. He put the glass of bourbon down on a little table and thought about what Jesse Shine

204

had just said.

"Perhaps you are right," he said to the kid. "They are both highly competent women. I am probably overreacting out of nervousness. Let's sit down over here by the side rail and talk awhile. Tell me about yourself, son. How do you happen to be here?"

The kid shrugged his shoulders. "Boss gave me a job when I asked," he said.

"You asked for a job?" Alvie Weather said to him.

"I needed work," Jesse said.

"And y'all are how old?"

"Almost nearly twelve."

"What about your schoolin'," Alvie said to Jesse Shine.

"What about it? I can do all sorts of things," the kid said. "I know how to take care of myself. Better'n you do, yourself."

Alvie Weather thought about that. "Well," he said, "is there something you can't do that you'd maybe like to do."

Jesse Shine wondered if it was a good idea to tell the truth to this odd man. I guess it can't hurt me much, he said to himself.

"I think I'd like to read and write," the kid said, "so I can know where I'm at and figure out where I'm goin'."

Alvie Weather was shocked by this unexpected and unemotional response from the boy. I was so poor as a child that I never had one blessed thing that belonged just to me, he thought. But I almost always went to school. What had happened to Jesse Shine?

Riley Satterfield and Tommy Too had gone through all of the marijuana that Riley had brought with him. At the moment, they were drinking the last two cans of beer from Ray Ray's refrigerator.

"We shoulda saved somethin' for the trip down the Waccamaw," TT said to his friend. "I'd appreciate some mellowness, I get nerved up."

"There's a few good dime bags of trainwreck in the trailer," Riley Satterfield said. "And about fifteen hundred cash money in the lockbox. It'll only take a half hour to drive there and back."

"Hell, let's go," Tommy Too said. "Ain't nothin' like a boat ride stoned."

It was eight-thirty at night, and they would be picking up the ransom money left in the hollowed-out tree in the pocosin at a little after ten o'clock, after which they would head down the Waccamaw River until its name changed to the Little Peedee and its state changed from North to South Carolina. Both men were excited. They walked toward Ray Ray's Impala to head for the old single-wide Marlette on Lula Trail.

"Hang on a minute, Riley," TT said. "Let's dump the woman now. Then we can come straight back to the airboat after we pick up the stuff at the trailer."

"A righteous idea," Riley said.

"There's a deep ditch about a half mile to the right of the big barn where she's at now," TT said. "It'll work, we tape her mouth. I expect they'll manage to find her, we give them a hint. But it'll take a while; give us all the head start we need."

"Pack some food in a sack, TT, and a couple pairs of Ray Ray's jeans," Satterfield said. "And whatever you do, don't forget the guns. We don't never want to be without guns. I'll be back in ten to pick you up. I can deal with the woman."

———————————

The two deputies that Billy Conroy had dispatched to guard Dutch Boutelle's trailer in Shallotte were resting inside the mobile home. One was in the living room. One was in the back bedroom. Their car, which was a plain, unmarked Ford, was parked by the side of the road. Riley Satterfield saw it first.

"Whoa," he said to Tommy Too. "Looks like somebody's inside tryin' to rip me off. See that car? See that little light inside the trailer?"

"You know the car?"

"Ain't never seen it before, but it's a cheap one. Might be a wannabe player out of Wilmington. They are mostly young bloods without the brains to defend themselves because they are addicted to knives. Your gun loaded?"

"I'm cocked and ready," TT said.

Both men exited the Impala, and the sound of the car doors closing startled the deputy in the living room. "Heads up, Ricky," he said to his fellow officer in the back room as he drew his gun. "Somebody's comin'. Look alive."

That was the next-to-the-last word heard by any of the men involved in the shootout that happened the second Riley Satterfield yanked open the trailer door, yelled "Geronimo you motherfuckers," jumped in, and fired a single shot into the trailer. The heavy volley returned by the two deputies, one from right in front, the other from the rear, dropped Satterfield and Tommy Dauterive where they stood, just barely inside the single wide. They were dead before they hit the floor, one on top of the other.

"Holy fucking shit, Ricky," said the deputy in the living room. "We just killed two men."

"Not worth worryin' on," his partner said. "They fired first. Check who they are and notify the Sheriff. We did our job."

Sheriff Billy Conroy put down his cell phone, sighed deeply, and walked to the kitchen of the cottage on Beach House Lane where Sarah Ehrenson was in the process of making sandwiches for the two of them.

"We have got a massive problem," he said to her.

Sarah stopped what she was doing and turned to him. "It seems to be the day for it," she said. "Tell me."

"Two of my deputies just shot and killed Riley Satterfield and Tommy Dauterive," he said. "They must have gone back to the trailer to pick up the money and the pot. Bitch of it is, now we got no idea where Mallory Weather's at, unless they already took her to the shed in the swamp."

"Jesus Christ," Sarah said. "How the hell did this happen?"

But Billy Conroy was already dialing his phone. He put it on speaker.

"What?" his daughter whispered, when she answered.

"Where are you?" the Sheriff said.

"Watching the shed, waiting for them to drop Mallory. Why?"

"They're not going to be dropping her," he said.

"Why not?"

"Because they are no longer breathin'. Can you reach Cooper and Jefferson before they deliver the ransom money?"

"What in the hell is goin' on, Daddy?" Stella said out loud.

"Call Coop. Then y'all meet me and Sarah at 2218 Lula Trail in Shallotte. And shake a stick, Stella. We'll fill in the blanks when you get there."

CHAPTER THIRTY FOUR

When Stella and I pulled up to a rusting old mobile home on Lula Trail in Shallotte, Billy Conroy was directing traffic. A crowd had gathered at the scene, and an ambulance was trying to maneuver through them without causing any more damage than the two dead men. I looked into the exposed front room of the trailer and saw a couple of cops hefting a body bag while two others were stuffing a second body into another one. The glimpse I caught of the dead man's face told me it was Riley Satterfield. His wide open eyes were as vacant as they had been on his driver's license photograph. Even his violent and unexpected death hadn't interested him.

"Pull up behind your father's car," Sarah said to Stella. "Did you reach Coop and Jefferson?"

"They are on their way," Stella said.

"Meanwhile," said Sarah, "we've got a mob of spectators and local law enforcement on our hands."

As we exited the Mustang, the ambulance made its way to the trailer where deputies began loading the two corpses into the back of the vehicle.

"What happened," I asked Sarah.

"Billy had stationed two of his men here in case anyone returned, something that he did not expect to happen. Well, Satterfield and his friend, who Billy says is that guy Tommy Dauterive, defied his expectation and did just that. His deputies told him that Satterfield opened the front door, yelled something about motherfuckers and fired a shot. You can easily imagine the response this garnered from the two deputies. Billy says the back half of Dauterive's head is now painting two walls in the trailer's living room. Satterfield took six shots through his left side and chest. I doubt they drew another breath once the bullets struck them."

"And once again," Stella said, as she lit a cigarette, "we are left to wonder where in this world they have stashed Mallory Weather."

"How did they get here?" I said to Sarah. "They didn't walk."

"No," she said. "The car they came in is over there on the other side of the road. That old Impala."

I could see Billy Conroy in the near distance talking with his two deputies. One of them was waving his arms around as though to protest whatever the Sheriff was saying. I thought about the irony involved in the deaths of these two men and how the value of foresight is so integral to the human race. Plan and be prepared, the brain tells us. However, there is no accounting for impulse and its unintended consequences. That is, of course, unless you are religious: then whatever happens is God's will. But religion, with its negative corollaries of war, bigotry, crude misogyny, and immutable intolerance, is an extremely expensive fix for the rampant and powerful energy that pervades the universe.

"Cash," Stella said to me, startling me out of my reverie. "You wanna take a look at their car? It might give us something."

"Yes, I do," I said and started to cross to the Impala.

"Billy says it's locked," Sarah said.

"Grab that coat hanger you keep in the trunk of your car," I said to Stella.

I was fiddling with the hanger on the driver's side of the car when a local cop walked up to me and put his left hand on my arm.

"Not the best idea you've ever had, break and enter right in front of the law, young lady," he said to me. I looked at him. He wasn't smiling, and his right hand was resting on his gun.

"It's all right, Chet," Stella said when she noticed what was happening. "Check with the Sheriff. He'll fill y'all in."

"I can't be sanctioning any nonsense right now, Stella," the cop said. "This is a damned crime scene, not some sorority girls' high jinks affair."

"Do I look like a sorority girl to you after all these years, Chester Hollings," Stella said sweetly to him with a small smile on her face. "I am truly flattered." That sort of response from Stella is usually a clue to get the hell out of the way of her trajectory.

"Why're you here, anyway," he said to her, ignoring her parry. "This is just two dead numbskulls messed up with drugs. Hardly seems like your sort of case at all, Stella. I will say, though, y'all do look a mite untidy right now." I had to agree with the man. Our boots were muddy, our slacks were wet, and both of us would have benefitted from soap and water applied to our hands and faces. But this is what happens to your grooming when you spend a few hours in the Green Swamp.

By this time, Sarah had made her way to Billy Conroy, and the two of them were hurrying over to where we were.

"Chet," the Sheriff said to the cop who was still eyeing me with suspicion. "I've got them aiding me in a little side investigation that hinges on these two men. I'll fill you in later. Right now I don't have a lot of time to waste. Why don't you see can you help break up that crowd. We need to clear this scene. And I have this other situation to handle before the sun comes up."

The two men looked at one another. If they were friends, you couldn't have told it right at this moment. Finally, the cop relented, tipped his hat at me and walked away.

"Did you set him off again, Stella," Billy Conroy said heatedly to his daughter. "I can't be mendin' fences you are always tearin' down."

"It was me, Billy," I said quickly. "He saw me trying to open this car door with a coat hanger. It unsettled his sense of propriety." I popped the lock on the door and opened it. "We thought it might tell us something."

"And for your information, Daddy," Stella said evenly to her father, "I haven't laid eyes on Chet since I cleared that case he couldn't begin to fathom three years ago. I am not responsible for the man's endless wounded pride. There oughta be a damn pill for men to swallow, help them get over themselves. It'd sure go a long way with the women in this world."

I opened the trunk on the Impala, and Stella and I went to take a look. There was a flat tire along with a bunch of tools and an empty box. Next to the box was a role of heavy gray masking tape and two black hoods. A duffle bag held two pairs of jeans and a gallon bottle of mountain dew, some potato chips in an old canister, two bags of pork rinds, a jar of peanut butter, a loaf of white bread, and a huge bag of red twizzlers.

"Redneck soul food," Stella said. "They were all fixed to make their escape, they picked up the money."

"This car is registered to Raymond Dauterive," Sarah said, "although the registration expired two years ago. Who is he to Tommy?"

"His brother," the Sheriff said.

"So maybe that's where they were keeping Mallory," I said, "when they sent us that last photo."

"And maybe that's where she's still at," Stella said, "because they damn sure did not drop her in that shack in the swamp. Y'all know the place, Daddy?"

"Not off hand," he said. "But I can find out right quick."

I watched him walk away and dial his phone. I was also watching some distant lightning creep closer. It was in the low forties tonight, and a winter downpour was possible.

When Billy walked back, he said to Stella, "He lives between Ash and New Britton, on the Waccamaw River side, closer to Ash. It's probable Tommy kept his airboat there. My secretary Louise says Ray's mailbox is in the shape of a nude woman. She says we can't miss it. Coop and Jefferson will most likely drive right past it. See can you catch them before they do. Sarah and I will meet you there."

As we all headed for our cars, I looked at the sky again. The lightening was much brighter, and I could hear the distant claps of thunder.

"That sound is not good," Stella said to me. "Rain in November is hardly ever a shower. It's more like a deluge. I hope to hell she's somewhere inside."

But every bone in my body told me she wasn't. I knew in my gut that time, if it hadn't already, was quickly running out for Mallory Weather.

CHAPTER THIRTY FIVE

"Give me a hand out of this runabout," Cooper Grey said to Jeff Davis. "My left knee feels like a soft basketball. It must be getting ready to rain."

"I didn't know you had arthritis," Jeff said to his friend. "You're awful young, aren't you?"

"It started after I took that bullet back in 2004," Coop said. "It's not too bad, but when the humidity cranks toward 100, I feel it."

The two men pulled the 14-footer up the bank of the Waccamaw and secured it to a tree. When they reached Coop's Altima, he threw the bag of ransom money into the trunk. Then they drove away from the landing at New Britton and headed for Raymond Dauterive's house, which Stella had said was just before Ash, on highway 130.

"We see a mailbox that's a woman, we're there," Jeff said. "It'll be on our right."

"I don't want to be standing too close to Stella when she lays eyes on that mailbox," Cooper Grey said. "She'll be inclined to light it up and bullets can ricochet."

"She'll have other things on her mind," Davis said.

"Maybe that's true. But it won't make any difference."

An unidentified object started to take shape in the distance. "I think I see the mailbox," Davis said. "Slow down. We don't want to drive right by it."

A couple of minutes later, the shape of a naked woman with a mailbox for a head became clear.

"That's it," Cooper said.

"What the hell's the message," Davis muttered. "Women are empty-headed? I think you're right, Coop. If Stella doesn't blow that thing to hell and back, Katherine surely will. We might as well park in the driveway. They'll be right along."

"What driveway," Cooper Grey said. He had pulled to the side of the road. About two hundred feet in, he could see a ramshackle house that leaned left and two small outbuildings. A huge barn on the right of that was missing half its roof.

"Can you get any closer to that big barn," Davis said, shining his portable spotlight toward it. "It might be the place they were holding her when they sent that last email. Those high narrow windows remind me of that photograph."

Cooper Grey eased the Altima onto the sandy lot and drove slowly past the mailbox. He got about fifty feet shy of the barn when his wheels began to slip in the sandy soil.

"This is as far as I want to go and still back out," he said.

"Let's take a look," Davis said.

As they were exiting the car, another vehicle pulled in behind them.

"The girls are here," Davis said, pulling a well-worn fisherman's rain hat on his head. A cold rain had begun to fall.

———————————————

Mallory Weather was nearly awake from whatever drug she had ingested last, and the first thing she realized was that she was wet. Then she realized why: it was raining. It was also pitch black, and she was leaning against something. A tree. Her wrists and ankles were bound, and there was a piece of tape across her mouth. It also seemed to her that she was in a hole of some kind because it didn't matter whether she looked left or right, all she saw was dirt and debris and sketchy grass. She decided she must be in a ditch. She wondered where.

When she took a second to consider how she felt, the urge to vomit was strong. She had never felt so awful in her life. She hurt everywhere. She glanced at the running clothes that she had now been wearing for nearly a week. All she saw was filth. And they smelled to high heaven. Still, she thought if she could crawl up one of the sides of the ditch and get to level ground, she could eventually locate someone to help her. She considered how to move and decided to see if she could shinny backwards up the tree. A few minutes later, she knew she couldn't; her legs were no longer sturdy enough. And her wrists and the palms of her hands were bleeding from contact with the rough bark of the tree.

She rolled to the right of the tree and fell forward. Then she struggled to her knees and rested a few seconds to make sure of her balance. She had about a four-inch spread on the cord that was binding her ankles. Then she studied the incline in front of her. It looked like she'd need to climb up about twenty feet to get to ground level. She chose an area a little to her left where she could see places that might serve as footholds, along with the tops of rocks and the trunks of very small trees that she could use to lever and brace herself as she climbed. She refused to acknowledge the near impossibility of her task without the use of her hands and arms.

Her first attempts were unsuccessful. She fell back every time she tried. But then she made a little progress and found herself braced against a rock that did not give way under her weight. As she lay resting before beginning again, she heard first one car, then another, quite close by. Doors opened and closed, and she heard several indistinct voices which sounded high-pitched. Women, probably. All they will want to do is get out of the rain as quickly as possible, Mallory Weather thought to herself. And I can't blame them for that. It's cold out tonight.

"Where do you want to start," Cooper Grey said to Cash Delaney. "All of these buildings need to be gone through. And Jeff thinks that barn looks like where they were when they sent that last photograph."

"I don't think she's inside anywhere, although that's just my intuition talking," Delaney said. "But you're right. We need to check. You and Jeff start with this barn and finish up the other three as quickly as you can. When Billy and Sarah get here, they can help. Stella and I are going to take a look around the outside."

Stella was holding two pairs of goggles. "What've you got?" Davis said to her, as he and Grey headed for the barn.

"Night vision goggles," she said, handing Delaney a pair. The women slipped them on and activated their flashlights. "Whaddya think," Stella said.

"I think if she's here, they didn't leave her in front, in plain sight," Cash Delaney said. "And we've got to realize just what a big 'if' that is, Stella. They could have driven her anywhere. But let's walk behind this barn. If it is where they've been keeping her, and they did just dump her outside, they can't have carried her too far. You go left, I'll go right. Holler if you find anything."

By now, the rain was heavy and steady, the lightning was close, the thunder was loud, and both women were soaked. When Cash Delaney heard a sound of something rolling down the side of a ditch, she figured it was a small animal. Then she heard a soft sort of noise, like a grunt, and another sound that she knew could be dirt and rock displacement.

"Stella," Delaney yelled, starting to run toward the sound. "I think I may hear her."

Mallory Weather couldn't believe her ears and then her eyes. A woman she had never seen before in her life was sliding down the side of the ditch and getting behind her and pushing her up the wall of the incline until she lay prone on the level ground, where another woman was lifting her to a sitting position, gently removing the masking tape from her mouth, all the while saying softly, "It's all right, Mallory. You're safe now, baby. Cash and I have got you."

Mallory Weather felt a flood of relief she had never before experienced. This release from fear was followed by an overwhelming gratitude for these two women who had found and rescued her. Then, she just allowed herself to collapse in the woman's arms and truly, really cry.

CHAPTER THIRTY SIX

"Your wife is severely dehydrated, undernourished, and her electrolytes are nowhere near close to normal," the doctor on call at the emergency room of New Hanover Regional Medical Center said to Alvie Weather. "Does she have any other conditions I should know about?"

"Conditions," Alvie said uncertainly and looked at Stella. He was so anxious to see Mallory he had completely lost his ability to focus. I figured we were lucky he hadn't fainted.

"Like is she anemic or depressed or allergic to anything; stuff like that, Alvie," Stella said to him.

"I don't know," he said. "I don't think so. She's delicate. I know that."

"Delicate isn't a condition, Mr. Weather," the doctor said patiently to him. "Although it can be reflective of something more serious. What medicines does she take routinely?"

"Ambien," Alvie said. "Most every night."

"Well," the doctor said, "that's a sleeping pill. If that's all she takes, I'm inclined to discount any other serious medical problems." He looked at me. "Are you in pain?" he asked.

I'm not used to doctors noticing me if and when I grimace so he caught me off guard. "It's an old injury," I said to him, and realized I'd been scowling and rubbing my bad leg where I'd taken a debilitating bullet a couple of years ago.

"What happened," he said, glancing at my leg.

"I was shot," I said. My response startled the man, although he tried to hide it. By this time, Alvie was literally dancing on his tiptoes, as though he was in desperate need of a men's room. "I think my friend would like to see his wife," I said to the young doctor.

"Well, she's sedated, probably asleep" he said to all three of us, "but you can certainly look in on her. It's just this way."

"I'll stay here," I said to Stella and Alvie, "and wait for everybody. You two go ahead." What I wanted more than anything was to tear off these soggy clothes of mine, climb into a steaming hot bath, drink a glass of wine, and listen to Billie Holiday tell me some stories; but all that would have to wait awhile. I closed my eyes.

When I opened them, Sarah was sitting next to me reading a magazine. "What did I do," I said to her. "Fall asleep?"

"For a little bit," she said. "You need to get out of those clothes. I was thinking of having you admitted so you could. But I didn't think they'd go for it."

I grinned at her. "Where are Billy and the boys?" I said.

"Billy's finishing up his report about Mallory," she said.

"Which is?"

"She was out running, fell, hit her head, lost her memory temporarily, and wandered around until she fell into a ditch where we found her. Something like that, anyway. If anybody found it hard to believe, nobody said so. It's difficult to argue with a well-respected county sheriff."

"What about Coop and Jeff?"

"I told them to go back to the Portofino to relieve Tally and Junior. What shape is Mallory Weather really in?"

"As you might imagine," I said, "she's sort of a wreck, but I don't think it's going to prove to be life-threatening. My guess is she can get out of here in a few days and finish recuperating at home." I noticed that Sarah was looking past me. I followed her gaze and saw Stella walking with Alvie, who appeared distrait.

"How is she," I said when they got close enough.

"Out cold," Stella said. "I told Alvie we should let her sleep, see her in the morning when she's feeling more like herself. He can bunk with the boys tonight." She looked hard at Sarah and me.

"That's a good idea," Sarah said.

"I don't know," Alvie said. "It might could be she'll wake up, wonder where I am. The last thing I want to do is cause her anymore distress. She's hooked up to a lot of tubes full of stuff. It might scare her, she wakes up and doesn't understand why."

"That's what nurses are for, Alvie," I said. "And the nurses here are wonderful. You can trust them to take care of her."

That seemed to mollify the man, so the four of us walked out of the hospital. The only thing I really noticed as we all climbed into Stella's car was that the winter rain had stopped. I often notice the little things in life. It's probably what keeps me sane. It's certainly not the big things.

When Mickey Huntley answered her cell phone at nine a.m. on the morning after Mallory Weather had been rescued, she was sitting at the kitchen counter in the cottage on Beach House Lane drinking coffee and eating a bagel with cream cheese and lox.

"Mickey Huntley," she said.

"This is David Keating," the FBI agent said. "I'm trying to locate Alvie Weather to speak with him about a certain incident I'd like more information on. He isn't home, and he isn't at his place of business. Do you have any idea how I can get in touch with him?"

"Perhaps I can shed some light on whatever incident you're referring to, Agent Keating," the lawyer said easily, stalling for time while she thought of a suitable response to his query.

"Well," David Keating said, clearing his throat, "I have it on good authority that he, along with some of his friends, paid a recent visit to Maurice Washington. I'd like to know why, and whether it's connected to the explosion at the port."

Mickey Huntley chuckled. Then she said, "It's probable that Alvie was assuring Mr. Washington that the car he had ordered was not being stored in the shed when it blew up. It was a courtesy call."

David Keating thought for a few seconds before he said, "You do understand how it looks to me, don't you, counselor?"

"Perhaps you'd better enlighten me," the lawyer answered.

"Maurice Washington is one of Wilmington's biggest drug lords. We've been building a case against him for over a year now and I seriously doubt I'm telling you anything you don't already know. So what I'm saying is that while I understand your explanation for the visit makes sense, I'd still like to speak with Mr. Weather directly. If you can just tell me how to reach him, I won't bother you further."

"I don't keep track of my clients on a daily basis, Agent Keating. Let me see if my assistant can find him. I'll get back to you ASAP. Is the number on my screen the best way to reach you?"

"It is. And thank you."

"You're welcome," she said, disconnecting the call. The next number she dialed rang five times before a voice said, "Hello, what?"

"Where's Alvie," Mickey Huntley said.

"Coop's drivin' him to the hospital. They left five minutes ago," Jeff Davis said. "Why?"

"That FBI agent wants to talk with him about the visit he and Cash and Stella made to Maurice Washington. The one that broke the case."

"Who's Maurice Washington?"

"Big Daddy," she said. "Wilmington's north side."

"Oh, the drug dealer."

"Exactly."

"Alvie's scattered this morning. He's worried about Mallory. Now's not the best time to put him with the law, especially if he's got to prevaricate a bit."

"I understand that, Jeff. Get in touch with Coop. Tell him to stay with Alvie, and then drive him back to the boat when he's ready. And Jeff, I would encourage him to be ready after an hour. Okay?"

"I got it," Davis said.

Mickey Huntley was finishing her breakfast when Sarah Ehrenson walked into the kitchen wearing the clothes she'd had on last night.

"When did you get here," Sarah asked.

"A while ago. You were asleep and looked as though you needed to be. And I read your note, so I'm up to speed."

"How're you doing, honey," Sarah said, putting her arms around the lawyer's shoulders.

"I'm okay," Mickey said. "Better now that you're awake."

CHAPTER THIRTY SEVEN

"What happened to me, Alvie," Mallory Weather said to her husband. "First, I was in my kitchen making coffee after my morning run and then I wasn't." She was feeling a lot better and had just finished a bowl of cereal and a cup of tea.

Her husband smiled at her and took her hand. "It looks like my manager had some real money problems he wanted to get away from," Alvie said. "And he needed to raise a bunch of cash quick to make that possible. So he decided to hire some men to kidnap you and hit me up for a huge ransom."

"That nice man George?" she exclaimed.

"The very same. Turns out he was quite a gambler. In deep debt to the tune of a half million dollars or more. But we don't need to talk about such unpleasantness right now, sweetie pie. In fact, I don't want anybody here to know anything about it. You're safe. That's all that matters."

Mallory Weather shook her head. "I know you told me last night to tell whoever asked that I don't remember anything, Alvie, and that's what I did; but I want to talk. I've been drugged and alone and frightened out of my mind for days now. Do you know that two women I have never seen in my life found and rescued me?"

"That's what I hired them to do, Mallory," Alvie said. "And you did run into one of them a few years ago at one of my company parties. Stella Conroy is her name. She and her partner, Cash Delaney, run an investigative services business in Carolina Beach. I've known Stella for years. We went to school together."

"I want to meet them," Mallory said. 'I want to thank them. I think I want to see if they might agree to be my friends. I don't believe I have ever encountered anybody quite like either one of them."

Alvie Weather considered the rather sheltered upbringing his wife had always enjoyed. "No," he said to her gently, "I suspect you never have."

Mallory Weather smiled and raised her husband's hand to her lips and kissed it Then she said, "So did they arrest George?"

"No. He's dead. And there was never any official presence of the law in this, darlin'. I was told if I brought in the law, you would be killed. So the official story is exactly what we told y'all last night: you fell and hit your head while running and lost your memory. Please do not stray from that story. All you need to remember is that you don't remember."

"So nobody got arrested? Where are the other kidnappers? There were always two of them whenever I woke up."

"Nobody got arrested is exactly right. Those other two men are also dead. I really think we've talked about this enough for one day, especially here."

A nurse walked into the room. "Your wife is scheduled for some tests this morning, Mr. Weather," she said to Alvie. "You can come back later this afternoon if you like."

"Any idea when she may be released?" he asked.

"Not yet. We'll know more when we get the results tomorrow morning."

When I finally woke up in my own bed, my little table clock said it was noon, and there was something that sounded like a radio from somewhere nearby, maybe the living room, maybe a car passing by the cottage. I just lay there deciding whether or not to go back to sleep until I realized I had a sore throat, a deeply sore leg, and possibly a fever.

"Sarah," I said as loudly as I could manage. My voice sounded like a high croak.

In a few seconds, Sarah came to my door. "What's up?" she said to me.

"I'm sick," I said. "I hurt all over and I think I have a fever."

"Jesus Christ," she said and walked over to me and put her hand on my forehead. "Well," she said, "you are a tad warm. Might be a hundred or so. What do you mean, you hurt all over? Are you achy or in pain?"

"Both. My throat's sore. My right leg's pounding out its syncopated version of chopsticks."

"That's why your mother always told you to stay out of a cold rain," she said to me.

"What's the problem," Mickey Huntley said. She was standing at my bedroom door, holding a glass of white wine.

"Baby's sick," Sarah said to her. "Get me a big glass of orange juice and four fast-acting ibuprofen."

"Put some vodka in the juice," I hollered after her.

"You should not mix booze and pills," Sarah said.

"If I were at all interested in feeling the way I do right now, I wouldn't think of it," I said to her, and sat up in bed. I was wearing a pair of underpants and one of Jefferson's old work shirts. When my juice and medicine entered the room, Stella was carrying them.

"Who fixed the juice," I said to her.

"I did," Stella said.

"Good," I said and swallowed the four pills and half the vodka laden screwdriver. "Why're you here," I said to Stella. "Is something wrong?"

"Not really," she said. "Mickey and Sarah and I are just out on the deck talkin' about that endlessly nosy FBI agent and Alvie."

"Why?"

"Because the man somehow knew that we visited Big Daddy, and he wants to hear from Alvie exactly why we did."

"They probably tap a few of Big Daddy's lines," I said to her. "And he probably knows it. He's a smart, savvy guy, Stella. I would guess he dropped that information into the conversation strictly as a misdirection play." I quickly drank the rest of the screwdriver.

"Y'all want another?" Stella said to me.

"Yes. Let me take a shower and get dressed, and I'll be out to join you in a few minutes."

Fifteen minutes later I was enjoying my second screwdriver, eating a fried egg sandwich, feeling better, and sitting in the warming sun with the girls.

"Just have Alvie repeat what you told Agent Keating," I said to Mickey. "After all, it could be true. He can handle it."

"Now that Mallory's back, I suspect our Alvie can handle most anything," Stella said. "Coop told me he is actin' like a completely different man."

"Well, we can each decide that for ourselves, momentarily," Sarah said. "Here he comes right now."

When I looked, there was Alvie, walking quickly down the beach, wearing a pair of hot pink Bermuda shorts, a white long sleeved polo shirt, knee high black socks, and a pair of sandals.

"Call GQ," Stella said and grinned. "I'll alert the local media."

"Good morning, ladies," Alvie said and bowed. "May I join y'all?"

"Please do," Mickey Huntley said.

"Where are the rest of the boys," I asked him.

"I believe they are all on their way to Varnamtown. They implied they had some business to conduct with someone over there. They left around eleven."

I looked at Stella. She was scowling. "Stella?" I said.

"You know what they're gonna be up to," she said to me.

"Not really," I said.

"They are on their way to confront Jesse's father," Sarah said. "He's a serial abuser, and this whole thing does not sound kosher to me."

"Is this the man who is ultimately responsible for the death of Jesse's sister?" Mickey Huntley asked her.

"Yes," Sarah said, as Mickey's cell phone started to ring. She looked at the number and put it on speaker.

"Mickey Huntley," she said.

"Boss, we got some trouble," said Darius Millar.

"Explain," the lawyer said.

"A man's in intensive care, a boy's wounded, another man's got a broken shoulder and ankle, and a man's in jail," he said.

"Darius," she said, "either you explicate or you're fired."

"Hollis Shine's in Dosher Memorial Hospital in critical condition. He's Jesse's father. Jesse's got a side wound and is in the hospital emergency room. Jeff's got a broken shoulder and ankle, and he's in the same hospital. And Coop's in the Brunswick County jail. He shot Hollis Shine."

"God damn it," Stella said, standing up. "We gotta go, Cash," she said to me.

"Who called us?" Mickey said to Darius.

"Coop." said her assistant

"Where's the Sheriff?"

"Coop told me they said he was somewhere fishin' with a friend of his."

"Is there bail?"

"I don't know," Darius said. "They booked him on attempted murder one."

"I'll drive the van," Sarah said. "We'll all go."

"I'm on my way," was what Mickey Huntley said to her assistant. "You get back to Coop and tell him to do nothing 'til he hears from me."

"I've always loved that song, boss," Darius Millar said, disconnecting the call.

CHAPTER THIRTY EIGHT

It took Mickey Huntley eight hours to bail Cooper Grey out of jail, primarily because nobody could locate a judge to hear the arguments for and against it. Finally, Stella reached her father, who reached a judge named Stone, who agreed to leave his poker game early and hold the hearing. Bail was set at a whopping half million dollars, a sum that was guaranteed by Alvie Weather.

"I could have gone his bail," Jefferson Davis said to me. He was lying in an awkward position in a hospital bed with his left shoulder immobile in a cast and his left leg up in the air. His ankle was in a temporary cast that somebody would remove with a sort of saw early tomorrow, after which they would knock him out again and give him a permanent one. He'd be wearing both casts for at least six weeks. "Where's Jesse at?" he said to me.

"He's with Sarah, and Mickey is working with some children's agency and the courts to see about removing him from his parents' custody, although heaven knows his poor mother played no part in his abuse except to be unable to prevent it."

"Katherine," he said in a strained voice. "You cannot imagine the hideous circumstances of that boy's life. His home was a nightmare. Trash and dyin' trees and dead animals all around the front sandlot that passed for a lawn. I could not believe what I was lookin' at when we drove up to what he called his home."

I was wondering how much he remembered of what had transpired. "Can you tell me what happened?"

"I wanted to talk with the man," he said to me. "I felt like I owed him an explanation regardin' the whereabouts of his son. My first mistake was not realizin' right off how drunk he was. My second was when I turned my back on him to walk back to the car, and he decided to knock my shoulder into center field with a baseball bat."

"You could have been killed," I said, "if he'd swung at your head instead."

"If Coop hadn't shot him, most likely I would have been. It's crazy that those deputies arrested him," Jeff said to me. "He only nicked the man in the hand that was holding the bat."

"That's not exactly true, Jefferson," I said.

"I was there, Katherine," he said to me. Then he frowned. "Although I may have been less observant than usual. The pain I was experiencin' was a bit overwhelming."

"You may well have been unconscious for more than a few minutes," I said. "Because, as you know, Hollis wasn't satisfied with breaking your shoulder. He broke your ankle next. That's when Cooper shot the bat out of his hand. But that didn't stop Jesse's dad. He grabbed his rifle."

"What?" Jeff exclaimed.

"Cooper shot him a second time and hit him in the chest. The one shot Hollis Shine managed to get off went astray and took a sliver out of Jesse's torso."

"Jesse got shot?" He sounded amazed.

"Yes, and he's fine. There's nothing to worry about as far as his physical well-being is concerned. I can't speak to whatever emotional scarring he may suffer. Not too many fathers shoot their sons."

"And Hollis?" he said to me.

"The man is being kept alive by a machine that breathes for him," I said, as a nurse walked in the room.

"I will be getting ready to check his catheter," she said to me. "Then he'll be sleeping for a while." She smiled at both of us. I nodded.

"I'm going to leave you in her capable hands," I said to Jeff. "I'll be back tomorrow."

"Katherine," he said to me as I was heading for the door. I turned. "I wish y'all would kiss me," he said. "I would surely benefit from that kiss."

I looked at him, and then I looked at the nurse. "It might be good for his blood pressure," she said. She winked at me.

So I walked back in and kissed him. If it wasn't the best kiss he'd ever gotten in his life, you couldn't have testified to that by looking at his face.

"I love you, Jefferson,' I said, as I turned again and headed for the door.

"When the man told you he was a legitimate bail bondsman, and that he was defendin' the life of his friend, was there a reason y'all ignored him?" Sheriff Billy Conroy said to the guy who was in his office, standing restlessly in front of him.

"I couldn't sort out the particulars right then, Billy," the deputy said. "A man was bleedin' to death, another one was all broken up on the ground, a kid was screamin', and the guy left standin' was holdin' a gun. I hadda do the best I could with what I saw in front of me."

"Uh huh," the Sheriff said. "So you threw my son-in-law in jail and left him there until I could find a judge."

"I didn't know he was related to y'all. He never intimated such a thing. And he didn't have no papers to prove what he said was true."

Billy Conroy sighed as he looked at his young deputy. "All right, Harris. I can see your point. And no doubt your adrenaline was on overload. But if you run across Mr. Grey again, you might want to consider an apology, hear?"

"Yes, sir."

A minute after the deputy had gone, Billy Conroy heard a knock on his door. "Louise?" he said.

The door opened, and a woman he had worked with for twenty years poked her head in. "We got a complaint of vandalism on that place with the nude female mailbox," Louise said to him.

Billy Conroy chuckled. "No doubt," he said. "Did you accidentally run over that abomination on your way to work this morning?"

"Not me," she said.

"Well, then, who complained and what happened?"

"Ricky Titus complained. He just got back this morning from one of his cross-country truck deliveries. He told me he liked, and I am quoting here, those big beautiful knockers. Apparently what happened is that the female form itself is gone and the mailbox has been blown into kingdom come by a barrage of bullets."

"You tell Ricky we can't be wastin' time chasin' down people who target practice on mailboxes," Billy said. "He has a problem with that, he can see me."

"Yes, sir," Louise said.

When Mickey Huntley presented her petition for temporary legal custody of Jesse Shine, she was also prepared to present a separate petition for temporary physical custody of the boy to Mr. and Mrs. Alvie Weather of Landfall, Wilmington, North Carolina. And after the judge had heard testimony from all parties called to testify, including a timid plea by a married sister of Jesse's, he granted legal custody to the lawyer and asked to speak with Alvie, from whom he had been buying his cars for eight very satisfactory years.

"I am seeking temporary physical custody of the child, your honor," Alvie said, "because I have a deep appreciation of the severe damage that poverty inflicts on children. I came from extreme poverty, myself; however, unlike this child, I had loving parents who cared for me in ways that this boy has never experienced. And that mitigating circumstance has made all the difference in my life. My wife and I are delighted to open our home to Jesse and to see can we improve the quality of his young life. He is a bright boy with many needs, including a proper education. We are prepared to meet those needs."

Five minutes later, temporary physical custody was granted to the Weathers and court was adjourned with the understanding that these issues would be revisited and evaluated in six months.

CHAPTER THIRTY NINE

"The more I think on it, Alvie, the more I am wonderin' about that old car that's in one of the sheds at Tommy Dauterive's place," Billy Conroy said to Alvie Weather. "It might could be one of yours that Riley Satterfield stole from that shed and drove over there."

"Sir?" Alvie said. His wife Mallory was leaning against her husband, sipping a sweet iced tea, with a look of total contentment on her face.

We were gathered at the Sawtelle place in Sea Breeze because Tallahassee Bodine and Junior Fisk had caught a huge mess of spots and decided to have a fish fry. Sarah and Mickey were due to arrive with a lot of other side dishes in about an hour. Stella and Coop were playing a fast game of catch with Jesse Shine.

"It's a bucket of rust, far as I'm concerned; but you're the car man," Billy said.

"What does it look like," Alvie said to him.

"It looks exactly like what it is: a very old BMW," the Sheriff said.

Jeff and I had been listening to this conversation, and when Billy said that last bit, Jeff poked me in the ribs with his good arm and muttered, "I just don't believe this."

"Believe what?" I said to him.

"Give me a push over to the bar," he said. "I'd like a drink."

So I turned his wheelchair around and did just that. "That's the car that's holding a huge uncut diamond in one of its wheel wells," Jefferson said to me, taking a couple of glasses and pouring some merlot.

"What? How would you know something like that," I said.

"Alvie told me and Coop that night when we took him for a walk," Jeff told me.

"This doesn't sound as though it bears any resemblance to anything that's legal," I said to him.

"That's right," he said, and took a decent sip of the wine.

"So give me the shorthanded version," I said. "And let it go at that."

"Mallory does onsite inspections of whatever locations are involved when she writes her romance novels. Those locations range for a week's stay anywhere from Alexandria, Egypt to Paris, France to the Amalfi coast, to Monaco," he said. "Her last book cost Alvie around a million dollars. He found himself dipping into capital."

"That's really all I want to know about this," I said.

I wheeled Jefferson back to where we'd been. Alvie was still talking to Billy as though the only thing on his mind was one of many automobiles he'd lost in the explosion. It fortified my belief that he had missed his calling as an actor. "I will have my shop manager retrieve that car in the morning," he said to the Sheriff. "It is true that it's old. But restored it is worth a good deal of money. I want to thank you, Billy."

"Glad to help," the Sheriff said.

I drained my glass of merlot and decided to pour myself another one.

"Me, too," Jefferson Davis said.

———————————————

Sarah Ehrenson was handing covered dishes to Mickey Huntley. She'd spent the morning fixing various sides to accompany the fish fry, and the van was fast filling up with her creations.

"How many did you do?" Mickey said.

"About a dozen," Sarah told her. "I just felt like it. You know I love to cook. And we've all got things to celebrate."

"Yes, I know. But when it comes to your cooking, that can be dangerous; and I have the extra five pounds to prove it."

"You were too thin a year ago," Sarah said, walking out with a last tureen of spinach soufflé. She was closing the rear door on the Mercedes van when a man walked up to her.

"Hello, beautiful," he said to Sarah. "You remember me?"

Sarah turned and looked at him. "Not off hand," she said. "Should I?"

"I gave you a fish quite a while ago," the guy said. "A speckled trout."

"Of course," she said, snapping her fingers. "Down at the pier."

"That's right," he said. "And then I sort of took advantage of you."

"Really?" Sarah said, glancing at Mickey Huntley, who was listening carefully to this conversation.

"Well, yes," he said a bit sheepishly, "I'm not only a fisherman. I'm a street artist. And six months ago a lady asked me to create a portrait for her to use on one of her book covers. She wanted what she called 'a strong and totally ravishing beauty'. And there you were, indelibly imprinted on my memory. You're impossible to forget. She paid me five thousand dollars, more than I've ever made before. It's keeping me housed and fed this winter. I feel like I owe you a lot."

Sarah Ehrenson looked at the guy, and then she turned and looked at Mickey Huntley. "So that explains it," she said to her lover.

"It certainly does," Mickey said and grinned at both of them.

Sarah turned to the man before getting into the van. "Here's what we'll do," she said to him. "You keep me in speckled trout this winter and we'll consider you are paid in full. Do we have a deal?"

"We sure do," he said. "Matter of fact, I'm going out tomorrow."

As Sarah turned the big van onto Carolina Beach Avenue, heading for Snow's Cut Bridge, Mickey Huntley said, "That fellow was right, you know."

"About what?" Sarah said.

"About you," the lawyer said. "You really are unforgettable."

CHAPTER FORTY

Three days before Christmas, everybody involved in the rescue of Mallory Weather was invited to a get together at the Weather's home. So Stella and Coop and Jeff and I and Sarah and Mickey all piled into the big Mercedes and repeated the drive that had started out at four-thirty in the morning a number of weeks ago. Billy Conroy, who had asked Louise to join him, was following. What a difference a month can make.

The Weather's property was a spectacular sight. Every window in the house held tall, bright candelabra nestled in greenery. The spreading bare branches of the huge oak trees that shaded the front lawn in summer were aglow with what looked like miles of white lights, and a beautiful wrought iron rendering of a group of carolers was poised as though to greet us as we all headed for the front door.

"Welcome to our home, and happy holidays," Alvie Weather said with gusto, opening the double front doors. "Let's repair to the living room, where my wife and Mr. Jesse are eagerly waitin' to offer you some of their best food and drink."

"Wow, this is some foyer, Alvie," Cooper Grey said to him. "It could be as big as my entire condo."

"It's most likely bigger, Coop," Jeff said.

"Boss!" yelled a young, excited voice from the living room. "Are y'all finally here?"

"We are," Jeff said, heading for the living room. He was managing to support himself with one crutch under his good arm while he limped along with a heavy cast on his broken ankle. "Be careful you don't mow me down in your excitement."

When I walked into that room, which earlier Sarah had called a clown school, I wasn't prepared for what I saw. Neither were Stella and Sarah and Mickey.

"Where the hell are the clowns?" Stella said in astonishment.

But Jesse wasn't waiting for her question to be answered. He jumped up out of the chair he was sitting in and ran to Jefferson and threw his arms around his waist and held on for dear life. Jeff staggered a bit as I reached to brace him at the small of his back.

"Let's get a look at you, son," Jeff said. Jesse was wearing a pair of brown wool slacks and a raw silk white shirt with the red sweater, which Coop and Jeff had bought him on the day he had wandered into our lives, tied around his neck. He had a pair of black socks and tan leather loafers on his feet, and the watch on his left wrist was gold. He was sporting a great big grin and a fabulous haircut.

"Well," Jeff said to him, "y'all don't look like Tom Sawyer anymore, and that is for certain. You are quite the handsome young man."

"Jesse wasn't comfortable with the harlequins," Mallory Weather said quietly to all of us. "So we removed them and had the room painted this peaceful ivory color. It is a much more inviting place than before." She looked as ethereal as ever in a long flowing white dress that reminded me of an old Wilkie Collins novel.

"It's lovely," Sarah said, handing her coat to Alvie, who was making a collection of our outer garments.

"Yes," Mallory Weather said. "It's something we probably should have done years ago. But one gets used to things. And change is not an easy issue with which to grapple, is it? My, my," she added, looking directly at Sarah. "That book cover of mine perhaps does not do you justice, Ms. Ehrenson. Had I known of your existence I would most assuredly have asked your permission before I used it. I apologize."

"Please call me Sarah. My mother is comfortable being known as Ms. Ehrenson. I'm not."

"Listen, sweet pea," Alvie said to his wife, "Why don't you and Mr. Jesse get your offerings together in the kitchen. You know I am anxious to speak with these good people for a few minutes about that matter you and I discussed."

"We got a lotta good stuff," Jesse said, taking Mallory Weather's proffered hand in his. "Y'all better be hungry."

Billy Conroy and his date Louise had walked over to the grand piano.

"I need your attention, Sheriff," Alvie said to him. "Let's all grab a seat over this way. There're some things I need to get off my mind." I glanced at Jeff, who shrugged his good shoulder.

"What's goin' on, Alvie?" Billy Conroy said to him, taking a seat next to Louise on the sofa.

"I am in need of confessin' to some chicanery," Alvie said. "Although I can't exactly say that I'm seekin' absolution as the Catholics would call it, I am goin' to relieve my mind."

"What are we talkin' about here," Billy Conroy said cautiously. "Am I gonna have to make a legal judgment of some sort?"

"I leave that determination in your reliable hands, Billy," Alvie said to him. "Makin' a long story short, that old BMW you so kindly told me about held an uncut diamond that is worth in aggregate about ten million dollars. And I knew it was there. I just assumed it'd been blown to bits along with the other vehicles I lost."

"Whoa, Alvie, stop, do not proceed," Stella said sharply. "You might wanna talk to your lawyer, who is sitting right next to you, before you go any further. You can't be askin' law enforcement people to be disinterested in anything illegal."

"Stella's right, Alvie," Mickey Huntley said. "I suspect you haven't thought this through. There are consequences to a confession when it's addressed to a Sheriff rather than a priest."

"I need to make this right," Alvie said stubbornly. "You people have treated me with nothing but respect. I need to return that somewhat rare consideration. I am willing to accept the consequences."

"Alvie agreed to launder a colleague's money in exchange for the diamond," Cooper Grey said evenly. "His wife's novels cost him a fortune because she visits all of her locales, which include places like Monaco and Paris, and Alexandria, Egypt. He told Jeff and me that he agreed so long as the money was not the result of any illegality."

"What is it the result of," Mickey Huntley said to Alvie.

"Legitimate income," Alvie said. "But my friend is a Dane. Does that mean anything to any of you?"

"Well, yes," his lawyer said. "He's taxed at nearly 60%."

"What? How much?" Billy exclaimed.

"It's expensive to maintain a society that affords all of its citizens multiple safety nets from birth to death," Mickey said. "What percentage of his income did you agree to launder, Alvie?"

"About a quarter. He's a yacht builder, but his real love is architecture. The diamond in the wheel well was partial payment on a ship he was designin' for one of his Saudi clients."

"So the Danish government is out some money," I said.

"Yes," Mallory Weather said, jarring us out of our conversation. No one had heard her return. "I am the person responsible for this. If it weren't for me, Alvie wouldn't have agreed to such a thing. I had no idea what my casual desire to visit scenes from my imagination was doing to Alvie's bottom line."

Alvie Weather stood up quickly and went to his wife. "Where's

Mr. Jesse?" he said to her.

"He's upstairs gathering everyone's present," she said.

"Well," Mickey Huntley said, "this is not the first, nor will it be the last time a government agency has been thwarted in its ability to collect taxes from people."

"Are you all right, Billy?" Sarah said to him.

"It's not my business," he said to her. "Right, Mickey?"

"It's a federal matter," the lawyer said. "We won't be seeing a need to enlighten them, however."

"We have decided on another more serious use for the money the diamond will bring," Mallory Weather said. "We are going to construct a private academy for underprivileged youth. We really were never aware of the desperate need before. However, it is very clear to each of us now."

"We're calling it 'The Sunshine School'," Alvie Weather said proudly.

POSTSCRIPT

A few days before New Year's Eve, Sheriff Billy Conroy was in his office in Bolivia, North Carolina when his office phone rang.

"Conroy," he said.

"Y'all still alive up there in the northwoods," said a voice in a drawl he recognized immediately.

"And kickin'," the Sheriff said. "How goes it, Manny? You stayin' even with the criminals that yearn to run Louisiana?"

"Lord knows we try," Lieutenant Manny Mora said. "But that's not why I'm callin', Billy. I got that information y'all been lookin' for."

"Shoot," Billy Conroy said.

"Pete and Ray Ray Dauterive left Morgan City early this mornin'. I expect they'll hit home early tomorrow. Be my calculated guess they are carryin' a truck full of black market handguns."

"Beautiful," the Sheriff said. "I owe you one, partner."

"I'll be collectin' sometime in May when the Spanish are runnin' wild. Speakin' of runnin' wild, how's Stella?"

"As unpredictable as ever. She's got a kind of counterbalance these days, though," Billy Conroy said.

"Oh?" said Mora.

"A gal from up north. Name of Cash Delaney. They're teamed up and I see a lot of good in it. But let me assure you, my friend, my life is never boring."

"I really like that daughter of yours," Mora said.

"Well," Billy Conroy said to him, "unfortunately for you, Manny, so does her husband."

"C'est la vie," his friend said. "It is a sad truth that I am often a day late and many dollars short."

"Aren't we all," said Billy Conroy. "Aren't we all."

ABOUT THE AUTHOR

Beverlee Hughes lives in Carolina Beach. This is her second published novel and also the second in a series of Cash Delaney mysteries. She is currently at work on a third, entitled Labrador Drift.

www.ingramcontent.com/pod-product-compliance
Lightning Source LLC
Chambersburg PA
CBHW031313170626
46807CB00001B/408